Books by A

McIntyre Security Bodyguard Series:

Vulnerable

Fearless

Shane (a novella)

Broken

Shattered

Imperfect

Ruined

Hostage

Redeemed

Marry Me (a novella)

Snowbound (a novella)

Regret

With This Ring (a novella)

Collateral Damage

Special Delivery

McIntyre Security Protectors:

Finding Layla

McIntyre Security Search and Rescue Series:

Search and Rescue

Lost and Found

A Tyler Jamison Novel:

Somebody to Love

Somebody to Hold

Somebody to Cherish

A British Billionaire Romance:

Charmed (co-written with Laura Riley)

Audiobooks & Upcoming Releases:

For links to my audiobooks and upcoming releases, visit my website:

www.aprilwilsonauthor.com

Finding Layla

McIntyre Security Protectors

Book 1

by

April Wilson

Copyright © 2021 April E. Barnswell/
Wilson Publishing LLC
All rights reserved.

Cover by Steamy Designs
Photography by Eric David Battershell
Model: Mike Chabot and Sally Nofal
Proofread by Amanda Cuff (Word of Advice)

Published by
April E. Barnswell
Wilson Publishing LLC
P.O. Box 292913
Dayton, OH 45429
www.aprilwilsonauthor.com

ISBN: 9798794386196

No part of this publication may be reproduced, stored in a retrieval system, copied, shared, or transmitted in any form or by any means without the prior written permission of the author. The only exception is brief quotations to be used in book reviews. Please don't steal e-books.

This novel is entirely a work of fiction. All places and locations are used fictitiously. The names of characters and places are figments of the author's imagination, and any resemblance to real people or real places is purely coincidental and unintended.

Character List

Main Characters

- Layla Alexander, 21-yr-old university student
- Jason Miller, 28, professional bodyguard; former Army medic and former paramedic; works for McIntyre Security, Inc.

Other Characters

- Ian Alexander, 28, Layla's brother
- Tyler Jamison, 42, Ian Alexander's boyfriend
- Judge Martin Alexander, 58, Layla's father
- Ruth Alexander, 56, Layla's mother

1

Layla Alexander
One Week Ago

I don't know what's real anymore and what's not. The voice in my head is screaming hysterically, and my mind is fractured into so many pieces I can't count them all. Everything around me is utter chaos. I hear the other girls screaming, crying, begging for the men to stop. But they don't. And the screams continue.

As I lie chained to a metal cot, naked and bruised, all I can do is concentrate on trying to breathe through my nose. I feel sick, but there's nothing left in my stomach to throw up. It's for the best, because the one who likes to choke me shoved a ball gag in my mouth to shut me up. If I vomit, I'll likely choke to death.

I know why they gagged me and hid me away in this windowless storage room. It's because, even though I haven't been raped like all those other girls—they said I'm worth a lot more untouched—I'm the one who screams the loudest.

The door opens, letting in a shaft of blinding light. I squeeze my eyes shut tight. It's him. I can smell him, vile and sour. My stomach churns.

He climbs onto the cot and rubs himself against me. And then he wraps his fingers around my throat and squeezes until bursts of light start flashing behind my eyelids.

I can't breathe.

Maybe this time is it. Maybe this time I won't come to.

The last thing I register is a painful prick on my arm. The room begins to spin, and then I—

2

Jason Miller

Eight o'clock Saturday night, right on time, I show up at Tank's Pub downtown. A quick glance around the bar tells me I'm the first to arrive, so I grab a table with a good view of the large flatscreen that's replaying last week's baseball game.

A gorgeous blue-eyed blonde in a tight T-shirt stops by the table to take my drink order. "Hi. I'm Robyn." She points to her name tag, which is positioned right over top a very large breast. Kinda hard to miss. "What can I get you?"

I automatically glance at the door to see if any of the others have shown up yet, but no. It's just me at the moment. "Whatever you've got on draft is fine. Thanks."

She smiles at me, tilting her head slightly as she wraps a strand of curly shoulder-length hair around an index finger. "Is there anything else I can get you?"

Her heated gaze roams down my arms. Since I'm wearing a short-sleeved T-shirt, there's a lot of skin exposed. Some girls really go for tattoos, some don't. This one clearly does.

"I like your ink," she says. "You work out a lot, don't you?"

"A bit. Thanks."

"So, is there anything else I can get you?" She lets the question hang in the air. The inuendo in her voice is thick enough to cut with a knife.

I smile. "Just the beer, thanks."

She purses her lips. "Let me know if you change your mind. I get off at midnight."

Just as she's walking away, her lush hips sashaying in skin-tight blue jeans, I feel a pair of strong hands clamp down on my shoulders.

"Jason!" says a familiar voice from behind me. "Don't start the party without us."

I glance back at Liam McIntyre, who pats my shoulders as he nods toward the retreating figure of the server. "Who's your friend?"

Miguel and Philip are right behind him. Looks like the gang's all here.

"She's not my friend," I say as the three of them take their seats.

"I'll bet you wish she was," Miguel says with a grin.

Philip laughs as he nudges Miguel with his elbow. "I'll bet you do, too."

"But not you," Liam says to Philip. "Because you're *saving yourself* for Haley."

Now it's everyone else's turn to laugh. Poor Philip gets teased a lot because the daughter of one of our co-workers has a big crush on him. The truth is, he has an equally big crush on her. But she's only seventeen and still in high school, while Phil is twenty-four. That makes her off-limits. And since Phil doesn't want to make an enemy of Mack Donovan, her father, he's biding his time until Haley turns eighteen.

"Come on, guys. Don't tease him." I pat Philip's back. "I think it's cute."

"At least one of us has romantic prospects," Miguel says.

Robyn, our server, drops my beer off at the table and takes the other guys' orders.

"Three more beers, coming up," she says before heading back to the bar.

These three guys have become my closest friends since I started working at McIntyre Security after leaving my job as a paramedic. Before that, I was an Army combat medic for a tour in Afghanistan. Between my time in the Army and my job as a Chicago paramedic, the PTSD got to be too much, and I decided to go into private security instead. The pay is better, and it's less stressful. Win-win. Unfortunately, I still have the PTSD, along with a bad case of insomnia.

The four of us are in our twenties. Miguel Rodriguez and I are both twenty-eight, and we're bodyguards for McIntyre Security. Liam McIntyre's twenty-four. He's the head martial arts instructor for the company. Liam specializes in some serious ass-kicking mojo. Philip Underwood, also twenty-four, works on Jake McIntyre's surveillance team. The four of us all started working at McIntyre Security around the same time, and we all live in the same apartment building. It kinda made sense that we all became friends.

"I'm starving," Philip says as he reaches for a well-worn laminated menu.

Liam laughs. "Dude, when are you not hungry?"

Philip's a big guy—like seriously big. He's always hungry because it takes a lot of calories to fuel that big body of his. He's six-four and built like a tank. His arms and legs are massive. The rest of us are about the same size—six feet tall, lean muscles—but next to Philip we're pipsqueaks.

"I'm serious," Philip says as he skims the menu. "I did a twelve-hour surveillance shift today, with no breaks for food. I ran out of coffee and snacks by noon. It was brutal."

Robyn returns to pass out the rest of the beers. "Can I get you guys something to eat?"

"Hell yes," Philip says. "I'll take a dozen hot wings, a double cheeseburger, and loaded fries. And how about some nachos? I'm starving."

Miguel shakes his head. "Dude, you can really pack away

the food."

Philip leans back and slaps his solid abdomen. He's big, but it's all muscle, and not an ounce of fat. "What can I say? I have a big metabolism."

I practically choke on my beer laughing at that understatement. "You think so?"

It's a regular thing with us—my buddies and I meet on Saturday evenings to unwind after the work week. Usually everyone makes it, unless they're on assignment. As for me, I just finished up a full-time assignment not long ago, and I've been floating ever since, filling in as a temporary bodyguard where needed.

The rest of us put in our food orders, and we munch on the free peanuts while we wait for our meals to be delivered. It's not long before our food arrives, and everyone digs in.

When my phone chimes with an incoming text message, I check the screen. It's from my boss, Shane McIntyre.

Shane: I have a full-time protection assignment that requires medical expertise. I'll e-mail you the details. Let me know this evening if you want the assignment.

Jason: Will do.

"What was that about?" Liam asks as he sticks a fry in his mouth.

"A new assignment. Shane's e-mailing me the details."

"Who's the client?" Miguel asks.

I shrug. "He didn't say. He only said medical expertise is required." As the only bodyguard with any serious medical training, it's sort of my area.

I enjoy the rest of the evening with the guys, eating good food, drinking lots of excellent beer, and watching the game. I might as well get the most out of my free time before my new assignment begins. I'll have very little of it for the foreseeable future.

After I leave the bar, I sit in my car and read Shane's e-mail.

Layla Alexander, 21 years old.

I've never met her, but I've heard a lot. That poor girl. She's been through hell and back. The papers were full of stories about how she was rescued recently from a local sex trafficking ring.

I text Shane back, telling him I'll take the job.

Shane: Great. Come to my office at eight am tomorrow to meet her parents.

* * *

The next morning, I walk into the front lobby of the McIntyre Security office building on N. Michigan Avenue, downtown Chicago. Since it's the weekend, the place is pretty deserted. Once I'm waved through the front lobby by the guards on duty at the front desk, I take an elevator up to the twentieth floor, where the executive offices are located. Shane's door is partially open, and I hear muffled voices coming from inside.

I knock, and Shane meets me at the door. "Jason. Thanks for coming."

"No problem." Shane's not just my boss; he's also a friend. After all, I delivered the man's first child under severe duress. It's fair to say we bonded over that traumatic experience.

"Come on in," he says. "Mr. and Mrs. Alexander are keen to meet you." He steps aside for me to enter his high-rise corner office.

The parents are seated on chairs facing Shane's desk.

Shane nods to me as he takes his seat. Behind him is a panoramic view of downtown Chicago. "This is Jason Miller, the bodyguard I was telling you about," he says to the parents. "He has extensive medical training, which makes him ideally suited to take over Layla's protection. Have a seat, Jason."

Martin Alexander—*Judge* Alexander—offers me his hand. "Hello, Jason." His voice is deep and authoritative. "Thanks for coming."

"Good morning, Your Honor," I say as we shake hands.

"This is my wife, Ruth Alexander," the man says as he nods to the woman seated beside him.

I shake her hand as well, nodding curtly. Her grip is firm and confident. According to Shane's e-mail, she's a district attorney here in the city. "Ma'am. It's a pleasure."

These two are a power couple in the local Chicago legal circuit.

Based on the information Shane shared with me, the Alexanders are in their late fifties. They have two children—a twenty-eight-year-old son, Ian; and their twenty-one-year-old daughter, Layla. Both children are adopted. I happen to know Ian personally; I've met him many times before, and we have friends in common. I've never met the daughter, though.

I've been a bodyguard for a few years now, but this is the first time I've been interviewed by a prospective client's parents. I don't blame them for their heightened concern. I know what their daughter has been through. I read the stories in the news. Not only was she abducted into a sex trafficking ring, but her bodyguard was killed right in front of her. I can only imagine what that poor girl went through.

Her brother, Ian, and his partner, Tyler Jamison, a former Chicago homicide detective, were the ones who rescued Layla, and in the process uncovered a sex trafficking ring. Over a dozen young women were saved that night. Sadly, many of them had already been horrifically abused.

Layla has a complicated medical history, which is now compounded by her recent abduction. Even though she was discovered in less than a day, the physical and emotional damage she suffered was severe.

Martin turns toward me. "I know Shane has updated you on Layla's situation. I'm sure you know that, in addition to her recent trauma, she is a type 1 diabetic and she suffers from auditory hallucinations. Her diabetes is back under control, but the hallucinations—the voice she hears—has been particularly bad lately."

The judge looks to his wife.

"Unfortunately, Layla's not doing well at the moment," the mother says. "She's currently under a psychiatric hold at the hospital while her psychiatrist determines if it's safe to release her. Layla has a past history of inflicting self-harm, and that's only been exacerbated by recent events. Right now, my daughter refuses to speak to anyone outside of the family and her doctor, so you'll have your work cut out for you."

I nod. "Understood. I realize it'll take time for me to earn her trust. I'm prepared for that."

Ruth Alexander's blue eyes fill with tears. "I don't know how much Shane has told you, but Layla's previous bodyguard, Sean, betrayed her—he sold her out to his drug dealer, who in turn sold her to the sex traffickers. She has good reason to be distrustful. Your job, besides keeping her safe, is to teach her that it's okay to trust again. That's all we ask."

I can hear the pain in the parents' voices. The love they have for their daughter is palpable. "I promise I'll do everything in my power to earn her trust."

"Thank you, Jason," the father says. "She knows you're officially coming on board today as her new full-time bodyguard. We asked her to meet with you at the hospital today, but she refused. Please don't take it personally."

I nod. "How long do you think she'll be hospitalized?"

"We hope she'll be released soon," Mrs. Alexander says. "Other than having a multitude of bruises, she's medically fine. Her psychiatrist is working on getting her emotionally stabilized again, as much as possible. We've obtained permission from the hospital administrator for you to remain on-site until she's released. The press has been an issue lately—they keep hounding us for interviews and comments. The photographers are particularly bad. Images of our daughter are very profitable right now given the circumstances. We're trying to shield her from as much of that as we can."

"Our daughter is an extremely wealthy young woman," the father says. "And that makes her the target of unscrupulous people. Her health conditions only complicate the risks. Your job is to keep her safe, while at the same time letting her live as normal a life as possible for a twenty-one-year-old university student. Her mother and I work hard to balance her freedom with safety. It's a fine line to walk, and it won't be easy, but we're counting on you to make it work."

The parents rise to their feet, as do I. Shane stands as well. Looks like the preliminaries are over, and it's time for me to get to work.

Mr. Alexander pulls a keychain out of his trouser pocket and hands it to me. "Here's a key to our home. Let us know if you need anything else." He eyes me hard. "We're counting on you to live up to your reputation. Your boss speaks very highly of you. Don't let us down."

"I won't."

I've made a lot of promises in my life—to the US Army, to Shane McIntyre—but this one weighs particularly heavy on me. There's a lot at stake here. This girl has already suffered more than most people will in a lifetime. If there's anything I can do to make her life a little bit easier, I'll gladly do it.

After the parents take their leave, Shane says, "This is a challenging assignment, Jason. We're all counting on you to keep your client safe. Her former bodyguard failed her miserably. We won't make that mistake."

I nod. "I won't let you down."

"I'm counting on it."

* * *

When I arrive at the hospital, Ian Alexander and his partner, Tyler Jamison, are sitting with Layla in her room in the psych ward. I knock on her door, and Tyler steps out into the hallway with me.

"I'm glad you're here, Jason," he says, offering me his hand. We shake. "I was hoping Martin and Ruth would take my advice and hire one of Shane's bodyguards. With your medical background, you're perfect for the job."

I peer around Tyler, through a partially-open door, into a quiet, dimly-lit room. It looks like any other hospital room, lots of beige and white. There's a single bed in the room, surrounded by monitors and cabinets. There's a utilitarian guest chair next to the bed and, across the room is a sofa that undoubtedly pulls out into a bed.

The room is eerily quiet, and most of the lights are off. I can just make out the form of Ian seated next to the bed, facing his sister and holding her hand.

"How is she?" I ask Tyler.

It's weird seeing Tyler in civilian clothes—jeans and a button-up shirt. I'm used to seeing him dressed in a black suit and tie, all part of his former homicide detective persona. My understanding is he's been fired for violating the conditions of his administrative suspension. It's a shame. Chicago lost a highly-experienced, veteran homicide detective all because of a technicality. Tyler, along with Ian, rescued over a dozen young women that night. He deserved a medal, not termination.

Tyler frowns. "Medically, she's fine. Her vitals are stable, and none of her physical injuries are life-threatening. It's going to take some time, though, for the physical reminders of her ordeal to fade. She's covered in bruises. As for the emotional damage—there's no telling. She doesn't have much of an appetite, so she's not eating well, and that's wreaking havoc on her blood sugar. She's had multiple lows. The alarm on her monitor has gone off several times in the past few days. Everyone's pretty stressed out."

I nod, knowing exactly what a lack of food will do to a type 1 diabetic. "She knows about me? That I'm here?"

"Yes."

"Can I see her?"

He sighs heavily. "You can come in and say hi, but don't expect much."

I nod. "I understand. Baby steps, right?"

"Right."

I follow Tyler into the room and close the door behind me. It takes a few seconds for my eyes to adjust to the darkness. Layla is lying under a mound of blankets. All I can really make out is a pretty oval face and long, dark hair that spills across the stark white pillowcase.

I stand at the foot of her bed. "Hi, Layla. I'm Jason Miller, your new bodyguard."

She doesn't respond, which doesn't surprise me. Instead, she turns her face to the wall.

"It's okay if you don't feel like talking," I say, hoping to reassure her. I keep my voice low and even. No pressure. "I just wanted to come in and say hi. We can talk later, when you feel like it. I'll be hanging around in case you need me."

Still no response. She lies completely still, as if she didn't hear a word I said.

As my eyes adjust to the dim lighting, I start to make out the bruises on her pale, battered face. It sickens me to think about what she's been through. And the fact that her former bodyguard—someone who was sworn to protect her—betrayed her is unthinkable. I don't blame her one bit for being wary.

I nod to her brother. "Hey, Ian. I'll be right outside the door. Let me know if she needs anything."

Ian nods. "Thanks. We'll keep you posted."

Tyler walks me out into the hallway.

"What's with all the blankets?" I ask.

"She couldn't stop shaking. I think the weight is helping."

"Sure, like a weighted blanket. They're supposed to help with anxiety."

He nods. "This is going to take time, you know. We're taking it hour by hour."

"It's fine. I have nowhere else I need to be. When she's ready, I'll be here for her."

Tyler pats my shoulder. "I can't imagine a better bodyguard for her than you."

After Tyler disappears back into Layla's room, I pace the hallway as I process what I just saw—a beautiful, vibrant young woman reduced to a frightened shell. I'll do whatever it takes to bring her out of the darkness and back into the light where she belongs.

3

Layla Alexander

"You can trust him, Layla," Ian says as he rubs my arm through the bedding.

I'm still cold, but the extra blankets are helping.

He's lying. You can't trust anyone. They all lie.

That's not true. I trust Ian and Tyler. I trust my parents.

He'll betray you too, just like Sean did. You're so stupid.

Shut up.

Ever since I was abducted, my auditory hallucinations have been on overdrive. The voice has been at it nonstop for days—bombarding me with negativity and doom. Normally, I can block her out a lot of the time, but right now I'm exhausted.

As Tyler comes to stand behind my brother's chair, he lays his hands on Ian's shoulders. "I know Jason personally, Layla. You can trust him. I'll vouch for him myself."

Ian brushes my hair back from my face. "You know we wouldn't recommend someone to be your bodyguard unless we had full faith in him."

My gaze goes from Tyler to Ian. I never liked my previous bodyguard, Sean. I thought he was a jerk. But I never dreamed he'd betray me the way he did—sell me out to his drug dealer. Drug addiction makes people do crazy things.

And now Sean's dead. Karma got the last word on him. He was shot in front of me by his roommate and drug dealer—Chad.

That's when the real nightmare began.

As I watched Sean fall to the ground and blood begin to pool beneath his body, I started screaming. And then Sean's roommate injected me with something that made my mind float out to sea. After that, I don't have much recollection of what happened. Just bits and pieces. Flashes of memory. Mostly terror and pain. I do remember the sound of all those other girls screaming. I don't know what those men did to them, but I can imagine.

"I'm tired," I say, and then I roll onto my side to face the wall. I just don't care anymore about whether I live or die.

No one cares. You're a waste of a human being. Useless. An idiot.

Normally, I'd fend off her attacks, but I just don't have the energy.

You'd be better off dead. Your whole family would be better off. Just get it over with.

Shut up.

Ian pats my shoulder. "Okay, sis. We'll let you rest."

* * *

Darkness.

Bone-chilling cold.

Uncontrollable shaking.

And terror. So much terror.

I can't think straight. I can barely hear over the sound of the voice screaming in my head. Or maybe that's me screaming. I can't tell.

I want to disappear. Vanish. To not exist any longer, because this misery is worse than death.

I hear a loud clang, and the metal platform beneath me shudders.

"How the fuck do we shut her up?" a man says, his voice gruff and hateful.

"I don't know. Have we got any more sedatives?" another says.

"I'll get some. We've gotta do something. She's spooking the *other girls. And someone might hear her."*

"Here, use this," a third man says. "This'll shut her up."

Rough hands pry open my jaws, and a hard rubber ball is shoved into my mouth and strapped tightly in place.

I can't do more than whimper now.

I gasp for air and nearly suffocate until I relax enough that I can breathe through my nose.

"Man, it's too bad she's off-limits," the first man says. "I'd love to have me a piece of that."

I feel a hard hand grip my naked breast, squeezing painfully. Another hand slides between my legs.

I scream over and over.

"Layla!"

My eyes flash open as panic swamps me. I shoot up into a sitting position, but before I can scramble off the bed, firm hands hold me steady.

"It's okay, sis," my brother says. "You were having a nightmare."

The door to my hospital room swings open, and light from the hallway floods the room. A tall, dark figure stands in the opening, tense, poised as if ready to go to battle. He's backlit, so I can't make out his facial features. I just get an impression of a lean, muscular build.

"Is she okay?" he asks, his deep voice laced with concern.

"She had a bad dream," Tyler says as he hovers behind my brother. "She's okay."

The tension in the man's posture eases a bit. He studies me

a moment before he steps back out into the hallway and lets the door slowly close.

Jason. My new bodyguard.

He'll betray you, too. Just like Sean did.

Shut up.

You know it's true. They all do eventually.

I'm ignoring you.

You're an idiot if you think this one will be any different.

I spend a lot of wasted time arguing with the voice in my head. She's mean. Hateful. And she never lets up. It's like she knows every deep-seated fear I have and rubs my face in them.

Ian presses his palm to my forehead. I'm sweating and shaking, light-headed.

An alarm sounds on his phone, and he grabs it and looks at the screen. "Shit."

"I'll get something," Tyler says. He opens the top drawer of the cabinet beside my bed, pulls out a little carton of apple juice, opens it, and hands it to me.

A moment later, Ian's phone rings, and he answers it immediately. His gaze goes to me as he says, "Hi, Mom. Yeah, she's fine. Don't worry. We were awake when the alarm went off. She's drinking some apple juice."

Whenever my glucose monitor alarm goes off, both Ian and my mom are notified. My poor mom was probably awakened from sleep by her phone screeching at her, which means my dad was awakened too. "Tell her I'm sorry. I should have been paying better attention." I'm supposed to be checking my sugar levels regularly.

I hate worrying my parents. They both have high-pressure jobs, and I don't want to add to their stress.

After reassuring our mom that I'm okay, Ian ends the call. "Do you want anything else?" he asks me.

"No, I'm okay." I hand him the empty juice box, and he tosses it into the trashcan. "The juice should hold me over until breakfast."

"You promise you'll eat something then?"

I nod. "I promise."

After a short while, Ian checks the glucose monitor once more. "Your sugar level is starting to go up."

I notice he's wearing a pair of flannel PJ bottoms and a T-shirt. Tyler's wearing the same. I glance over at the sofa bed. "I'm sorry I woke you up."

Ian leans close to kiss the top of my head. "It's no problem. Try to go back to sleep."

Ian and Tyler return to their makeshift bed. I roll over to face the wall and close my eyes, pretending to sleep.

You're such a burden to your family.

I know.

* * *

That evening, my parents come to the hospital as soon

as they get off work, still dressed in their professional attire. They both look exhausted, and I know I'm the cause. I hate being a burden to them. I wish they'd forget about me and go do their own thing, but I know that's not an option. They'd never give up on me.

You don't deserve them.

Shut up.

Since my parents are here for a couple of hours this evening, Ian and Tyler leave to have dinner. It's become the routine—my parents take the evening shifts, babysitting me after they get off work so that Ian and Tyler can have a break. They're afraid to leave me alone because they're afraid I'll hurt myself. I'm in a psych ward at the moment. There's nothing sharp in my room. No belts or ties either. Nothing I could hurt myself with. At least I'm allowed to wear my own clothes—a pair of light gray flannel PJ bottoms and a white tank top.

You should hurt yourself. You're a complete waste of everyone's time.

Stop it.

You're dragging them all down with you. Is that what you want? You selfish idiot.

Shut up!

"How are you feeling, sweetheart?" Mom asks as she sits down in the chair beside the bed. She's dressed in a sapphire blue business suit and jacket with a tailored white blouse. Her blonde hair is shoulder-length, and she's wearing a familiar gold heart-shaped locket on a chain around her neck. In the locket are pictures of me and Ian when we were young. She's a great mom, and I hate the fact that she worries about me.

"I'm feeling better." It's not really true, but she'll feel better if I say that.

"How have your levels been today?"

"Fine." That's true for the most part. I did eat three decent meals today, even though I had zero appetite. And I ate a few snacks when my blood sugar levels dropped.

Mom already knows what my levels have been all day. She has the Dexcom app on her phone, and it shows her the history of my glucose readings around the clock.

"When does your pump need to be changed?" she asks.

"Not until tomorrow." I wear an Omnipod insulin pump. It usually lasts two to three days before I have to replace it.

"Make sure you're eating well and checking your glucose level regularly." She glances at my dinner tray, which is sitting on the bedside table.

I forced myself to eat most of it.

She reaches out and brushes my hair out of my eyes. "I'll be so glad when you're home. It'll be easier to monitor what you're eating."

I'm a type 1 diabetic, have been since I was a baby. It's why my birth parents put me up for adoption They were still in high school when they got pregnant with me, and apparently they didn't feel like they could handle my medical needs. I guess no one in my birth mom's family did either. All I know about my dad was that he was a foreign exchange student—I don't even know what country he was from. I doubt his family even knew I existed.

I went into state custody, and eventually I ended up with the Alexanders. They were experienced with at-risk adoptions. They already had a son, Ian, who came from a situation of severe abuse and neglect.

And somehow, piecing together all of us with our different medical and emotional needs and past traumas, my parents formed a loving, supportive family.

I love my *family*. I just feel bad that they're saddled with me and all my baggage. The diabetes is bad enough, but it's doable. We've gotten really good at managing it over the years. But the voice… the auditory hallucinations… *she* complicates everything. She's inexplicable. We don't know where she came from or why she's here. Most people who have auditory hallucinations do so because of past trauma, but I've been raised from birth in a loving family. Yes, I suffer from anxiety, and yes, I have low self-esteem. And recently, I survived a horrifyingly traumatic event, but I can't point at anything from my past as a source of trauma.

She first appeared about two years ago, after I graduated high school. She came out of nowhere, her biting criticism and scathing taunts filling my head, tormenting me, making my life unbearable at times.

A lot of people hear voices. Some hear just one, most hear many. For me, it's just the one—so far at least—and she's a mean, spiteful bitch. I think of her as *the monster* who inhabits my head. She exists just to cut me down, to ridicule me. I do my best to shut her out, but she's persistent.

In the beginning, I tried drowning her out with alcohol, but that only got me into huge trouble with my parents because alcohol combined with type 1 diabetes is especially dangerous. I've tried cutting myself, but that does nothing to quell the monster. It just hurts a lot, and my family goes into a tizzy when they find out. The only thing that helps me cope is listening to music. I use music to try to drown her out. I also run on the treadmill, as if I can outrun her. That never works, of course.

I take psychiatric medication, and that does help, but it doesn't eliminate the voice completely.

I notice my Dad's not here. He's usually wherever Mom is. I tease them about being attached at the hips. "Where's Dad?"

"He's out in the hall talking to your new bodyguard. Have you met Jason yet?"

I nod. "He came in yesterday to say hello."

"What do you think?"

Honestly, I wouldn't know. "It was dark last night. I couldn't really see him."

"Your brother and Tyler went home to do laundry and grab a bite to eat. Your dad and I will be here until around ten, when Ian and Tyler should be back. I wish we could be here more, but our work schedules don't allow it. I'm just grateful Ian and Tyler's schedules are more flexible at the moment."

I feel terrible for all the trouble I'm putting my family

through. Mom and Dad are spending their only free hours here with me, and Ian and Tyler are with me the rest of the time, day and night. It's not fair to any of them.

Why do you think they hired someone to babysit you? So they don't have to do it themselves.

I hate to admit it, but she's right for a change. I should just let the new bodyguard do his job. Then my family can go back to living their lives and stop sacrificing themselves for me.

4

Jason Miller

After Ian and Tyler return around ten p.m., Layla's parents leave. I feel like a fifth wheel hanging out in the hallway. I hate that I can't do my job, but she's just not ready. I requisition a chair from a nearby waiting room and get comfortable outside her door. I want to be close in case she needs something or asks for me. So far, no one's given me any grief about it. Layla's nurses smile at me as they come and go from her room. Except for giving me a few come-hither looks and one invitation to grab coffee after her shift ends, the nurses pretty much ignore me.

Ian and Tyler are sitting with Layla now, the three of them talking quietly. I can hear the murmur of their voices, but I can't make out what they're saying. If I had to guess, I'd say they're trying to talk her into seeing me again. Or at least letting me come into her room just to say hi.

So far, no luck.

I don't blame her. Tyler gave me the unedited rundown on what he and Ian found at the warehouse where the abducted girls were being held. When the cops raided the warehouse, they discovered over a dozen young women, naked and chained to beds. Most of them had been raped repeatedly. Layla was found in a storage room, naked, beaten, and chained to a bed. Fortunately, she hadn't been sexually molested, but the reason for her good luck sends a chill down my spine. Her abductors realized she was worth more as a virgin.

Just the thought sickens me. I'll never understand how humans can do this to the more vulnerable members of society.

She'd been found wearing a ball gag. The traffickers had likely been trying to keep her quiet, as the trauma of her situation had exacerbated her mental state. The other girls, who were later interviewed extensively by the police, reported that they heard Layla screaming and yelling.

It's a miracle she survived the ordeal. She'd gone nearly twelve hours without food or insulin, and she was forcibly plied with alcohol and drugs. The poor girl had lost all touch with reality. Now she lies quietly in a hospital bed, under constant supervision.

It should be me in there with her, but we're not quite there yet.

Layla's door opens, and Tyler walks out, closing the door behind him. He gives me a nod. "Jason." He scrubs his hands over his face as he exhales a long breath.

I detect exhaustion beneath that deep, gruff voice. I don't know how much longer he and Ian can keep up this grueling schedule. "How's she doing?"

He walks across the hall and leans against the wall directly opposite me. His black hair is disheveled, and he's wearing a pair of wrinkled black trousers and a white button-up shirt, no tie. There are shadows beneath his eyes. "We're all worried. She's withdrawn and depressed. Even Ian's having trouble getting through to her, and he's her favorite person in the world." He gives me a bleak look. "You have your work cut out for you."

"That's what her dad said."

Tyler nods down the hallway. "I'm heading to the vending machine to get coffee. Do you want some?"

"No, thanks. I'm fine."

He pushes away from the wall. "If Ian asks for me, tell him I'll be right back."

Tyler returns with two cups of coffee in hand. "Go home and get some sleep. There's nothing you can do for her tonight. You're going to have to be patient and wait until she's ready."

"That's okay. I'll stay."

He shakes his head. "There's no point in you staying. Come back in the morning. Maybe things will be different then."

I hate to admit he's right. I'm no good to her without any sleep. And I know she's safe with Tyler in the room—the man's a former police detective. "Are you sure?"

He chuckles. "Get out of here. We'll see you tomorrow."

"Call me if anything changes, no matter the time."

"We will."

Reluctantly, I head back to my apartment on Lake Shore Drive in the Gold Coast. I have a two-bedroom unit in my boss's apartment building. It's nothing fancy, but it's comfortable, and it has a fantastic view of Lake Michigan. It's a typical bachelor pad, with a treadmill and a set of free weights stashed in the spare bedroom. In the living room, there's a sofa and a huge TV on the wall, a coffee table, and a bookcase. There's a small galley kitchen, a tiny pantry, and a laundry room. It's enough for me. I often work long hours, so I'm not home that often.

I'm too wired to sleep, so I hit the treadmill and run a few miles to loosen up. Then I do my reps with the free weights. Afterward, I grab a quick shower, then crash on the sofa and turn on Netflix and skim through the offerings until I find a new sci-fi series that catches my eye.

My stomach starts gnawing on itself, so I place a delivery order for sweet and sour chicken and egg rolls.

Finally, after I've eaten and watched as much TV as I can stand, I head to bed.

As usual, I put off going to bed as long as I possibly can. Even though my body is ready for rest, my mind can't shut down. To distract myself, I climb into bed and download an e-book to my phone—it's a memoir written by a woman who hears voices. I can't imagine what that's like, but I'd better find out quickly because I'm about to become responsible for the safety and well-being of someone who does.

*　*　*

I quickly fall into a pattern over the next few days. My days and evenings are spent on guard duty in the hallway outside Layla's hospital room door, leaving only on the rare occasion to visit the bathroom or grab a bite to eat in the cafeteria.

Every day, it's the same routine. Nurses come in periodically to check on her. Therapists stop in to assess how she's doing. Her parents come sit with her in the evenings from around six to ten. The rest of the time, her brother and Tyler are with her. Sometimes they take turns. Sometimes it's both of them. Every night, they sleep in her room on the sofa bed.

On the third day, after the parents have left for the night and I'm about to head back to my apartment, Ian opens the door to Layla's room and peers out at me. "You can come in." The guy looks ragged. There are distinct shadows beneath his eyes.

I jump to my feet and straighten my shirt before I follow

Ian into a dimly-lit room.

Layla's sitting up in bed, leaning on a pile of pillows propped against the headboard. The mountain of blankets is gone, replaced by just a single one. I'm guessing this is progress.

Tyler's sitting on the sofa to the right of the bed, reading on a tablet.

Ian nods toward his sister. "Layla asked to see you."

This is definitely progress. I approach the foot of the bed, slowly so I don't scare her. After all, she doesn't know me from Adam.

"Hi, Layla," I say, keeping my voice low and even.

Her gaze lifts to mine, and the force of those midnight dark eyes hits me square in the chest.

"Hi," she says. Her voice is soft and hesitant.

Her dark hair is pulled back in a ponytail, and she's dressed in her own clothes—a T-shirt with some writing on it—not in a hospital gown. I wasn't expecting that. Her face is shrouded in shadows.

Ian points to the bathroom. "If you don't mind, I'll just—"

"Sure, go ahead," I say.

Ian opens the bathroom door and flips on the light switch inside, casting light into the room. For a moment, just a split second before he closes the bathroom door, the light shines on Layla, illuminating his sister's oval face. My breath catches as I make out her features.

She's stunning—hair black as night, eyes dark as coal and framed by thick dark lashes, a perfect blade of a nose, and a beautifully-shaped, lush mouth. My chest tightens.

I try not to openly stare at someone who could pass as a real-life Disney princess. I'm going to have my work cut out for me just trying to keep the guys away from her. I imagine she gets hit on left and right on campus. And that's *before* they realize she's at the top of the list of *Forbes*' wealthiest young Americans. She and her brother are heirs to a fortune larger than the coffers of some small nations.

When Ian closes the bathroom door, we're shrouded in semi-darkness once more. I stand glued to the floor at the foot of her bed, not daring to come closer. The last thing I want to do is scare this girl. "Thanks for letting me come in."

"I really didn't have much of a choice." She sounds resigned as she stares up at me from her bed. "I suppose you already know everything about me."

"Well, some things. At least the things I need to know so I can do my job. I guess I'll learn the rest from you."

She looks away. "I'm sorry you got stuck with me."

I shove my hands in my pockets and try to act casual so I can put her at ease. "I'm not complaining."

Her lips flatten. "Give it time. You'll change your mind."

Something tells me she's got it all wrong.

5

Layla Alexander

If I ignore him, maybe he'll go away. That's what I keep telling myself. He's going to start asking questions soon—they always do—and I don't want to answer them. I don't even want to talk about it. Not any of it. Not Sean, not the kidnappers. Not even my hallucinations.

In the past week, my mind has been ripped apart, and I feel like I'm bleeding out. I'm holding on by my fingertips to what little sanity I have left. I'm afraid if I let go, I'll be lost.

You're already lost.

I'm not. I'm holding on.

No, you're drowning in self pity. Do you really think this new guy will make a difference? Grow up. You're such an idiot.

Stop it!

When Ian steps out of the bathroom, light infiltrates my dark room once more, giving me another brief glimpse of my new bodyguard. I glimpse a handsome face, short dark hair, and a neat, trim beard. He's tall with lean, cut muscles. His arms and chest are muscular, and I imagine the rest of him is too. Clearly, he works out.

Jason looks to be about Ian's age—late twenties. The sleeves of his white shirt are rolled up almost to his elbows, exposing sinewy forearms that are heavily inked. He's wearing a chunky silver watch on his left wrist.

When he said hello, his calm, masculine voice sent a shiver down my spine.

He thinks you're pathetic. A mental case.

"Stop it," I snap as I look away. "You don't know that."

Jason shifts his weight on his feet. "You're not talking to me, are you?" he asks casually, as if it's no big deal I'm talking to myself. Or at least that's how it looks to the outside world. They aren't privy to the words and the conversation that goes on inside my head.

"No, sorry. I wasn't talking to you."

"Thanks for letting me come in." There's no judgment in his tone. Just a quiet acceptance of the fact I've kept him waiting out in the hallway like a servant for days. "I've been looking forward to getting to know you."

He's lying. You idiot.

I'm tempted to turn the lights up so I can see him better, but if I do, he'll see the bruises on my face and neck. I look away as shame heats my cheeks. *He knows what those men did to me.*

Jason seems perfectly relaxed, which is the opposite of Sean, who used to fidget constantly. Probably because he was frustrated with me all the time. Or bored.

Or disgusted. That's probably why he sold you to his drug dealer. Because you disgusted him.

"Shut up," I say, immediately regretting it. Usually I don't reply aloud to the monster that inhabits my head, but right now my reserves are low, and she's getting to me more easily than usual.

The room is so quiet you could hear a pin drop. I watch as my brother drifts over to the sofa to sit with Tyler. They both look haggard. I don't think they've had a good night's sleep since I've been here. The only time they leave me is when my parents are with me.

They think you're going to kill yourself.

Shut up.

You should do it. It would make everyone's life so much easier.

I said, shut up!

Jason comes around to the side of my bed and nods to the empty chair. "Mind if I sit?"

I shrug. "Suit yourself."

After he takes a seat, he nods toward Tyler and Ian. Lowering his voice, he says, "Those two look beat. How 'bout we let them go home and get some sleep? I'll stay with you tonight."

He said *we* so easily, as if it was second nature. As if *we* are a team. He's right, though. They're exhausted, and it's because of me.

It's your fault. Isn't everything?

I want desperately to tell him no, but that would be selfish. After everything Ian and Tyler have done for me, I owe them. "Okay."

Jason nods. "You heard her, guys," he says to my brother and his boyfriend. "Take off. Go get some sleep. We'll be fine."

Ian and Tyler study me closely, probably watching to see how I handle the idea of Jason staying with me instead of them. After everything they've been through, they're still worried about me. "Yeah, guys. Go on home. I'll be fine."

Ian gets up and approaches my bed. "Are you sure, sis?"

I sigh. No, not really. But what choice do I have? "Yeah, I'm sure."

Tyler joins Ian at the side of my bed. "We're just a phone call away." His deep voice is rough from exhaustion. "No matter the time, call if you want us, okay?"

"I will." I caught that he said if I *wanted* them, and not just if I *needed* them. There's a difference. Ian's always been here for me, since we were little kids. Now Tyler is too. I didn't expect that when they first got together. I was afraid Tyler would pull Ian away from me, but he hasn't. It's been quite the opposite. I didn't lose a brother; I gained one. "Thanks, guys." I paste a smile on my face as I try to hide the panic I feel at the thought of them leaving me here with a practical stranger.

Ian doesn't look convinced that I'm okay with them leaving. He leans in to kiss my cheek. "We mean it. Call and we'll come running."

"Thanks."

Jason walks them to the door, and the three of them stand out in the hallway to have a quiet conversation

They're talking about you.

Yeah, I know that.

Jason probably wants to quit.

No, he doesn't.

At least I hope he doesn't want to quit. The only way my family will get any kind of break from babysitting me is if I have a new bodyguard.

A few minutes later, Jason comes back into the room and closes the door before returning to sit by my bed. "Do you feel like talking for a bit?"

I shrug. "What about?" My stomach clenches tightly, souring as I contemplate being forced to reveal my darkest secrets to him.

He returns my shrug, perfectly at ease. He's so laid back. "I don't know. Whatever you want to talk about. We're going to be spending a lot of time together, so I think it'd be a good idea for us to get to know each other better. I'll go first." He pauses a moment as if collecting his thoughts. "I like classic rock and sci-fi movies. My favorite food is steak, but pizza is a close second. My favorite flavor of ice cream is chocolate. I drive a black Dodge Challenger. What about you?"

"A Dodge Challenger? That's very old school. You like muscle cars."

He grins. "Guilty. Now it's your turn."

I'm swamped with relief. He's not asking for anything hard. "Um, my tastes in music are pretty eclectic, but I have a soft spot for singer/songwriters from the seventies, like Carole King and James Taylor. I guess that kind of makes me old school, too. My favorite food is Mexican—I think Taco Tuesday should be a national holiday—but I'm with you on pizza. My favorite ice cream flavor is Neapolitan, but I have to be careful with ice cream. It sends my blood sugar levels through the roof. I'm a type 1 diabetic—a T1D—but you probably already know that."

He nods. "I do. But that's cheating."

"What is?"

"Picking Neapolitan as your favorite flavor. That's not just one flavor—technically it's three. You're getting chocolate, vanilla, and strawberry all in one. I call cheating."

I try not to smile. "Okay, then. Strawberry. But it has to be real strawberry, not fake."

"That's better. I like sci-fi and paranormal shows, like *The Twilight Zone* or *Supernatural*."

"See? You're old school. You probably prefer the original *Star Wars* movies over the newer ones."

He nods. "Yep. Guilty. What about you?"

"I like paranormal shows too, and superheroes. And medical shows, like *Grey's Anatomy*. My favorite TV series of all time is probably *Stranger Things*. I could relate to Eleven—being different, feeling out of place, like she didn't belong."

He nods. "Good one. I could have said *Stranger Things*, too"

He's so easy to talk to, not at all what I expected. Sean was always trying to show off, to impress me, or make me feel stupid. Jason's pretty chill, and I don't feel like he's judging me.

"Do you want to tell me about your insulin pump and glucose monitor?" he asks.

"I have an Omnipod." I lay my hand on my torso, to the right of my belly button, where my insulin pump is currently located. Then I point to the left side of my belly. "The Dexcom monitor is here."

He frowns. "I know your kidnappers removed your pod and glucose monitor." His voice is quiet, gentle. "I'm so sorry, Layla."

I shrug. "They probably didn't even know what the devices were for."

"And they didn't give you any food or water?"

I shake my head. "They forced me to drink alcohol, and they shot me up with drugs. Mostly sedatives, I think. To shut me up."

"God, they could have killed you."

"When the EMTs arrived, my sugar levels were dangerously low. They injected me with glucagon to raise my blood sugar level."

"As your bodyguard, I'll be monitoring your glucose levels." He pulls out his phone and shows me the Dexcom app. "I'm already set up to access your glucose monitor. I might as well get into the habit, right?"

"Sure."

The corners of his lips quirk up. "Please don't sound so enthusiastic."

An unexpected snort escapes me as I'm caught off guard by his droll sense of humor. I've only talked to the guy for half an hour, and he's already got me laughing. That's a surprise.

Is it wishful thinking on my part to wonder if my new bodyguard might not be so bad after all?

Yes, you idiot.

You shut up.

6

Jason Miller

Once Layla's sound asleep, I slip out of her room so I can phone Ian from the hallway. He made me promise to call him as soon as I got a chance.

He answers on the second ring, his voice drowsy. "Hey, Jason." He yawns. "Is everything all right?"

"Yes. Sorry. Did I wake you?"

"No, I was up waiting for your call."

"She's fine. She's sleeping."

He lets out a relieved sigh. "I'm so glad to hear that." Then I hear him whisper to Tyler, "Jason said she's okay. She's sleeping."

I hear the rustling of fabric. "Did I catch you at a bad time?"

"No. Perfect timing, actually. We're just getting into bed. I'm putting the call on speaker so Tyler can hear, too." He pauses for a moment. "She's still having nightmares and wakes up screaming, so be prepared. You know she witnessed the drug dealer shoot and kill Sean. She was drugged after that, so the rest is pretty much a blur. She remembers just bits and pieces of being held captive in the warehouse, but it all jumbles together. It's the stuff of nightmares, you know? Girls screaming, crying, begging. Layla was beaten repeatedly. She doesn't remember a lot of it, but she has the bruises and cuts on her body to show for it."

"I saw some of the bruises." My stomach knots when I think about the bruises around her neck. They look like they were made by someone choking her. "Thanks for the heads-up. I'll keep a close eye on her. You guys need to relax and get some sleep."

"Thanks, Jason," Tyler says. "Good luck tonight."

"No need to thank me." I feel honored to be the one chosen to protect this girl. I'll gladly be her guard dog. I won't let anyone hurt her ever again.

Just before ending the call, Ian throws out one more useful tidbit. "She keeps her phone and earbuds on the bedside table. Listening to music is one of her best coping mechanisms. If things get bad, turn on the music and put her earbuds in her ears."

After the call, I slip back into Layla's room to check on her, and I'm relieved to find she's still sleeping soundly. I head into the bathroom, leaving the door ajar so I can monitor her, and get ready for bed. I usually take a shower at night, but I decide to skip it. If she calls for me, I want to be sure I hear her.

Once back in the room, I make up the sofa bed. I've got my duffle bag with me, containing a few changes of clothes and toiletries. After changing into a pair of shorts and a T-shirt, I try to get comfortable on the mattress. This thing is rock hard, and I can feel springs poking me. I don't know how Tyler and Ian stood it for so many nights. I guess now it's my turn. Oh, well, I've slept in worse places.

As usual, sleep eludes me. My senses are focused on Layla who's sleeping ten feet from me. I'm hyperaware of her every movement, every breath and sigh, every rustle of the sheets as she changes position.

I often get like this on a new assignment, edgy and restless until I get a good read on my new client. Until I learn their habits inside and out, their likes and dislikes. What scares them. What worries them. This is the first time I've had a client who suffers from auditory hallucinations. I've been doing my research, reading everything I can find about the condition, from medical textbooks to science journals to firsthand accounts written by people who suffer from the condition.

Layla hears a *mean girl* voice. That's how she describes it.

I can't imagine what it's like to have a hateful, demeaning voice in your head day and night, tearing you down constantly, criticizing you. That's got to be hard on anyone, but especially on a young woman. Layla's just twenty-one. She's at a vulnerable age when people are trying to discover who they are and find their place in the world. Hearing voices that tear you down day after day doesn't make that easy.

After lying here for an hour and still unable to sleep, I open up the Kindle app on my phone and resume reading. If I'm going to help Layla, I need to learn everything I can about her condition.

Just as my eyelids start to grow heavy, and I'm thinking about putting away my phone, I hear a quiet sound. I lay my device down and listen.

Layla's breathing rate has picked up.

I sit up and watch the rise and fall of her chest. She rolls to her side, facing away from me, then she promptly rolls back. Her hands are restless, fidgeting. She makes a pained sound, a whimper.

She's having a nightmare.

I can relate. I have my own share of nightmares, but for a very different reason. Just as I rise from the sofa, she clutches her throat, grasping and pulling at something that's not there. She's actively struggling now, her body thrashing beneath the bedding.

I'm at her side a moment later, and I have to use considerable strength to pry her clawing fingers from her throat.

Layla screams as she sits up. She's panting, frantic. I reach over to switch on the light so I can see her better. Her dark eyes are wide with terror, and she's seeing something that's not there, something from the dark recesses of a nightmare.

I hold her hands securely in mine to keep her from hurting herself further. "It's okay, Layla. You're safe."

She blinks several times before focusing her frantic gaze on me. "What? Where—"

"You're in the hospital. You're safe."

It's only then that I get a really good look at her neck. The column of her throat is entirely ringed with bruises.

"I couldn't breathe," she says, sounding a bit dazed. She pulls her hands free and touches her throat, searching gently. "It still hurts."

"Someone choked you." I read it in the police report.

She nods. "I remember him the most. He liked it. He laughed when I choked and gagged."

My chest burns, and I see red. I'd give anything to get my hands on whoever did that to her. I'd like to see how he fares when the tables are turned and someone's choking him.

Layla snaps her head to face the wall, and she stares into space, suddenly distracted. When she shakes her head, I see glittering tears in her dark eyes.

"No," she hisses. She shakes her head vehemently. "No."

I know she's not talking to me. "What'd she say to you?"

Layla turns her startled gaze to me. "She said he should have choked me to death. Put me out of my misery and everyone else's."

On impulse, I reach for her hand. "She's wrong. Don't listen to her."

Layla looks skeptical. "You—" She falters.

"I what?"

"You believe me? You believe I hear the voice?"

"Of course I do."

She shakes her head. "Most people think I'm crazy. They think I'm making it up or imagining it."

I squeeze her hand. "You hear it. That's all that matters. The rest of us can't, so it's hard for us to relate." Her fingers are soft and warm in my grasp. I shouldn't be touching her—it's inappropriate—so I release her hand. "Sorry, I shouldn't have done that."

She gives me a small smile. "It's okay."

"Do you want to talk about your nightmare?"

She shakes her head. "Not really."

"Maybe it would help."

She laughs. "You sound just like Dr. Hartigan, my psychiatrist."

"Well, your psychiatrist is right. It does help to talk about the things that scare us the most."

"It was awful." Her voice cracks as she looks away.

I'm not sure if she's referring to the nightmare or her abduction. She's shaking now. When she lies back down, I cover her with the blankets and tuck her in. "You experienced something pretty awful, Layla."

"Yes, but it was my own fault."

"Why do you say that? None of it was your fault."

"Sean's dead because of me."

"No. Your former bodyguard got himself into trouble with his roommate, and it got him killed. That had absolutely nothing to do with you. And as for the abduction, for god's sake, that wasn't your fault. Human traffickers are human scum, and I hope they all rot in jail. You know, it's because Ian and Tyler found *you* that all those other girls were rescued too. So, when you think about it, you were responsible for saving all those young women."

"I never saw any of the other girls. I only heard their screams. I still hear them in my nightmares."

The pain and despair in her voice breaks my heart. "I'll never let anyone hurt you again. I promise."

She laughs bitterly. "Sean was supposed to protect me, and look how that turned out."

"I'm not Sean. And I won't let you down. Sean was controlled by his drug habit, and he made bad decisions because of it. I assure you, that won't happen with me."

Gradually, her shaking stops.

I pull out my phone and check her blood sugar level. On impulse, I reach out to brush her hair back from her face. "Try to sleep, okay?"

She nods. "Goodnight." When I return to my makeshift bed on the sofa, she says, "Thanks, Jason."

It's the first time she's used my name. I think we're making progress. "You're welcome, Layla. Goodnight."

7

Layla Alexander

The next morning, when I come out of the bathroom, I find a breakfast tray waiting for me on the table beside my bed. Jason's sitting on the sofa by the window, reading on his phone.

"Good morning," he says with a sleepy smile.

While I was in the bathroom, he changed into a pair of blue jeans, a long-sleeved black T-shirt, and a pair of running shoes. I'm bummed because I can't see his tattoos now.

I pick up the slice of wheat toast on the breakfast tray, take a bite, and make a face. It's dry, but I force it down anyway, along with the rest of my breakfast—cold scrambled eggs, diced fruit, and a cup of black coffee. I mentally calculate how many grams of carbohydrates I'm about to eat and enter the number into my pod. Over the years, I've gotten really good at counting carbs, and I do a pretty decent job of regulating my blood sugar.

I glance around this dreary hospital room and sigh. I miss my own bed, my TV, and my computer. I should be at home doing schoolwork. I've already missed over a week of the semester. "I really want to go home."

Jason lays his phone down. "My understanding is you can go home as soon as your psychiatrist gives the okay."

I nod. "I have an appointment with Dr. Hartigan this morning. If I can convince her I'm doing okay, she'll release me. I just want to get back to normal—well, as normal as I can be." I laugh. "That's not saying much."

There's a knock on my door, and Jason rises from the sofa and heads toward the door. "We all have our own version of normal, Layla. And we all have struggles. You're no different." He opens the door and steps aside to let my parents enter. I realize it's Saturday, and they don't have to work today.

"Hello, darling," Mom says as she comes over to hug me. "Did you sleep well?" She gently brushes my cheek. "You look rested."

"I did," I say, lying through my teeth. I give her a well-practiced smile. "I slept great."

I meet Jason's eyes, but he says nothing to contradict me

in front of my parents. I had two more nightmares last night, and with each one I woke up frantic and agitated. And each time, he talked me off the ledge. I don't think either one of us got more than a few hours of sleep last night.

"Good morning, Jason," Mom says to him. "I talked to Ian, and he told me you stayed with Layla last night." She smiles, clearly pleased by the news. "I'm so glad."

"Hello, sweetheart," my dad says as he leans down and kisses my forehead. "Are you ready for your appointment with Dr. Hartigan this morning?"

I suspect they're both anxious to find out what my shrink thinks about how I'm coping. "Yes. It's at ten." But I have a suspicion my parents already knew that.

"How lucky," Mom says as she checks the clock. "We're here just in time."

My parents never leave anything to chance. I know they timed their arrival with my psych evaluation. I'm sure they want to speak to Dr. Hartigan after she sees me.

I sit on the side of my bed. Mom joins me, leaning close so that our shoulders are touching. "How's it working out with Jason?" she asks quietly.

My dad is across the room having a conversation with my new bodyguard.

"He seems nice."

Mom frowns. "If you don't like him, honey, we'll—"

"No. That's not necessary. I like him just fine."

She purses her lips in thought, as if she's trying to decide if

I'm being truthful.

"Really, Mom. I like him."

"Okay. If you're sure."

"I am. I'm hoping Dr. Hartigan approves my release today. I want to start back to school on Monday." I've already missed over a week of classes.

"Honey, don't you think you should wait a while before you go back? Give yourself some more time?"

"But the more classes I miss, the more I'll have to make up."

"I know. But you can do your schoolwork from home, right? I'm sure your professors will work with you." She brushes her thumb gently across my cheek. "There are still so many bruises, honey. People are going to hound you more than ever with questions about everything from Sean to the abduction. I'm sure the university will agree to give you more time to recover."

She's right. I'm not ready to face any of that.

At ten that morning, Dr. Hartigan stops by my room. There's a lot riding on this assessment. I'm desperately hoping she'll approve my release.

She greets my parents and says hello to Jason. "You must be Layla's new bodyguard."

Jason nods. "Pleased to meet you." As he's following my parents out the door, he pauses to look back at me. "I'll be right out here if you need me. Just holler."

Dr. Hartigan takes the seat beside my bed. I like her. She's always been nice to me, nonjudgmental, but I still hate having to answer so many questions. *How am I doing? What is the voice saying? Is she telling me to hurt myself or someone else?*

That's what I hate the most—the idea that I would hurt someone. I would never do that.

Of course you would. You're crazy.

"So, what do you think of your new bodyguard?" Dr. Hartigan asks.

"He seems nice."

"Your parents seem to like him. Are you ready to let a new bodyguard into your life?"

I nod. "Sure." After all, that's what this meeting is about. They—she and my parents—want to know if I'm ready to trust someone new.

I can't be just a normal girl, living a normal life. So many things conspire against me—my diabetes, the monster in my head, and the fact that my bank account has more money in it than most people can comprehend. Even I can't wrap my mind around it.

Ian and I each inherited an enormous fortune from our paternal grandfather, who got rich by starting a telecommunications company in the early twentieth century. All that money makes me the target of unscrupulous people and brings me so much unwanted notoriety.

I'm famous for no good reason. I'm hounded by photographers looking to make a buck by getting candid photos of me. People sneak selfies with me and post the shots on social media.

People act like they want to be my friend, when usually they just want what they think I can give them.

Dr. Hartigan opens her notebook and makes a notation. "How are you doing?"

"I think I'm doing pretty well, all things considered."

"How's the voice?"

"It's about the same." It's not, but if I tell her the truth, she's likely to keep me here longer, and I just want to go home.

"Have you been taking your medication?"

"Yes."

"Is the voice saying anything different?"

"No, not really." *Yes, sometimes.*

"How are your coping mechanisms working?"

"Back to normal, I'd say."

"I'm glad to hear that." She makes more notations. "What about the nightmares? Are you still having them?"

"I had one last night." *Actually three, but who's counting?*

"What was it about?"

My heart starts pounding. "A man was choking me. I couldn't breathe."

"That pertains to the abduction, doesn't it?"

"Yes."

Her lips flatten into a line. "What happened last night, after the nightmare?"

"Jason woke me."

"I'm glad he was there for you. Were you able to go back to

sleep?"

I nod. "I did. I felt... safe... knowing he was in the room with me."

She writes something in the notebook. "I'm glad you feel safe with him. That's a very healthy attitude, Layla. Yes, Sean turned out to be untrustworthy, but not everyone is like that. I assure you, there are good people in the world."

"Are you going to approve my release? I really want to go home."

"Do you think you're ready?"

"Yes. Definitely."

No, you're not. You're crazy. You belong here.

Stop it.

I paste a smile on my face. *I'm fine. Perfectly fine.*

You're not fooling anyone. You're a nutjob.

Dr. Hartigan asks me a few more questions about how my parents are doing, how Ian's doing. The usual. Then she says, "Yes, I think it's okay for you to resume your normal activities, including school."

Relief rushes through me. "Thank you."

"No problem."

I give it a week before you're back in the psych ward.

As soon as Dr Hartigan closes her notebook and stands, I know our session is over.

"It was good to see you," I tell her, doing my best to sound normal.

"It was good to see you, too. Good luck with school. I'll see you next week in my office for your regular visit."

As soon as she's gone, the door opens and Jason walks back in. "How'd it go?"

I smile, feeling hopeful for the first time in days. "She's releasing me. I can go home."

Home.

Jason's going to come live with me at my parents' house. That seems unexpectedly appealing. I've always hated having bodyguards living with us, but it feels different this time. I don't think it will be so bad having Jason around.

The poor guy will be miserable living with you. You're so stupid. Such a loser.

Shut up.

But nothing she says right now is going to bring me down. I'm going home. I'm going to resume my life and try to be as normal as I can.

And I have a new bodyguard who isn't a jerk. I'm kind of looking forward to getting to know him better. It sounds like we have a lot in common.

He hates you.

8

Jason Miller

"That's your *house?*" I ask, stunned. The imposing white stone structure in front of us takes up an entire city block.

Layla smiles. "Home sweet home. It is rather large, but I grew up here, so I guess I'm used to it."

"How did you not get lost in there?"

"A lot of it is closed off," she says. "We mostly use the south end of the building, which is where the main living areas are located."

The stately old building is easily early twentieth century.

From the exterior, it looks more like an art museum than a private residence. And I'd be willing to bet my next paycheck that the interior does as well. Where I come from, born and raised in the middle-class neighborhood of Rogers Park, twenty families could easily live in this space.

After Layla's psychiatrist released her from the hospital, we packed up her few belongings in a fancy designer suitcase that her mother left for her. Her suitcase is in the trunk of my car, alongside my old Army duffle bag, which holds a few days' worth of clothes, some books, my laptop, tablet, and toiletries. This is the first time I've had a full-time live-in assignment, and I didn't know what to bring with me.

This is going to take some getting used to.

At least I won't get bored. Ian told me there's a fully-equipped home gym here at the house, as well as a home theater. I'm a movie buff, so that's promising. With working out in the gym, watching movies, and reading, I should be able to keep myself plenty occupied during downtime. If I need to leave for any reason, I can request a temp to fill in for me. Miguel Rodriguez, who's also a friend of Ian's, is on standby as a backup for me since he's already met Layla. She knows him, and she's comfortable with him.

As I cruise slowly past the house, Layla points straight ahead. "Drive to the end of the block, turn right, and then continue around to the back. There's plenty of parking in the rear for family and staff."

Staff? Jesus. Well, of course they have staff. The family is obscenely wealthy. I doubt they do their own laundry or cook their own food.

The back of the building is just as impressive as the front. There's a six-car garage back here, along with a small parking lot. I slip my black Dodge Challenger into a spot next to a cherry red Fiat—Layla's car. There's also a separate structure back here that appears to be a four-unit apartment building.

"What's that?" I ask, pointing.

"Those are the staff apartments. Margaret lives in one—she's our housekeeper. Charles, the butler, lives in another, as does Claire. She's our chef's assistant."

A housekeeper, a butler, and a chef. I've definitely moved up in the world.

As soon as I turn off the engine, Layla opens her door and hops out. I grab her suitcase from the trunk, as well as my duffle bag. "I guess I'll be staying in the fourth apartment," I say as I nod toward the smaller brick building.

She shakes her head. "No, you'll be staying in the house."

That's a bit of a surprise.

She heads for the back door. "Come on, I'll show you."

I follow her through a door that leads into a huge kitchen. There are three uniformed people working in here. An older man wearing a white chef's coat stands at the stove stirring something in a huge stainless-steel pot, while a young blonde woman is cutting up veggies on a butcher block counter. A silver-haired woman wearing a gray dress with a white apron is seated at a long wooden table, apparently doing paperwork.

Whatever's in that pot smells amazing. My stomach growls.

"Layla!" cries the older lady as she jumps up from the table and rushes toward us. She gingerly wraps her arms around Layla, as if she knows to be careful of her bruises. "I'm so glad you're home. We've all been terribly worried."

Layla returns the woman's hug. "Thanks, Margaret. It's good to be home."

Margaret steps back so she can get a good look at Layla's face. Here in the bright daylight, the bruises are far more visible. "Are you all right, dear?"

Layla puts on a brave face. "Yes, I'm doing well." Then she turns to me. "Margaret, this is Jason, my new bodyguard."

The woman scans me from head to toe, her sharp gaze assessing me critically. I get the feeling I'd better be on her good side.

"Margaret runs this house," Layla explains.

The housekeeper extends her hand to me, and we shake. Her grip is strong.

Yeah, she's definitely in charge here.

"Welcome, Jason," Margaret says. "We're happy to have you join the household. If there's anything you need, just let me know." She glances down at my old duffle bag. "Do you have luggage that needs to be brought in?"

"No, ma'am. I didn't bring much with me."

"Very well." She looks to Layla. "Are you hungry, dear? Dinner won't be served for another couple of hours. You've had lunch, I presume."

Layla frowns. "If you can call it that."

I choke back a laugh. "Layla wasn't too fond of the hospital food."

Margaret nods. "I'm not surprised. Not when she's used to André's excellent cooking." The woman nods toward the man standing at the stove. "Layla's parents recruited André all the way from Paris. Needless to say, he's a phenomenal chef. You'll be spoiled in no time, like the rest of us."

André smiles warmly at Layla. "Welcome home, miss," he says in faintly accented English. Then he tips his head to me. "And welcome to you, sir. We're glad to have you." He nods toward the young blonde woman chopping vegetables. "This is my assistant, Claire."

I'd put the man in his late fifties. He has a kind face, short light-brown hair and beard, both liberally threaded with silver, and blue eyes.

Margaret claps her hands once. "All right, then. Layla, why don't you show Jason to his room so he can settle in? If you need a snack before dinner, come back to the kitchen." Then she looks at me. "Dinner is served at six in the informal dining room. I'll have someone deliver your things to your rooms."

"Thanks, but that's okay," I say as I reach for the handle of Layla's suitcase and my bag. "I've got it."

"This way," Layla says as she heads toward a door that leads out of the kitchen into a long hallway.

Sure enough, the inside of the building is just as impressive as the outside. It's like something you'd see in an issue of *Architectural Digest*. Underneath our feet is a long burgundy floral runner, thick and plush, which lays over top dark, polished wood floors. Above our heads, hanging from a high ceiling, are crystal chandeliers lighting the way. The walls are decorated with ornately-framed paintings and mirrors, and there's the occasional marble statue sitting on a pedestal.

I follow Layla to the foyer, which is dominated by an impressive curved staircase leading up to the second floor. The stairwell showcases family photographs depicting the parents with their children at various ages. I stop at a photograph of Layla as a toddler, wearing a pale pink party dress and a child-size tiara. It must have been her birthday because she's holding the string of a helium balloon featuring a cupcake with a candle on it. Her dark eyes dominate her sweet face, and her mouth is a perfect little pink bow. She's adorable.

Once we reach the second floor, Layla turns to the right. We walk a few dozen yards before she stops in front of a white six-paneled door that is distinguished by the presence of a purple and white unicorn sticker. Beneath the sticker is a child's homemade nameplate featuring cut-out letters colored with bright markers: L A Y L A. I can't help smiling when I see it.

She gestures sheepishly to the child's artwork. "Obviously, this is my room."

"At least I won't have trouble finding you."

She laughs. "That's exactly why I made the sign when I was five—so I could find my own room. I guess I should have taken it down long ago, but I'm kinda sentimental." She points across the hall. "That was Ian's room when he lived at home. He now has his own house not too far away in the Gold Coast." Then she points to the door next to hers. "That's your room."

I glance down the long hallway, in both directions, seeing door after door. Good god, how many bedrooms are in this place? "Where do your parents sleep?"

Layla points to a room we passed earlier—one closer to the staircase. "I think they chose that room so they could monitor Ian at night. He had a habit of sneaking out of the house when the rest of us were in bed. He was a bit of a rebel."

Her parents seem like caring people, but I'm starting to wonder if maybe they're a little too protective of their daughter. I guess I can't blame them. Layla has a lot going against her.

She opens her bedroom door and walks into the room, flipping on a light switch. An ornate chandelier fills the room with light, rainbows of color streaming out of a multitude of small crystal pendants. The room, huge by any standard, is dominated by a white four-poster canopy bed along the back wall, flanked on both sides by massive floor-to-ceiling windows. The bedding is lavender, and the mountain of pillows are a mix of white, lavender, and pale green. It's a feminine room, a typical teenage girl's bedroom. I'm surprised there aren't posters of movie stars on the walls.

The rest of the bedroom furniture—a dresser, chest, and

nightstands—is white with gold knobs. There's a freestanding mirror in one corner of the room, a computer desk, and numerous bookcases. A burgundy University of Chicago banner hangs above the computer workstation.

There's a massive TV hanging above the stone hearth. A sofa sits at the foot of the bed, facing the TV. There's even a mini fridge in here, and a microwave. One door opens to a walk-in closet, and another door leads to her private bathroom.

Layla surveys her room critically. "I guess it hasn't changed much since I was in high school."

"It looks very comfortable," I assure her.

"Come on, I'll show you to your room."

I leave her suitcase near her closet, then follow her out into the hallway to the next room over. Pushing the door open wide, she motions for me to enter first. This room is equally large, big enough for four bedrooms if you ask me. The color scheme here is more muted—blues and browns. It's got a masculine vibe. Besides the king-size bed and matching mahogany dresser, there's a computer desk, bookcases, a TV, a fireplace, and a sofa. This room is also equipped with a mini fridge and a microwave. I guess it would be a long hike to the kitchen if I wanted something cold to drink in the night.

"This house didn't always have central heating," she explains as I eye the hearth. "When my grandfather was young, they used to heat the rooms with fire. I'll let you—" She stops midsentence and looks away, as if she's listening to something

I can't hear. I imagine it's the voice in her head. A moment later, she seems to snap out of it and picks up right where she left off. "I'll let you get settled in. If you need any changes to your room, just ask Margaret." Then she heads for the door.

"Layla, wait."

She stops and turns back to me.

"This place is big enough to get lost in. Why don't we exchange phone numbers, so I can text you." I pull out my phone. "What's your number?"

She rattles off her number, which I add to my contacts list. "I'll text you so you have my number, too."

"Sure." She nods, but then she looks away again and shakes her head. When she snaps back to me, she smiles apologetically. "Sorry. I'll see you at dinner. We eat in the informal dining room."

I grin. "You have more than one dining room?"

"Well, yeah. A formal one for entertaining, an informal one for family meals, and the big table in the kitchen, which is where the staff eat. It's also where I eat breakfast and lunch, if I'm at home."

"How about I stop by your room a few minutes before six? That way you can show me where this informal dining room is. I'd hate to get lost my first day here."

She cracks a tiny smile, displaying a hint of dimples. "Okay."

And then she's gone, leaving me to my own devices in a very large and very quiet room that's half the size of my entire apartment.

After acquainting myself with my new bedroom—which feels more like a guest suite in a Ritz-Carlton Hotel than a bedroom—I unpack the few belongings I brought with me and hang up my clothes in the large walk-in closet.

My phone chimes with an incoming message from Ian.

Ian: How's she doing?

I message him back, assuring him his sister seems to be doing well.

Ian: Keep me posted. Tyler and I are coming for dinner tonight.

The next couple of hours pass slowly, and I'm restless. I spend some time reading more about auditory hallucinations. This particular woman's story is pretty hopeful because after years of hearing voices, she's come to terms with them and has learned to work *with* them, instead of constantly fighting against them.

I watch a little baseball on TV. Then I get up and pace the room, stopping at one large window, then another, to survey the street. It's clearly an old-money neighborhood, consisting of huge private residences and expensive cars parked out front.

Since I haven't heard a peep out of Layla in quite a while, I send her a text just to say hi and ask how she's doing. I don't have a good feel yet for her mental state, so I don't know what's normal behavior for her and what's not.

When I get no response, I text her again.

Jason: Hey, what's up?

Still nothing.

Instinct has me exiting my bedroom and knocking on her door. After still getting no response, I knock again, louder this time. I suppose it's possible she left her room, maybe went back downstairs, and I just didn't hear her leave. But I can't help the feeling of unease I have.

I try knocking again, but when she still doesn't answer, I turn the knob and slowly open her door just enough that I can poke my head inside. "Layla?"

When I scan her room and don't see her, my pulse kicks up. What could have happened? I didn't hear her leave the room. Her phone is lying on the bed.

Suddenly, her bathroom door opens, and she walks out wearing nothing but a lacey pink bra and matching underwear. I get an eyeful of skin and long, supple limbs. Also a ton of bruises. She has her earbuds in, which explains why she didn't hear me knock.

Shit!

My heart thuds in my chest as I quietly shut her door before she notices me. Okay, that didn't go as planned. I definitely jumped the gun.

I return to my room, and a moment later, my phone chimes with an incoming message.

Layla: Sorry. I was in the shower. Didn't see your message. You ready to go down to dinner? I'll be dressed in a sec.

Jason: Sure. Come get me when you're ready.

As I sit on the sofa in my room and wait for her, I try not

to think about those curves I just saw. It was inappropriate as hell for me to walk in on her. While I'm trying to come up with a better way to handle a situation like that in the future, I hear a knock at my door. "Come in."

The door opens, and Layla steps inside. "Ready?"

My breath catches.

Holy crap.

I thought she was gorgeous before, but now she's stunning. It's her eyes. She's got a bit of eye make-up on, not a lot, just subtle shadows and eyeliner framing her large dark eyes, making them utterly mesmerizing. Her lips are pinker, glossier. And her hair—she put part of it up in a high ponytail, and left part of it down. She's wearing a dark purple tunic dress that hugs her curves, black leggings, and short black boots.

"Wow." The word slips out before I can engage a filter.

As she smiles, color blooms in her soft cheeks. "Thanks."

Then I attempt to do some damage control. "I mean... you clean up well." I glance down at my faded jeans and T-shirt. "Do I need to change for dinner? Am I underdressed? Maybe I should put on a velvet dinner jacket."

She laughs. "No. Dinners are informal. It's come as you are. You're fine."

I pretend to be relieved. "Good, because I left my formalwear back at my apartment." Actually, I don't even own a decent suit. I have an old one that dates back to high school, but I doubt it fits me anymore. I'm a hell of a lot more muscular now than I was then.

As we head for the stairs, I calculate how long it's been since she last ate—she had a snack right before we left the hospital at two-thirty. I pull out my phone and quickly check her blood sugar level. It's a bit low, but nothing crazy. It's definitely time for her to eat something. I'm not used to monitoring eating times so carefully; this will take some getting used to.

I walk with her down the carpeted steps to the foyer, with its black-and-white checkerboard floor.

Too rich for my blood.

Layla was raised in this house, and she takes it all in stride. "The family dining room is this way," she says, pointing back toward the kitchen.

Just as we reach the dining room, Ian and Tyler come into view, heading toward us. They must have come in through the kitchen.

"Ian!" Layla runs into her brother's waiting arms.

He wraps her carefully in his arms. "Hey, sis. How're you doing?"

"Fine," she says with a heartfelt sigh. "I'm glad to be home. And I'm even happier now that you're here. You, too, Tyler."

When Ian releases his sister so that Tyler can hug her, he looks to me for confirmation.

I nod. *So far, so good.*

9

Jason Miller

My idea of informal dining is eating while sitting on the sofa with my feet up on the coffee table, watching TV. That's not the case here. At the center of the family dining room is an antique cherry table that seats six. Martin Alexander is seated at the far end of the table, his wife at the other end. Ian and Tyler are just now taking the two chairs on one side of the table, leaving the other two chairs for me and Layla. I pull Layla's seat out for her, and she sits.

A moment later, Claire enters through a side door, pushing a cart laden with salad plates, a basket of rolls, and a large pitcher of ice water. While she dishes out the salads, conversation flows around the table. Mostly, everyone's interested in how Layla's doing.

After the salads, comes the main course—roasted chicken breasts, tiny steamed potatoes, and grilled asparagus in some kind of cream sauce. My idea of a nice dinner is going out for hot wings with the guys after a job, or staying in, watching baseball, and ordering pizza. This is way out of my league.

Claire asks us what we want to drink. Layla's parents, Ian, and Tyler all opt for red wine. Layla is automatically given a bottle of sparkling water that might have been imported from Italy, as the label is written in Italian and it's one I don't recognize.

"And for you, sir?" Claire asks me. "Would you care for wine, beer, or perhaps a soft drink?"

"I'll have what Layla's having," I say.

Layla looks a bit surprised by my choice. I imagine she's drinking water to better manage her glucose level, so I will too. Solidarity.

For dessert, we get individual little dishes of bread pudding with a warm rum butter sauce over top. Except for Layla. She gets a small bowl of strawberries with a tiny bit of whipped cream on top.

I watch as Layla programs an estimate of how many grams of carbs she ate for dinner into her Omnipod. Her pump will automatically calculate how much insulin to give her. I'll check her glucose level again about an hour after we eat.

After the meal, Tyler and Ian are telling us all about their new venture as private investigators. When Layla went missing, Tyler and Ian searched for her. At the time, Tyler was on administrative leave from his job in the police department while they investigated bogus assault charges brought against him by some asshole carrying a grudge. By investigating Layla's disappearance, Tyler violated the terms of his leave, and it got him fired. I don't blame him for the choices he made. He was searching for his boyfriend's missing sister. I would have done the same thing if I'd been in his position.

After we're done eating, Martin catches my gaze and nods toward the door. "If you'll excuse me, everyone," he says as he rises from his chair. "I'll be in my office. Why don't you join me, Jason?"

I can tell from the tone of his voice that it wasn't exactly an invitation. It was more of a demand. I stand, pushing my chair back, and lay my hand lightly on Layla's shoulder. "I'll be right back."

Layla's father is waiting for me in the hallway. "Come to my office," he says, nodding down the corridor. "I'd like a word with you."

"Of course." I follow him to a closed mahogany door. He opens it and motions for me to step inside. "Have a seat, Jason," he says, pointing at the chair in front of a dark wooden desk.

The room looks like what I'd imagine a judge's office would

look like. Most of the walls are lined with bookshelves filled with leather-bound books that look awfully official, not to mention expensive. These books probably contain the entire legal precedence of the United States.

I sit across the desk from him, and he studies me a moment before he opens a fancy wooden cigar box. "Care for one? They're imported from Havana."

"No, thank you, sir. I don't smoke."

"Neither do I." He pulls a cigar out of the box, cuts off the tip, and lights it. After taking a few puffs to ignite the tobacco, he lays the cigar in a glass ashtray. "I don't smoke them anymore—my wife made me quit years ago—but I like the aroma. They remind me of my father and grandfather. I don't think I ever saw my grandfather without a cigar between his lips."

He opens a bottle of Glenfiddich and pours a shot in a crystal tumbler. "How about a drink, then?"

"Thank you, sir, but no. I'm on duty."

He nods approvingly. "Good answer. I noticed you drank water at dinner."

"Yes, sir."

"Why is that? You could have had anything you wanted. Beer, wine."

"Because it was what Layla was drinking."

"And why do you think she drinks water at dinner?"

"To control her blood sugar."

He nods, then takes a sip of his Scotch. "Of course, with

your medical background, you already know that, don't you? I'm curious as to why you chose water."

"If I expect Layla to limit her sugar intake, then I think it's only fair that I do, too."

Again, he nods. "I'm impressed. Are you going to make choices like that all the time, or just when her mother and I are around to notice?"

I bite back a grin. The man is straightforward, and I respect that. "All the time, sir. It's only fair."

"Excellent. I like the way you think, Jason." He leans back in his leather chair and places his hands over his abdomen. "I'll get straight to the point. I need something from you."

"What's that, sir?"

"I need you to make me a promise."

"If it's in accordance with my professional duties, then yes. I'm happy to."

"Oh, I assure you, it is." He picks up his cigar, runs it beneath his nose, and inhales its slightly sweet floral fragrance. "Layla means the world to her mother and me. We were blessed to have been given the privilege of raising her. Her safety and well-being are paramount." He looks toward a window, staring off into space for a moment, then back at me. "As you are well aware, her last bodyguard betrayed her trust in the most heinous way imaginable. We don't want her to suffer another disappointment. Ruth and I are counting on you to maintain a professional relationship with our daughter. Am I making myself clear?"

"Yes, sir." I ignore the fact I watched her walk out of her bathroom in her bra and panties just an hour ago.

"I'll be frank. Layla is an attractive young woman. She's also wealthy beyond most people's imaginations. Add to that, she's vulnerable, emotionally as well as medically. Her mother and I can't be with her every second of every day, so we have to be able to trust her bodyguard. Can we count on you to be the person she needs?"

"Yes." I answer without hesitation.

Martin takes one puff of his cigar and then sets it back in the ashtray. He wags his index finger at me. "Don't tell anyone you saw that," he says with a self-deprecating grin. "I'll deny it."

I smile. "I won't, sir."

Martin gives me a hard stare. "Don't let us down, Jason. Shane swore to us you'd never abuse your position with Layla, that you'd safeguard her. Ruth and I are counting on that. I don't know how to be any clearer."

I nod, fully aware of the commitment and vow I'm making. "I won't let you down, I promise."

"You'd better not."

I leave the judge's office and head back to the dining room. What he asked of me is perfectly acceptable. As a professional bodyguard, I'm expected to conduct myself with the utmost integrity when it comes to the health and welfare of my clients. It burns my ass that Layla's previous bodyguard failed her, nearly costing her not only her freedom, but her life as well.

I follow the sound of voices, hearing Layla and her brother laughing about something. When I step back into the dining room, I spot Tyler leaning back in his chair, watching them with an indulgent smile on his face. Ruth seems happy and relaxed as she gazes contentedly at her two children.

"What'd I miss?" I ask as I return to my seat beside Layla.

Layla manages to stop laughing long enough to catch her breath. "Ian was telling us about the self-defense class he's taking in preparation for his new career as a private investigator."

"Honestly, I wasn't that bad," Ian insists, even as he himself can't stop laughing. "Two against one clearly isn't fair. Right, Tyler? You saw the whole thing. They ganged up on me."

Tyler picks up his glass of wine and takes a sip. He's grinning as he shakes his head at Ian. "No comment."

"Anyway," Ian continues. "I fell and bruised my coccyx." He reaches behind himself to rub the spot where his spine meets his ass. "Literally, I have a bruise. This is the first time I've been able to sit comfortably all day."

Tyler nearly chokes on his wine as he stifles a laugh. "I'm sorry, it's not funny." He reaches over to pat Ian's thigh. "I didn't mean to laugh."

"Does he really have a bruise?" Layla asks just before she pops a strawberry into her mouth.

"He does," Tyler says. "It's a lovely shade of purple."

"All right, enough about my ass," Ian says.

Struggling not to laugh, Ruth gives her son one of those

parental looks. "Language, dear."

"Sorry, Mom," Ian says. His attention pivots to his sister. "So, sis, when do you start back at school?"

"I hope Monday," Layla says, looking to her mom first, and then to me, as if she expects one of us to contradict her.

Ruth frowns. "Honey, are you sure you're ready? Perhaps you should sit out the rest of the semester and start over next term."

"No way!" Layla says. "I'm not sitting out the rest of the term. I had A's in all of my classes before this happened. I can make up what I've missed, and I'll deal with the questions as they come."

"And the pictures?" her mom adds gently. "You know they'll be posting images of you on social media. Are you prepared for that level of scrutiny?"

Layla's stiffens. "I'm not sitting out the rest of the term."

Ruth nods. "All right. But I think you should wait at least another week to give the bruises more time to fade. I'm sure, under the circumstances, your professors will let you work from home."

Frowning, Layla nods. "One week. But not a minute more."

After more conversation about Ian's exploits in his self-defense class, Ian and Tyler head home. Ruth disappears to her home office to do some prep work for an important case she's litigating in the morning.

I follow Layla up to her room and check her blood sugar as it's been a while since she ate dinner. It's a little high still, but it's trending down, so she should be okay. I'll check again in an hour, and I know she will too.

Layla stops at her room. "I'm going to work on homework now. You can go relax, or do whatever you like."

"Okay." I remember the promise her father extracted from me tonight—the promise to do my job well. Of course I have every intention of doing that.

As I leave her to her own devices and head to my room, I'm uncomfortably aware of the fact I'm already missing her. I enjoy her company, which is a good thing, as we're going to be spending a lot of time together. But I'm starting to wonder if I enjoy it a bit too much.

10

Layla Alexander

After dinner, I shut myself up in my bedroom and e-mail my professors to let them know I won't be back to class for another week yet and ask them to let me work from home until then. They know what happened to me. If they didn't catch it in the news, they certainly heard it from the university administration and the disabilities office because my parents notified the school that I'd be missing some classes. The last thing I wanted was to fail this semester.

I change into pajamas to get comfortable—flannel shorts and a white tank top—and head to the bathroom to wash my face and brush my teeth. I avoid looking at my reflection in the mirror because the bruises—especially the ones around my throat—are reminders of the worse experience of my life.

You can't show your face at school. You look hideous. Ugly.

I ignore her.

Unfortunately, my mom's concerns about me returning to school tomorrow are valid. Showing my face in public right now isn't a good idea. I don't want to talk about how I got the bruises, and I really don't want to talk about Sean.

Sean's death was reported in the news, and it's likely many of the students at my university saw the story. He was shot right in front of me, and that's only going to lead to more questions.

Sean's dead because of you.

That wasn't my fault!

Of course it was. If it weren't for you, Sean would still be alive.

I check my laptop to see if any of my professors have replied to my e-mail, but no one has. It's evening, though, so they're probably busy with their families.

You're going to fail the semester.

No, I'm not.

Yes, you are. You're going to fail. Because that's what you are—a failure.

I'm not.

Your parents know it. Your brother knows it. And soon Jason will know.

Stop it!

I stare at the laptop screen, willing one of my professors to reply, to tell me it's okay if I work from home for another week. But my e-mail inbox remains unchanged.

Failure.

I jump up from my desk and grab my earbuds, shoving them into my ears in hopes of blocking her out. She knows how to get to me. She knows my deepest fears—that I'll fail. That I'll let my family down. That I can't cope, can't manage.

As I listen to the music, I pace my room. And as I pace, my anxiety grows. What if my professors won't let me work from home? What if I fail all my classes this term? What if I get kicked out of school?

Failure.

I am not.

You are. Just imagine how embarrassed your parents will be.

My parents love me.

No, they don't. They barely tolerate you. Why do you think they hire people to take care of you? It's so they don't have to.

Shut up.

They regret ever adopting you. You've been nothing but a disappointment since the very beginning.

Stop it!

But she's right. I know she is. And the pressure inside me builds and builds until I feel like I'm about to explode. There's nowhere to run, nowhere to hide. Everything's crashing down around me, and I'm suffocating. I struggle to catch my breath. It's just like when that hideous man choked me.

He should have killed you.

Maybe you're right.

You know I'm right.

As I continue pacing, my skin starts prickling as if an army of ants is crawling over every inch of my body.

You'll feel better if you cut yourself.

No.

You'll feel better.

Stop it.

Get the knife.

No.

I have one of André's paring knives hidden in my closet. I snuck it out of the kitchen a few months ago when no one was watching. It's so well hidden that no one has ever found it, even though I suspect Margaret searches my room from time to time, especially if something sharp goes missing. I think my mom does, too.

Go on. Get it.

I walk into my closet, switch on the light, and close the door behind me. This is my private space, where no one can see me.

I always see you. You can't hide from me.

I take a pink floral cardboard box down from the top shelf

that contains essays I wrote in high school. Nestled amongst the papers, wrapped in a white linen napkin, is a sharp, shiny knife.

I sit on the floor with the box on my lap and stare at the knife. Then I gaze down at my arms which are mottled with splotches of fading purple, green, and yellow. These bruises are easy to conceal beneath my clothing, but the bruising on my face and throat is much harder to hide. Make-up can only cover so much. Even if I wait a week longer to return to school, my classmates are still going to see them.

Cut the bruises out so no one will see them.

She makes it sound so easy.

It *is* easy. Just do it. Don't be a coward.

I pick up the knife and feel its weight in my hand. For such a small knife, it's surprisingly heavy. And I know from experience that it's incredibly sharp. Hardly any pressure is needed to slice through skin.

As I stare at the knife, I'm flooded with guilt. If I cut myself, my parents will be brokenhearted. So will Ian. I promised them all I would never cut myself again. Even now, parts of my body are marked with faint scars from previous cuts. They've faded to white, but they're constant reminders of what I've done to myself.

My throat tightens as hot tears slide down my cheeks.

She's right.

I am a failure.

11

Jason Miller

It's still early in the evening, and I feel like I should spend some time with Layla. It's critical I form a relationship with her and start the slow process of building trust. She's been holed up in her room all evening, ever since dinner, and I'm trying to think of something that will lure her out. I wonder if she likes to play board games. I found a stack of them in my bedroom closet—Scrabble, Monopoly, and Yahtzee. Do girls her age still play games, or are they all about social media now? Maybe she'd like to watch something on Netflix with me. TV's still cool, right?

I knock loudly on her bedroom door. I'm not about to repeat the mistake I made earlier when I jumped the gun and rushed into her room uninvited. When she doesn't answer, I pull out my phone and text her.

Jason: Hey, Layla. You busy?

I wait a good two minutes, which feels like forever, but she still doesn't answer.

I'm having a serious case of *déjà vu*. Only this time I'm not going to barge into her bedroom like I did last time and get an eyeful of her half-naked body. I'm trying really hard to forget what I saw that last time, because it's damn inappropriate for me to be thinking about her that way.

I knock again, louder this time, and when that doesn't work, I try texting her again.

Still no response.

I'm sure she's in there. I would have heard her leave her room.

I press my ear to the door and listen, wondering if she's in the shower. But I don't hear water running. Instead, I detect a faint, muffled sound. Something akin to a gasp. It's the kind of sound that makes the hairs on the back of my neck stand up.

Fuck.

I turn the knob and push the door open enough that I can poke my head in. "Layla?" But I don't see her.

As I step inside, I quickly scan her room from left to right. Then I check her bathroom. The door's open, and the room is empty.

She's not here.

But that's impossible. I would have heard her leave, unless she intentionally snuck out.

Where the fuck could she be?

There's only one place I haven't checked.

When I open her closet door, my heart nearly stops at the sight of Layla's huddled form on the bare wood floor. Her knees are drawn up to her chest, her arms wrapped tightly around them. Her head is down, and she's rocking forward and back. Light glints off the blade of the knife in her hand.

Holy shit.

"Layla." Afraid of startling her, I crouch down behind her, poised to snatch the knife out of her hand. She has her earbuds in, and I can hear pop music blasting into her ears. Gently, I lay one hand on her shoulder, while my other hand slides down her arm to her wrist. I sweep the knife from her grip and after checking the blade for any sign of blood—there isn't any, thank god—I toss it far out of reach.

Startled, she pulls away so forcefully that she topples over, falling to the floor.

"Layla?"

Because of the music, she can't hear a word I say, so I raise my hands in a placating gesture. "Shh, it's okay." Slowly, so as not to startle her further, I pull the earbuds from her ears, reach for her phone, and turn off the music.

She stares up at me with wild eyes. At this moment, I'm

not even sure she realizes who I am.

"Layla, it's me, Jason."

A range of emotions flashes across her face, from shock to surprise to mortification.

I scan her arms looking for blood and don't see any, but that doesn't mean she isn't hurt somewhere. I've hardly been on the job for long, and already my client is attempting to cut herself.

How did I fuck this up so badly?

"Are you hurt?" I ask gently.

She looks away, her face flushed with embarrassment. "No."

"Are you cut?"

Tears are streaming down her face. Shaking her head violently, she says, "No! I swear. I didn't do it."

But she wanted to.

I move to sit cross-legged on the floor and gently take both her hands in mine. "Can you tell me what happened?"

She looks so lost. I feel like I've failed her already because I'm only now realizing just how much she's struggling.

I squeeze her hands. "Layla, please. What happened? Why were you holding a knife?"

She shrugs. "My skin was crawling, and it wouldn't stop. It just kept getting worse and worse, and then there were the bruises."

"What about the bruises?"

"They'll see them. They'll ask questions."

"Who will?"

"The photographers and the students in my classes. When they see the bruises, they'll ask questions I don't want to answer."

A sickening thought hits me. Did she really think she could cut the bruises out of her skin? "Layla, did *she* tell you to cut yourself?"

Her panicked gaze flashes up to meet mine, and even though she doesn't answer me, I can see the truth in her eyes. *She did. The voice told her to cut herself.*

Layla's shaking so badly, I can't help pulling her onto my lap and wrapping my arms around her. At first, she resists, stiffening, her spine going ramrod straight as she tries to put distance between us, but I just hold her and talk quietly in her ear. "Shh, it's okay. I've got you. You're safe."

Slowly she begins to relax in my arms.

"Please call me when you're having a difficult time," I say quietly. "Let me know when she tells you to hurt yourself. That's why I'm here. To protect you from things like this. Think of me as your support dog."

To my surprise, she snorts out an unexpected laugh.

I see a watery smile. "That's much better." I raise the hem of my T-shirt to dry her cheeks and dab at the corners of her eyes. Impulsively, I press my lips to her hair. My heart hurts for this girl, and I just want to make her feel better. "What started all this? You seemed fine at dinner."

She lets out a heavy sigh. "I e-mailed my professors to ask

if I could work from home this coming week. If they don't agree, I'll fail my classes."

"And that bothers you? The thought of failing?"

"Yes."

"You can always take the classes again next term."

She shakes her head. "You don't understand. I *can't* fail."

"Everybody fails sometimes. It's not the end of the world."

"It terrifies me. She said I'm a failure. That I'm a disappointment to my family."

She. She means the voice. "That's not true, Layla. You're not a failure. And you could never be a disappointment to your family. They love you unconditionally."

When she doesn't respond, I'm afraid it's because she doesn't believe me. So, I change the subject. "Tell me more about what you hear. Help me understand."

"You mean the monster?"

"Is that what you call it? Is it just one voice?"

"Yes. She's constantly tearing me down."

"And she told you to cut yourself?"

Layla nods.

"The next time she tells you to hurt yourself, I want you to come to me. No matter where you are or what you're doing, you call me."

"You don't want to be subjected to all my drama."

"I'm here to help you, Layla. You don't need to suffer alone."

Slowly, she leans against my chest.

As I tighten my hold on her, I do my best to ignore how

good her warm weight feels in my arms. "I want to help you, but you've got to let me."

"It's not easy for me to let people in. I hate when others know about the chaos inside my head." She turns to look up at me with a frantic gaze. "You're not going to tell my parents, are you?"

My heart stops in my chest. I knew this was coming. "Layla." The tone of my voice says it all.

She slides off my lap and kneels beside me to grasp my forearm. "Please, Jason, don't. They'll be so disappointed."

"Layla, I don't have a choice. It would be unethical of me not to report this. Your parents need to know. They're counting on me to do the right thing, and that includes letting them know of any potential risks. They're not going to be disappointed in you, I promise. They *love* you. They only want to keep you safe."

Seeing her in so much agony hurts, and knowing that I'm about to cause her even more pain guts me. I brush her tears away. "Layla, you have to trust me. I wouldn't tell them if I didn't have to."

As she looks away, the tears keep coming. She's still shaking, and I can't bear it. I rise to my feet and pull her up onto hers. "It's getting late, and you're exhausted. Why don't you get in bed?"

She still won't look me in the eye. "I won't be able to sleep."

"How about you lie down and rest? I'll stay with you until you fall asleep."

She nods grudgingly, and I follow her out of the closet. While she goes into the bathroom to get ready for bed, I retrieve the knife and take it to my room. I'll deal with it as soon as she's asleep. I'm not looking forward to telling her parents, but I meant what I said. I don't have a choice. I just hope Layla will eventually understand and that it doesn't damage our fledgling relationship.

I return to Layla's room just as she emerges from the bathroom dressed in her pajamas. The good news is she has stopped crying, although her eyes are rimmed in red. The bad news is she looks like she expects the sky to fall in on her at any moment.

"It's going to be all right, I promise," I tell her as she heads for her bed.

While she crawls beneath the covers, I pull an armchair up to the side of her bed and sit. My gaze lights on what looks like an antique book lying on her nightstand. "What's this?" I pick it up and glance at the front cover. *Jane Eyre* by Charlotte Brontë. There's a bookmark sticking out of it.

"It's a first edition copy that Ian gave me for my birthday. I'm reading it for English class. I have to write a paper on it this term."

I get up to turn off the chandelier and switch on the lamp on her nightstand. Then I open the book to the spot where she left off. "How about I read to you?"

Her eyes widen. "Really?"

"Sure. I used to read to my little sister when we were kids.

Our mom had to work nights, so I was the one who always put her to bed. I'd read to her every night until she fell asleep. I'll probably suck so bad you'll fall asleep out of boredom."

She cracks the tiniest of smiles. "I doubt that. You have a nice voice."

I laugh. "I'm not sure I'd agree with you on that. But hey, let's give it a try." I start reading about Jane and Mr. Rochester in their old, dark, drafty house, and the things that go bump in the night.

Twenty minutes later, Layla's fast sleep.

I tuck the bookmark in its place and lay the book down on the nightstand. Then I lean back in my chair and watch her sleep, mesmerized by her beauty. Despite the many bruises, she looks like an angel.

I hate leaving her, but I need to go talk to her parents now, before it gets any later.

After I let myself out of Layla's room, I head down the hall toward the parents' bedroom. I hate disturbing them at this hour, but it has to be done. I knock quietly on the door and wait.

The judge opens the door dressed in a dark blue robe. "Jason." He sounds surprised. "Is everything all right?"

"Everything's fine, sir, but we need to talk."

He frowns. "Just a moment." He closes the door, then reopens it a minute later. "All right. Come in."

When I step into the room, I find both parents in their robes. Mrs. Alexander is seated on a chair by the hearth.

Mr. Martin stands, facing me. "Go ahead."

Exhaling heavily, I shove my hands in my front pockets. I get right to the point. "I found Layla in her closet a short while ago with a knife she stole from the kitchen."

Mrs. Alexander gasps. "Did she cut herself?"

"No."

"Are you sure?" she asks.

"Yes. I checked for blood, both on her and on the blade. There was none."

"Where is she now?" her father asks.

"In her bed sleeping. She was pretty distraught after the incident, but I was able to talk her into going to bed. I stayed with her until she fell asleep."

"Thanks for telling us," the judge says. He meets his wife's gaze, and they share a moment. They both look worried.

"She's afraid you'll be disappointed in her," I say.

Mr. Alexander shakes his head. "We're not disappointed. We know she can't help it. We're just concerned for her safety. Where's the knife now?"

"It's in my room. I'll return it to the kitchen tonight."

The judge nods. "Thank you, Jason."

"I'm sorry, but I should have searched her room before now, and I didn't. That's on me. I'll do random sweeps from now on. It'll never happen again, I promise."

Mrs. Alexander nods. "That's a good idea. Margaret and I check her room regularly, but we obviously missed this knife. I would appreciate your help as well."

"Yes, ma'am."

"Please, Jason," she says. "Call me Ruth."

I nod. "Ruth. Got it."

Layla's father claps me on my shoulder. "You did the right thing by telling us. We'll talk to her tomorrow."

I nod, because I know he's right. But that doesn't make this any easier. "Please don't be hard on her, sir. She's already afraid of disappointing you and being seen as a failure."

"Martin," he says. "Call me Martin. And we understand that. But we do need to address the issue with her, and with Dr Hartigan. We can't just sweep it under the rug."

I nod, understanding their position. But I can't help finding myself on Layla's side.

After returning to my room, I retrieve the knife and take it down to the kitchen, where I wash it and stow it away with the other cutlery.

I hope tonight doesn't damage the progress I've made with Layla. I can't help her if she doesn't trust me.

12

Layla Alexander

Memories of last night come rushing back, and I'm absolutely mortified that Jason saw me like that. Other than during the abduction and my recent stay in the hospital, I haven't had an emotional meltdown that bad in a long time. I'm glad my parents didn't see it. They'd be frantic with worry—especially my mom. And so disappointed.

Everyone's disappointed in you. You're pathetic.

I check the time. It's a quarter after seven—still pretty early. My parents have already left for work, I'm sure. They're both high-achieving workaholics. I think they do a good job of managing their work-life balance. I've never felt slighted.

I need to get up and get ready before I'm due downstairs for breakfast at eight. If I don't make a prompt appearance, Margaret will come looking for me.

I race to my bathroom and shower quickly. Then I head for my closet and get dressed. I search the closet floor for the knife, but I can't find it. I check behind my shoes and purses and under piles of discarded clothes and other accumulated stuff, but it's nowhere to be found. In a panic, I head to Jason's room.

He answers the door wearing nothing but a pair of faded blue jeans that hang low on his waist. My gaze travels down his chiseled chest, past his pecs, to his washboard abs. Is that a six-pack? Or eight? There's no time to count them because I'm distracted by the thin line of dark hair that runs down from his belly button and disappears beneath the waistband of his jeans. My mouth goes dry. OMG, his hips are lean, and he's got a V, just like the male models on social media. He's freaking ripped.

"Sorry," he says as he rubs his damp hair on a towel. "I just got out of the shower."

"It's okay." My voice comes out weak and breathy as I try not to stare at his body. "I don't mind."

He grins at me. "What's up?"

Suddenly I remember the reason why I came. "Where's the knife? I can't find it." I can tell from the look on his face that

I'm not going to like the answer.

He drapes the towel around his neck. "I returned it to the kitchen last night, after I spoke with your parents."

My stomach drops. "So, they know?"

He nods. "Have they said anything to you this morning?"

"No. I haven't seen them today. I'm pretty sure they've already left for work."

"They said they were going to talk to you." He reaches out to touch my arm. "Hey, relax. They promised me they wouldn't give you a hard time about it."

"Thanks," I tell him. "I'll let you finish getting dressed. Breakfast is at eight."

As I turn to walk back to my room, I see my mom heading toward me. She's dressed for work in a suit and blouse. My pulse picks up speed. *Oh, crap, here it comes.*

"Good morning, sweetheart," she says when she reaches me.

"I thought you'd already left for work."

"Your dad left a little while ago but I thought I'd stay and have a little chat with you before I leave." She nods to my door. "Can we sit in your room?"

I open my bedroom door and follow her inside. "It's about the knife, isn't it?"

She sits at the foot of my bed. "Jason told us what happened last night."

"I didn't cut myself, I swear."

She gives me a sad smile. "I'm really glad to hear that,

honey. But what concerns your father and me is that you had a knife in your bedroom to begin with. We've talked about this many times before, and you promised us you wouldn't hide sharp implements."

"I know. I'm sorry. But I didn't use it."

"Did the voice tell you to cut yourself?"

I nod.

"We're glad you didn't, but I hope you can see why we're so worried. If Jason hadn't come along when he did, we don't know what might have happened."

I sit beside my mom and stare straight ahead. "I haven't cut myself in a long time."

Mom puts her arm around me and pulls me close. "I know, sweetie. And I'm very proud of you. So is your dad." She's silent for a moment. Then, she says, "I've asked Jason to search your room periodically. You know that Margaret and I do as well."

"Yes."

"I have a feeling he'll be far more thorough than we are."

"Are you mad?"

"No, honey, we're not mad. We love you, and we're concerned. We just don't want you to get hurt. And please don't be mad at Jason for coming to us. He did the right thing, even if you don't think so."

I sigh. "I know. He told me he had to. I get it. I just hated the idea of you guys knowing."

"But the important thing is, you didn't cut yourself. The

next time she tells you to hurt yourself, or you feel the need, tell someone. Either your dad or me, or Jason. Can you do that?"

"Yes."

She kisses the side of my head. "I'm going to work now. Will you be okay at home today? I'm sure Jason will keep you company."

I hug my mom, grateful that she's not more upset at me. "I'll be fine. I promise."

13

Jason Miller

A few minutes before eight, I head to Layla's room and knock on the door. It opens right away this time—that's definitely an improvement. She's wearing jeans and a long-sleeve T-shirt with a UChicago logo on it. I caught her in the process of brushing her teeth.

"Almost ready," she mumbles.

Layla motions for me to come inside, and then she retreats to the bathroom to finish getting ready. I walk through her bedroom, just nosing around and stop to scan the titles of the books on one of her huge bookcases. Lots of familiar pop culture favorites—*Hunger Games, Twilight, Divergent, Game of Thrones, Fifty Shades of Grey*—whoa—are mixed in with classics by Jane Austen, Charlotte Brontë, and Jules Verne. There must be hundreds of books on these shelves. And then there's an entire bookcase of nothing but romance novels. I pull one off the shelf and roll my eyes at the image of a bare-chested man on the cover.

"Do you like to read?" she asks as she comes out of the bathroom.

Her hair is freshly brushed and pulled back into a ponytail, making her look even younger than her twenty-one years. When she smiles at me, my chest tightens. She's the most beautiful girl I've ever seen. As soon as the thought enters my head, I squash it. She's my *client*. That's all she can ever be to me, and thinking of her in any other way is pointless.

I mentally shake myself and focus on her question. "Yeah. I read sci-fi and military thrillers. As a kid, I devoured books by Jules Verne and Edgar Rice Burroughs. I wanted to travel to the center of the earth and find living, breathing dinosaurs."

She reaches for a book on one of the shelves and holds it out to me—*Journey to the Center of the Earth*. "This is one of my favorites. Have you seen the movie version starring Brendan Fraser?" Her smile makes my breath catch.

"No, I haven't."

Her eyes widen in surprise. "Oh, my god, it's so good. We have to watch it sometime. He's also in *The Mummy*? Have you seen that one?" Her excitement is infectious.

"Sounds like we're in for a movie night."

Layla's face lights up like I just promised her the moon, and suddenly I want to make it my life's mission to give this girl plenty of reasons to smile. She's such a surprise. She has more money than she could possibly know what to do with. She could have literally anything she wanted, and she gets excited because I agree to watch a movie with her.

"Sounds like a date," she says. And then her eyes widen in embarrassed shock. "I didn't mean a *date* date. You know what I mean—just friends watching a movie. That kind of date."

I try not to smile at how flustered she is. "I know what you mean, and yeah, I'm looking forward to it. All right, it's getting late. Are you ready to go down to breakfast?"

We head downstairs, and when we walk into the kitchen, there's plenty of activity going on. André is at the stove, as usual, and Claire is at the island counter kneading dough. Margaret's eating breakfast at the big kitchen table.

"Good morning, Layla," Margaret says with a smile. She nods to me. "Jason. I hope you both slept well. Help yourselves to breakfast." She points toward the buffet table, which holds several stainless-steel warming trays. "André made his famous French crepes this morning. They're delicious served with whipped cream and fresh sliced strawberries."

There's a huge spread of food and beverages available this morning including crepes, scrambled eggs, bacon, sausage, fresh fruit, orange juice, coffee, and hot water for tea.

Layla walks over to the buffet, picks up a plate, and starts helping herself.

I grab a plate for myself. One of the perks of living in a five-star home is that I get to eat like a king. André's cooking is a far cry above the frozen breakfast sandwiches and cold cereal that I'm used to.

When we sit down to eat, André and Claire join us.

While Layla inputs the estimated grams of carbs she's eating into her device, I check her current reading.

Of course she went with the crepes. That girl never passes up a chance to have strawberries. As I eat, I listen to the conversation flowing around me. It's obvious that Layla gets a lot of love from the people who work for her family. Margaret and André both clearly look out for her.

After breakfast, I follow her out of the kitchen and down the hallway. "So, what's on the agenda for today?" She's not starting back to school until next week, so I imagine we'll be hanging out here at the house most of the time.

"I'm behind on homework. I need to finish reading *Jane Eyre*, and I have an anatomy exam to study for."

Layla's dedication to her schoolwork is admirable. But in the short time I've been here, I've seen a lot of studying and not a lot of play. "When was the last time you got out of the house?"

She frowns. "Not since before—you know."

Yeah, I know. She can't bring herself to say abduction, and I don't blame her. When I think about what she went through, I see red. The idea that her bodyguard could have betrayed her is unthinkable.

"Since you don't have classes today, why don't we go out? I don't think it's a good idea for you to stay cooped up in the house. A little fresh air and sunshine works wonders."

She shakes her head. "What if someone recognizes me and takes pictures that end up on the Internet? I can't risk it."

I understand her concerns, but there's got to be something fun she can do without running into gawkers or photographers. Of course, with all the smartphones, everyone is a photographer these days. "If you could go anywhere, where would you want to go?"

She answers without hesitation. "To the beach. But the beaches on Lake Shore Drive are crowded this time of year. Everyone wants to enjoy the outdoors, and I don't blame them. But I don't feel comfortable around so many people."

"I know a quiet beach north of downtown that's far enough off the beaten path that you won't run into many people. It's hardly ever crowded."

She looks hopeful. "Really?"

I nod. "Yeah. And if you wear a hat, no one will recognize you. We could walk along the beach and then maybe grab some lunch. There's a great café in the area. How about it? You need to get out and have some fun."

She looks tempted. "You sure it won't be crowded?"

"We may come across a few people, but not many."

"We can try it."

As we head out the back door to the parking area, I dig the

keys to my Challenger out of my pocket and unlock the front passenger door. She slides in and buckles her seatbelt while I walk around to the driver's side.

It's a nice summer morning, and the sun has warmed the interior of my car. Outside, there's not a cloud in sight. It's a perfect day to walk along the beach and soak up some sun.

I head for Lake Shore Drive, and then we go north, away from downtown.

"Where are we going?" Layla asks, watching the shoreline that runs parallel to the highway.

"There's a public park ahead, not too far. It doesn't get a lot of foot traffic, but it has a nice beach with a great view of the lake."

When we arrive at our destination, I park in a small gravel lot beneath the shade of a large oak tree. Then I reach into the back seat and grab a Chicago Cubs baseball cap, which I set on Layla's head. I tug the bill down low, practically covering her eyes. "There. No one will recognize you."

She pulls down the visor in front of her so she can see her reflection in the mirror and smiles. Apparently, the cap meets with her approval.

We cross the parking lot and a small patch of grass to reach a paved walking trail that meanders along the edge of the lake, just a dozen yards from the edge of the water. The only sound we hear are birds chirping in the trees and the waves lapping against the sand as it ebbs in and out. The shoreline is littered with strands of green algae and pieces of driftwood. The only two people in sight are a middle-aged couple on their bikes heading north, away from us.

"See?" I say. "We have the whole place to ourselves."

Layla looks around as if to make sure that's the case. Then we start walking, heading north as well. The wide path meanders through some trees as it follows the edge of the lake. We hear the occasional shrill cry of gulls following boats as they chase after their next meals. Farther out on the lake, sailboats and motorboats cruise up and down the shoreline.

We walk for about twenty minutes along a paved path that runs along the shoreline, underneath a canopy of lush, green trees. We stop a minute at a small public ramp where people can put their boats in and out of the water. There are half a dozen cars in the parking lot, all empty.

We pause to watch two teens dressed in wetsuits play around on their jet skis. The girl shrieks when the boy runs circles around her, splashing her. Layla smiles wistfully as she watches them.

How many opportunities does Layla get to simply play and have fun? I'm starting to think not many. She's almost a prisoner of her own notoriety.

We continue walking along the path, passing a young couple pushing two toddlers in a double stroller. Their exuberant Golden Retriever runs ahead of them, off leash, stopping to smell every tree and shrub along the trail.

When the friendly dog bounds over to Layla, she holds out her hand so the dog can sniff it. I stand at her side in case I need to intervene, but it's pretty clear the dog wouldn't hurt a fly.

"Sorry about that," the young woman says as she calls her dog back.

"It's okay. I don't mind," Layla says as she tugs the cap down lower over her face.

After the family passes us, Layla says, "Thanks for suggesting this." There's a contented smile on her face. "It's beautiful here. I always thought I'd like to have a house on the shore. I'd love to be able to walk out my back door and down to the beach to enjoy my own little bit of paradise. I can't even walk outside my own house without the neighbors staring at me."

She can certainly afford a house on the lake. "Why don't you?"

Layla could easily buy a property on the lake—hell, she could buy a hundred of them. She's loaded, and yet she doesn't act like it. I don't think the money is all that real to her.

She shrugs. "I guess I never felt ready for something like that. I can't live at home with my parents forever. Eventually I'll want to move out and live on my own. It seems like such a big step. Maybe someday. It's definitely on my bucket list."

We come across a small wooden pier that stretches out a few yards over the water. She walks toward it and steps out onto an old, rickety dock that bobs on the waves. I follow her.

She strolls to the far end of the platform and looks out over the water. "I wish we could swim."

"We should come back soon and bring our swimsuits."

She shakes her head. "I can't wear a bathing suit in public."

"Why not?"

She rubs her arms through her long sleeves. "I have scars."

That's all she says—it's all she needs to say. Scars from cutting herself.

"Then you need a house with a private pool," I say. "Preferably one right on the lake. Then you could kill two birds with one stone."

Standing at the end of the dock, we watch sailboats, pontoons, and small yachts as they cruise up and down the shoreline.

"Ian has a boat," she says wistfully. "A small yacht. We should ask him to take us out on the lake sometime."

A fish jumps out of the water, causing quite a splash, startling Layla, who jumps back in surprise. The sudden movement causes the dock to rock violently, and she loses her balance and careens into me. I grab hold of her and pull her into my arms to steady her.

She latches onto me, and as she peers up at me, her dark eyes widen in surprise. My breath catches, and I find myself unable to look away.

"I'm so sorry," she gasps as she finally pulls away. Clearly flustered, she hurries past me and back onto solid ground.

I follow her back to shore, my heart pounding as I watch her retreating form. I'd say we're both a bit shaken. The look of naked desire in her eyes floored me. I think it took her by surprise, too.

It's noon when we come across a quaint little café in a small shopping district. We go inside, happy to see it's not very crowded, and are seated at a small table for two.

The same young girl who seats us hands us worn, laminated menus. "I'll be right back to take your orders." Her gaze is locked on Layla for a long moment.

"Thanks," I tell the girl.

Layla picks up her menu and uses it to shield her face from our curious server. The girl stares at Layla a moment longer before she walks away.

Layla glances back at the retreating girl. "Do you think she recognized me?"

"Maybe." Actually, I'm thinking probably, but I don't tell Layla that. She's already self-conscious. "Maybe she just thinks you're really pretty." I reach over and squeeze her hand. "You don't need to hide your face, and don't worry about the bruises. They're not that noticeable. You look beautiful." And man, is that an understatement.

Layla attempts to hide a smile behind her menu. "Thank you."

14

Layla Alexander

As I skim the menu, I'm reeling from my encounter on the dock with Jason. I can still feel his strong arms around me as he held me close and saved me from falling into the frigid waters of Lake Michigan. I wanted to lose myself in his gaze. I wanted him to... I don't know. *Kiss me? Touch me?*

I've never felt this way before, not about any guy. We haven't known each other that long, and yet I feel like I've known him forever.

I feel like I *know* him.

Is that even possible? How can I feel that way about someone I've just met? This has never happened to me before, and I don't know what to make of it. Is this what they mean by love at first sight? Is that even a thing?

Our server comes back to the table to take our orders. I ask for a bottle of sparkling water because I want to save my carbs for my meal. Jason orders the same. He tends to drink the same thing I do. I think he's doing it to be nice.

While we're waiting for our drinks and perusing the menu, he picks up his phone and glances at the screen. "Your glucose level is kinda low," he says. "Do you feel all right?"

"Now that you mention it, I do feel a bit light-headed, but it's nothing serious."

Our server returns almost immediately with our chilled bottles of sparkling water and silverware wrapped in paper napkins. "Do you know what you want?" she asks, her overly-curious gaze lingering on me first, and then on Jason.

I opt for the lunch special, which is a grilled turkey and cheese on wholegrain bread, served with homemade potato chips and a cup of fresh fruit. Jason orders a burger and fries.

"Would you mind bringing her fruit out right now?" Jason asks our server.

"Sure, that's no problem," she says as she jots down our orders. Her gaze bounces back and forth between the two of us. Then she looks right at me. "I don't mean to be nosy, but you're Layla Alexander, aren't you?"

My pulse slams into my throat. "Yes."

Her blue eyes widen. "I thought so." Then she looks at Jason. "And this is your new bodyguard? I read you had a new one." She grows a bit flustered as her gaze returns to me. "I follow your Instagram account. I read about what happened to Sean. That's so horrible. I can't believe you saw that with your own eyes. You must have been scared to death."

I don't have an Instagram account, but there is a fan-made account that pretends to be me. My heart starts pounding. This is exactly what I'm afraid of—unending questions.

"Excuse me, it's Amy, right?" Jason asks as he points toward our server's name tag.

Amy's gaze bounces eagerly back to him. "Yeah?"

He gives her a polite smile. "Layla would like to eat her lunch in private. Do you mind?"

"Oh, sure." Blushing, she nods. "I'm sorry. It's just that I've never seen you in public before. You're even prettier than you are on social media." Flustered, she tucks her notepad and pen into her apron pocket. "I'll go put your orders in. And I'll bring her fruit right away." After one last look, Amy hurries off toward the kitchen.

"That wasn't too bad," Jason says. When his phone chimes with an incoming message, he checks the screen and smiles. "It's your brother, checking up on you."

"Tell him I'm doing great."

That girl is still staring at you.

I turn to look behind me, and sure enough, our server is watching us from behind the lunch counter. She quickly turns away and busies herself with folding napkins.

She saw your face. The bruises. She thinks they're ugly. You're ugly.

I sit so that she can't see my face. And then I notice that Jason's frowning as he watches me.

She lied. You're not pretty. You're ugly.

I do my best to ignore her. Jason's still watching me closely, as if he knows what's going on inside my head. It's only making me even more self-conscious.

"Everything okay?" he asks.

I nod. "I'm fine." Nervously, I unwrap my silverware—a fork, spoon, and a knife—and lay the utensils on the napkin, mostly just to have something to do.

Grab the knife. Take it. Hide it.

I glance down at the serrated knife at my place setting. Then I notice Jason watching me. "I'm fine," I snap, then regret talking to him that way. "Sorry."

"Here you go." Amy sets a fruit cup on the table in front of me. "Let me know if you need anything else," she says before she walks away.

I stab a chunk of watermelon with my fork and stick it in my mouth and chew. Just in time. I'm starting to feel the effects of low blood sugar. It makes me shaky and cranky to start with. It gets worse from there.

By the time I've finished with my fruit, I'm already feeling better. The rest of our food arrives not long after, and I busy myself with eating.

"Can I have a fry?" I ask Jason as I look longingly at the mountain of thick-cut French fries piled high on his plate.

Grinning, he holds his plate out to me, and I snag three fries.

Jason reaches across the table for my hand. "Tell me what she said to you just now."

"Who?" I ask, pretending not to know who he's talking about.

"You know who. Tell me what she's saying." He studies me. "I'm learning to read your body language, Layla. I can tell when she's getting to you."

"She said our server is staring at me." It's only half a lie, because she did say that earlier. I don't mention the knife.

Jason laughs. "Of course she's staring at you. You're gorgeous."

I open my mouth to speak, but nothing comes out. Does he really think so?

He laughs. "To be honest, sometimes I have trouble trying *not* to stare at you. You've looked in a mirror, right? Surely you know you're stunning."

He's lying. You're ugly.

When I look away, he tugs on my hand to draw my attention back to him. "She's doing it again. What'd she say?"

I figure I might as well tell him because he's going to keep asking. "She said I'm ugly."

He breaks into laughter. "You tell her for me that *she's* ugly.

Go ahead, tell her."

I bite back a grin as I play along. *He says you're ugly.*

"Did you tell her?" he asks.

"Yes. I can't believe we're arguing with an auditory hallucination." Smiling, I stick another fry in my mouth and chew.

"Hey, it's two against one," he says. "We've got her outnumbered."

How does he do it?

How does he make everything better?

Jason reaches over and steals a potato chip off my plate. "You owe me for the fries."

"Help yourself. I don't mind sharing." Still smiling, I pick up my sandwich and take a bite. For a few moments, I'm able to just enjoy myself, enjoy being with him, and not worry about what others think.

Once we're done eating, our server returns to the table and asks us if we want any dessert. Jason catches me eyeing the display card on the table that advertises their seasonal special—strawberry shortcake with whipped topping and strawberry glaze.

"You want to split one of those?" he asks me.

He's a mind reader. I nod guiltily. "Yes."

"We're gonna share one of those," Jason says, pointing at the advertisement. "Good luck estimating the grams of carbs in that thing," he tells me after our server walks away.

"I know it's bad." I do my best to guestimate the carbs in that dessert and plug the info into my device. Then I check my current glucose level, which is climbing just from what I've already eaten for lunch. "It's already high. I'll have to check again soon."

"Don't worry. I'll keep an eye on it," Jason says as he checks his phone.

It's nice to know I'm not in this alone.

* * *

After eating my half of the most delicious dessert I've ever had, we walk back to the car. The exercise will help my body use up some of this excess glucose, but I imagine I'm going to need more insulin soon. I enjoy watching the lake as the wind ripples across the surface of the water. Bright white sails stand out against the horizon. Tourist ships cruise along the shoreline, along with smaller speedboats and yachts.

When we reach the car and buckle in, I take the baseball cap off and drop it in my lap. I pull down the visor mirror to straighten my hair. "Thanks for the hat. It helped a lot."

"Anytime, princess," Jason says as he takes the cap from me and tosses it in the backseat.

I laugh. "I'm no princess."

"You sure look like one," he says as he starts the engine and backs out of our parking spot.

I try not to smile as we head home. I get compliments from guys all the time, but none of them ever made me feel the way this one did.

When we reach home, we walk in through the back door, into the kitchen. I grab a bottle of sparkling water from the fridge. Jason follows me up the stairs and down the hall to my room.

"So, what's on the agenda for the afternoon?" he asks me at my bedroom door as I open my bottle of water.

"Homework."

He pulls out his phone and checks my glucose monitor. "It's still a little high, but that's not surprising after what we ate. You need more insulin."

I nod. "I'll take care of it."

He looks like he wants to say more, but instead he points to his room. "I'll be right next door. Holler if you need me."

"I will." As he starts to walk away, I call him. "Jason."

He turns back. "Yes?"

"Thanks for today. I had a wonderful time."

He smiles. "My pleasure." He stands there for a moment, looking as if he wants to say more, but he doesn't. He nods toward his own door. "I'll leave you alone so you can do your homework."

I nod, hating to part from him. "Thanks. I guess I'll see you at dinner then."

He's not your boyfriend.

I know that.

Then stop making a fool of yourself. He doesn't even like you.

I let myself into my room and close the door behind me. I grab my anatomy textbook and study for an upcoming quiz. After I'm done with anatomy, I pick up my copy of *Jane Eyre* and curl up on the armchair in front of the hearth and open to the bookmarked spot. This must be where Jason left off reading last night. At least, I think it's where he left off. I fell asleep, so I'm not quite sure where he stopped.

I turn back a few pages just to make sure I don't miss anything. I've read this book a dozen times already, and I've watched all of the film versions, but this story never gets old. I'm a sucker for romance, and Mr. Rochester is a divine, dark romantic anti-hero. He harbors so much pain and suffering, and his longing for Jane is palpable.

After having such a big lunch, it's not surprising my eyelids start to grow heavy, and I'm having trouble concentrating on what I'm reading. I lay my book down and close my eyes, just for a minute.

The sound of my glucose monitoring app alarm wakes me with a start as it warns me of a dangerous blood sugar low. *Crap!* I must have overestimated the amount of carbs in my lunch and my pod delivered too much insulin.

My head feels fuzzy, and my heart is racing. I try to stand, but I'm so dizzy I fall back onto my chair. I'm shaking and perspiring, my skin clammy. These are all symptoms I know well.

I keep a stash of apple juice boxes in my nightstand drawer for occasions like this, but my legs are so weak I don't think I can walk that far.

My bedroom door crashes open, and Jason storms in, his expression tight. He received the alarm on his phone, as did my mom and brother. *Great.* Now I've worried everyone.

I point to my nightstand. "Juice box, top drawer."

Jason retrieves the juice box and stabs the straw into the opening before handing it to me.

I suck down half the juice in one gulp and then lean back in my chair to catch my breath. "Thanks."

He crouches down beside me and pulls out his phone. "I'll text your brother and your mom to let them know you're okay."

As soon as he says that, both our phones start buzzing with incoming messages. "It's Mom and Ian." I text them both back, telling them I'm okay.

Jason checks his watch and then lays his hand on my knee. "Dinner is in twenty minutes. Perfect timing because you need to eat. Let's go."

"Just one second. Let me check my e-mail." I get on my laptop to see if my professors have replied. "Yes! They've all agreed to let me work from home another week." *Thank goodness.* "I just need to hear from two more, and then I'm going to be all right."

* * *

Later that evening, after dinner, I talk Jason into watching one of my favorite film versions of *Jane Eyre*—the one with Toby Stephens and Ruth Wilson.

Before we start the movie, we run down to the kitchen to grab some snacks. My blood sugar level is correct now, and Jason's been watching it like a hawk all evening.

"So, what do we want?" Jason asks as we walk into the pantry lined with shelves. "How about protein? I think you've had enough carbs today."

"Okay, fine." So we put together a platter of cheese and mixed nuts. "How about a little bit of popcorn?" I ask, grabbing a bag of pre-popped white cheddar popcorn off the shelf.

"Just a little bit," he says as he grabs two bottles of sugar-free lemonade out of the fridge.

As we head for the door, my dad enters the kitchen. "Hey, guys," he says as he eyes our loot. "What are you up to?"

"We're getting some snacks," Jason says.

Dad frowns. "Her glucose alarm went off earlier."

"It's under control," Jason says. "She's fine now. We're watching it closely."

"We're going to watch a movie, Dad," I say. "Snacks are a necessity."

My dad doesn't seem to agree. "Well, be careful with what you eat."

We carry our haul back up to my room. Jason sits beside me on the sofa, and we both kick off our shoes and prop our feet on the coffee table.

I hold the platter of snacks on my lap. Jason opens the

bottles of lemonade and sets them on coasters on the coffee table. Then he opens the small bag of popcorn.

"All right," he says, grabbing the remote. "Let's see this Mr. Rochester in action. I want to know what all the hype is about."

By the time the movie comes to an end, the popcorn is gone, and our lemonade bottles are empty. Most of the cheese and nuts are gone, too. Jason picks up his phone and checks my glucose level for the third time since the movie started. I've already programmed the carb amount into my device.

"Good movie," Jason says as the credits roll.

"Toby Stephens makes a great Mr. Rochester, don't you think? And I love the actress who played Jane. She's got this otherworldly vibe, like Liv Tyler in *Lord of the Rings*."

Jason rises to his feet and stretches his arms and shoulders, groaning at the effort. I find myself staring at his body as he flexes his muscles.

He checks his watch. "Wow, it's late. I should let you get some sleep."

"Thanks for watching the movie with me."

"Anytime. Let's do it again soon."

"You can pick the movie next time."

He smiles. "It's a deal." He reaches down and brushes my cheek with his knuckle. "G'night, Layla."

"Goodnight."

He hesitates a moment, just watching me, before he turns and heads for the door. He stops halfway out the door and looks back at me. "I'll see you at breakfast."

I watch him until he's through the door, and sigh when it closes behind him. I've never had a relationship with a bodyguard like I have with Jason. I've had six previous bodyguards in my life. The first couple, I don't even remember—I was too young. They accompanied me to school and waited for me outside my classroom door. The last two, Rob and Sean, were both jerks. God, especially Sean. But Jason? He's not just a bodyguard. He's quickly becoming a real friend. Someone I like hanging out with. Someone I look forward to seeing each day.

Someone you're crushing on.

We're just friends.

You're lying.

After getting ready for bed and turning out the lights, I crawl beneath the covers with my phone to watch some Tik-Tok. That usually relaxes me. But tonight, my thoughts keep drifting back to the day I spent with Jason. It was probably the best day I've had in a really long time.

I lay my phone on my nightstand and roll onto my side, wrapping my arm around the spare pillow. My cuddle pillow.

I can still feel Jason's gentle touch on my cheek.

Why can't I meet someone like him? Someone who accepts me as I am. Who makes an effort to understand me and my issues. Is it too much to ask for a normal life and to do normal things, like meet guys and go on dates?

Am I too much for someone to deal with? Too much of a freak?

Yes.

Shut up.

She'd been pretty quiet during the movie, probably because my attention was split between watching the film and secretly watching Jason's reaction to it. It had been a very relaxing and enjoyable two hours.

He hated the movie. He was just being nice.

Oh, for god's sake, would you stop?

You like him.

I ignore her.

Too bad he barely tolerates you.

I can't help wondering if she could be right. I mean, it's his *job* to spend time with me. That doesn't mean he wants to.

For a moment, I wish things could be different. I wish Jason was here because he wanted to be.

He hates you.

Oh, shove it, will you?

He's so far out of your league.

She's probably right about that.

15

Layla Alexander

*I*t's pitch black, and I'm freezing cold. I can't stop shaking. I can't think straight. I can't hear anything over the screaming in my head. I want to disappear. I want to vanish into thin air and not exist any longer. This misery is worse than death. It has to be.

I hear a loud bang, and then the bed shudders.

"How the fuck do we shut her up?" one man says, his voice gruff and hateful.

"Give her more sedatives."

I feel a sting on my arm, and then the room begins to spin. I'm *going to be sick.*

I can't breathe!

The men just laugh.

"Told you it would shut her up."

When I feel a hand between my legs, I try in vain to scream, but nothing comes out.

"Layla, wake up!" Strong hands grip my shoulders firmly, shaking me. "Come on, honey, wake up."

I shoot up into a sitting position, knocking my forehead into a hard, muscular chest. Jason sits back to give me room, but his hands are still on me, holding me steady.

Frantic, I search the dark shadows of the room for those awful men.

"What are you looking for?" Jason asks.

"They were here, just now. I heard them."

"Who was here?"

"The ones who hurt me. They drugged me." I rub my arm where the needle went in.

"There's no one here but us, Layla." He captures my hands and holds them tightly to his chest. "It was just a dream. You're safe."

I glance up at Jason, whose short, dark hair sticks up in places. "I'm sorry I woke you."

"Hey, it's okay." He releases one of my hands so he can brush the hair from my hot face. "Don't move," he says, frowning. He reaches over to switch on my bedside lamp, then studies my throat, tipping my chin up so he can see better in the dim light. "You scratched your neck."

"I couldn't breathe."

He thinks you're crazy.

Stop it.

He's going to quit because you're a nutjob.

"I said stop!"

Jason's brow furrows for a split second until he realizes my outburst wasn't directed at him. He sits back, putting some space between us. "Feeling better?"

"Yes."

He pulls his phone from his pocket and checks my sugars. I lie back down with a sigh. "I'm sorry I woke you."

He brushes my hair back from my face. "You don't need to apologize. I'm here to help you. I *want* to help." He straightens my bedding. "Better?"

"Yes." *No.* I always feel unsettled after a nightmare.

"Do you need anything?" he asks. "Some water maybe?"

"No, I'm fine." *Don't leave me.*

You're pathetic. He's paid to take care of you. He's not doing it because he wants to.

He studies me closely for a second, as if he's trying to solve a puzzle. "What's she saying?"

My heart jumps in my chest. "Nothing."

He frowns. "Layla, I can't help you if you're not honest with me."

"It's just the usual bullshit. That I'm pathetic and you—" I falter, because I don't want to say the words out loud. I don't want to put the idea in his head.

"I what?"

"She says you don't really want to be here with me."

His lips flatten as he shakes his head. "Layla, I wouldn't be here if I didn't want to." He cradles my hand in his, holding it to his chest. "I promise. Are you okay to go back to sleep?"

I have a hard time getting back to sleep after a nightmare, but it's late—three o'clock in the morning. I can't keep him up half the night. "I'll be fine."

He doesn't look convinced. "Do you want me to stay with you for a little while? Just until you fall back to sleep?"

My pulse jumps at his offer. I never once asked Sean to sit with me. I never trusted him that much. But I trust Jason. "Would you mind? For just a little while?"

"I don't mind." He motions for me to scoot over and then he crawls in beside me, on top of the blankets. He arranges two pillows beneath his head, settles in, and sighs. "Did I ever tell you about the time I delivered my boss's baby?"

"No." I fold my hands over my belly and feel the tension leave my body.

"Yeah, I delivered Shane and Beth's baby in the attic over a convenience store."

"How in the world did she get up there?"

"Crazy, right? It was during an armed robbery. They were taking a little road trip, along with Beth's bodyguard, Lia, who happens to be Shane's youngest sister. When Shane stopped to get gas, Beth and Lia went inside the convenience store, I'm guessing to get snacks. While they were in there, armed robbers attacked the store. Lia was able to sneak Beth—who was not quite eight months pregnant at the time—into the rear storage area, where they found stairs leading up to an unused attic."

Jason reaches over and lays his hand on mine. It's a simple touch—just skin and warmth—and yet it comforts me.

He goes on. "Beth went into labor, and—to make a long story short—Shane and his team managed to get me up into the attic with her while the robbery was going on downstairs, and I delivered her son, Luke. He was six weeks premature, and I had a heck of a time getting him to breathe. It was touch and go for a while, but ultimately, he started breathing, and then we whisked him off to the hospital."

I stifle a yawn. "Was he okay?"

"Yeah, he did great. He's fine now, just over a year old. He's a cute little kid. You should meet him sometime."

Jason continues on, talking in a low voice I find soothing. My eyelids grow heavy, drifting shut as I concentrate on his words.

"She was lucky to have you there," I say.

As he proceeds to tell me all about the little boy he helped deliver, my muscles ease and my mind begins to float as sleep takes me over.

16

Jason Miller

Layla and I settle into a comfortable routine over the next week. She spends each morning catching up on her schoolwork while I work out in the home gym. In the afternoons, I try to get her out of the house as much as possible because I think it'll do her a lot of good. We take long walks in the park, and we visit the zoo. We go see a Cubs' game at Wrigley Field. She wears my baseball cap low over her eyes, and not a single person recognizes her.

One evening, we go to Ian and Tyler's townhouse and hang out with them up in their rooftop greenhouse. Tyler cooks burgers on a gas grill, while the rest of us enjoy the view of Lake Michigan in the distance.

Ian stands and nods toward the door. "Hey, Jason, come down and help me in the kitchen."

I glance at Layla, who's busy chatting with Tyler. "Sure." I follow him downstairs.

Ian digs around in the fridge and pulls out prepped ingredients for a salad. He grabs a bowl and starts tossing ingredients in. "Layla seems in good spirits."

"It's been a good week. We've been to the park and the zoo. I've been working on getting her out of the house a little each day."

"Mom and Dad say she's doing pretty well, all things considered."

"She is. She's had a few nightmares this week, and of course there's always the voice to contend with, but she's coping."

Ian shakes a bottle of homemade vinaigrette. "You're good for her."

His compliment surprises me. And it feels good. "We're good for each other." And it's true. I truly enjoy being with her. It doesn't feel like a job. It feels natural. Like I'm hanging out with a friend.

Ian gives me a curious look as he tries to read between the lines. But there's nothing to read. There can't be.

I shrug. "I keep her out of trouble, and she keeps me employed. It's a win-win."

Ian laughs as he hands me a platter of burger toppings and

a bag of buns. "You carry that up. I'll bring the salad."

*　*　*

The bruises on her face are fading nicely, and it won't be long before they're gone completely. The hope is that by the time she returns to campus on Monday, they'll be pretty faint.

Layla's name remains plastered all over the news, her privacy nonexistent. News of Sean's violent death doesn't seem to be dying down either. I can just imagine all the questions she's going to get when she returns to campus on Monday. Unfortunately, she's just going to have to deal with it.

In the evenings, we watch movies in her room, or we walk on the treadmills in the workout room at her house. We play games. She kicks my butt at Scrabble every time, but I usually beat her at Monopoly. She's got a better vocabulary than I do, but I'm better at strategy. Yahtzee can go either way, as it's mostly a game of chance.

Layla manages her diabetes extremely well. She's pretty good at estimating her carb consumption. Occasionally, she has blood sugar lows, or highs, but we usually catch those *before* the alarms go off on our phones.

Ruth and Martin have been sending glowing reports back to Shane, who in turn pats me on the back—figuratively. The reason I know this is because I've been hearing about it from Shane himself.

"Keep up the good work, Jason," he tells me during a weekly status phone call. "Her parents are thrilled with the progress she's making. They say they can't remember a time when she was so relaxed, and they attribute that to your influence. Just keep doing what you're doing."

* * *

It's Sunday evening after dinner, the night before she's scheduled to return to campus. It's only eight o'clock, and she's got a couple of hours to kill before bed.

We climb the stairs together, side by side. We're walking so close that occasionally one of us will accidently brush against the other. When we touch, I feel things I shouldn't feel.

When we reach her bedroom door, she says, "I'm probably going to watch some Netflix. What about you?"

We've been spending nearly every minute together the past few days. I'm thinking I should give her some space. "I have some reading to do."

"For work, or for fun?"

I shrug. "A bit of both."

"I guess I'll see you in the morning, then," she says.

I don't know if it's my imagination, or wishful thinking on my part, but she sounds reluctant to part company. I know the feeling.

"Text if you need me," I tell her before I head to my room.

I take a quick shower and change into sweats. Then I get comfortable on the bed, resting against a stack of pillows propped against the massive headboard. I've probably only been reading twenty minutes or so when I hear a quiet knock. "Come in."

The door opens just enough for a pretty face to peek inside. "Can I come in?"

"Sure. You're always welcome."

Layla steps into the room and closes the door, her phone clutched in her hands and earbuds in her ears. She smiles apologetically. "Can I hang out with you?"

My first response is to redirect her back to her own room. I'm not sure how her parents would take it if they found Layla and me alone in my bedroom. But when I see that her earbuds are in, I suspect she's having issues with the voice. She's probably feeling anxious about returning to campus tomorrow.

I can't turn her away. She's clearly looking for companionship. "Sure." I pat a spot beside me on the mattress.

She doesn't need any further encouragement. She crosses the room and climbs up onto my bed. After plumping a couple of pillows behind her, she reclines against the headboard and immediately turns her attention to the TikTok videos playing on the screen of her phone.

I go back to reading on my tablet, and we lie together companionably, each of us doing our own thing. Occasionally, I'll hear a quiet snicker or a snort of laughter coming from her, which makes me smile. When she's happy, I'm happy.

And the converse is true. When she's hurting, so am I.

She puts her phone down and sighs. "Do you feel like watching something on Netflix?"

I lay my tablet down and smile. I knew it was only a matter of time. "Sure. What do you want to watch?"

"*Stranger Things.*"

We both love that show. "Okay." I grab the TV remote and find where we left off the last time we watched it. We end up watching two episodes before she starts yawning.

"You need to get some sleep," I say. "Tomorrow's going to be here before you know it. When do we need to leave? What time is your first class?"

"My first class is at ten. Parking can be tricky, and I like to arrive in plenty of time so I don't feel rushed. We should leave by eight-thirty."

I nod. "Eight-thirty it is."

When she yawns again, I laugh as I shoo her off my bed. "Go. I'll see you at breakfast."

"Okay. G'night."

"Goodnight. Sleep well."

After she leaves my room, I immediately feel the loss of her presence. I wish—*no*. I'm not even going to think it, because it's pointless.

We can't ever be what I wish we could be.

After Layla goes back to her own room, I lie awake for a long time, watching the minutes tick by. The minutes turn into hours, and sleep eludes me as it often does. I'm not sure if I can't sleep, or if I'm avoiding it.

Layla's not the only one who has nightmares. More often than not, when I close my eyes at night, I see the faces of the people I couldn't save. I hear their cries for help. And I feel a crushing sense of responsibility for those I lost.

I see the faces of fellow soldiers who didn't make it back home. I see limbs torn from bodies because of road-side bombs. I see my fellow soldiers who were so broken, I couldn't hold them together long enough to get them the help they needed.

Even back home, as a paramedic, I saw sights that I can't forget. Women, men, even children who died horrible deaths in car wrecks and fires. When it got to be too much, I quit my job as a paramedic and went into private security. It's not a walk in the park, but at least it's better.

17

Layla Alexander

When my phone alarm goes off Monday morning at seven, I hop out of bed, eager and excited to be getting back to campus and my friends. Well, my *one* friend anyway. Charlene is also a psychology major, and she's in two of my classes. That's how we met. I consider her a real friend. Actually, she's more like an older sister who has taken me under her wing.

You don't have any friends.

Yes, I do. Charlene's my friend.

She only pretends to like you because you're wealthy.

That's not true. She's never asked me for anything.

Just wait. She will.

I'm in too good of a mood today to let *her* get to me. And anyway, she's wrong. I do have friends. Charlene, for one. There's Tyler, too. Yes, he's my brother's boyfriend, but he also counts as a friend. And now I have Jason. I consider him a friend as well.

No, he's your paid companion. Big difference. If he weren't paid, he wouldn't be with you.

That's true, but I ignore her.

After a quick shower, I dry off and switch out my insulin pod. Each pod lasts two to three days, and then it's time for a replacement. Once that's done, I blow dry my hair.

Today, I'm wearing one of my favorite comfy outfits—black leggings, short black boots, a black skirt, and a sapphire-blue silk blouse with long sleeves. It's too hot out for long sleeves, but I can't bare my arms. I pull my hair up into a high pony so it's out of the way and put on a pair of gold hoop earrings. A light foundation of make-up does a decent job of covering the bruises on my face.

I study my reflection in the bathroom mirror from multiple angles and count the number of bruises that are still visible, even after almost two weeks. They look like faint shadows on my face. Lastly, I apply kohl eyeliner, some smokey-blue eyeshadow, and a bit of lip gloss.

When it's time to go downstairs, I grab my backpack and

go get Jason. Just as I'm about to knock on his door, it opens, and there he is dressed and ready. As soon as he spots me, his dark eyes widen, and I'm not sure if it's because he thinks I look good, or because I look bad.

You look hideous. Ugly. So ugly.

Self-consciously, I touch my face. "Does it look bad?"

He shakes his head. "No. You look... wow." Then he glances away, almost bashfully. "What I mean is, good job with the make-up. I can hardly see the bruises."

Jason is dressed in blue jeans and a gray T-shirt that is molded to his torso. The shirt clings to his muscled chest and the outline of his chiseled biceps. His arms are bare and his tattoos are visible for a change.

My heart flutters in my chest as my pulse kicks up, and suddenly I'm finding it difficult to catch my breath. It might be low blood sugar, but I think it's more likely just the effect he has on me.

He checks his watch. "Perfect timing. I was just coming to get you. Ready to go?"

I nod, not trusting myself to speak. "Mm-hmm."

"Let's go, then." He switches off the light in his room as he follows me out the door. We head toward the stairs. "I'll carry that," he says, slipping my backpack off my shoulder and onto his. "How'd you sleep last night?"

"Fine," I answer, surprised that it's true.

"I'm glad to hear it." We take the stairs. "Please tell me we're grabbing some breakfast before we leave for campus. I'm famished, and you need to eat."

I laugh. "Margaret won't let me leave the house unless I've had breakfast. And I have to take my meds."

We head for the kitchen, where we find Margaret seated at the table.

"Good morning," she says with a smile. She waves toward the buffet. "Help yourselves."

I head for the breakfast spread and grab a plate and move down the line, taking a little bit of this and a little bit of that—mostly protein, one slice of buttered toast, and a tiny bit of fruit. I fill a tumbler with iced coffee, to which I add some non-sugar sweetener and sugar-free caramel creamer.

Jason loads up a plate with eggs and bacon and pours himself a cup of straight black coffee.

"I'm already spoiled," Jason says as he takes the seat beside mine. "Before coming here, I was lucky to get cold cereal for breakfast."

"Not in my kitchen, young man," André says from across the room, waving a spatula in the air as he speaks.

Just as we start eating, Jason pulls out his phone to check my sugar level. He does it so quickly and quietly that I almost don't notice. But going by the satisfied smile on Margaret's face, she does.

After I eat, I take my psych medication. It helps lessen the frequency of the auditory hallucinations, but it doesn't eliminate them completely.

Twenty minutes later, with my backpack slung over Jason's shoulder, we head out the back door to the parking area.

"We'll have to take my car." He reaches down and pats his ankle holster. "I can't carry my gun on campus, so I'll have to lock it in the car safe."

Jason opens my car door for me, and I slide in. Then he walks around to the driver's side and climbs in. While he's adjusting the driver's seat, I receive a text message from my brother.

Ian: Good luck on your first day back to school. Tyler sends his love.

Smiling, I text him back.

Layla: Thank u both! What are you doing today?

Ian: Shooting practice at the range. LOL Me with a gun. Very entertaining for Tyler, trust me. And possibly dangerous.

I think it's wonderful. He's never even held a job before, and now he's fully embracing his new career as a private investigator.

Layla: Good luck. And be careful!

"Who's that you're texting?" Jason asks as we pull into traffic.

"Ian. He's wishing me good luck today."

Jason shoots me a quick glance. "You don't need luck. You're going to do great."

"I appreciate your optimism." But I frown.

"What's wrong?"

I pull the visor mirror down in front of me and examine

my face. "No amount of make-up can completely hide these bruises. People are going to talk. And take pictures."

Jason reaches over and pats my knee. "It's going to be fine. If anyone asks about Sean, tell them you traded up." And then he winks at me.

I do my best to smile, but the memories are still too painful.

Jason's not fooled. "Sean betrayed you in the worst way possible. He doesn't deserve your sympathy."

I gaze out my window at the passing scenery.

Jason's voice is gentle when he says, "Do you want to talk about what happened that morning?"

I haven't talked about that morning with very many people. I had to tell the police, of course. And I told my parents, Ian, and Tyler. But that's all.

Jason squeezes my hand. "Tell me, Layla. I know the gist of what happened, but I'd like to hear it from you."

A painful knot forms in my throat as the memories come rushing back—memories I've tried so hard to forget. "We were heading to campus when Sean said we needed to make a pitstop at his apartment. I told him no, because I was afraid I'd be late to class, but he insisted. He said he'd make it quick. And there really wasn't anything I could do about it since he was driving. I was more or less at his mercy. When we pulled up in front of his apartment building, he made me come inside with him. I wanted to wait in the car, but he said he couldn't leave me out there alone. He did live in a pretty sketchy neighborhood. So I went in with him. We walked into his apartment building, and his roommate, Chad, was waiting for us."

I have to stop then as I feel tears gathering in my eyes.

"You don't have to go on if you don't want to," Jason says.

I swallow hard. "It's okay. You should know. Sean brought me there on purpose, to hand me over to Chad. Basically, he sold me to Chad to pay off his drug debt. Chad pulled a gun on Sean and shot him in cold blood, right in front of me. I remember screaming as the pool of blood spread out beneath his body. He was dead already. I was hysterical, in shock."

In a daze, I shake my head. "I honestly don't remember much after that. I was screaming, and then I felt a pinch in my arm. Chad injected me with something, some drug. Everything got fuzzy after that. My legs gave out on me, and I fell to the floor. The rest was surreal. I do remember Chad helping me out to my car, and we drove off. Then there was another man and a different car. They took me to a warehouse where I was stripped and chained to a bed. All I could hear was crying girls." I shudder violently. "It was awful. No human being should ever be treated like that. It was inhumane."

Jason links our fingers together. "I'm sorry, Layla. I wish I'd been there."

His fingers are longer than mine, warm, and slightly calloused. It's comforting. "I wish you'd been there, too." If he'd been with me that day, none of that would have happened.

I'm quiet for the rest of the drive to school. We arrive on campus at nine-thirty. Campus parking is at a premium on

Monday mornings. He cruises up and down the lanes looking for an open spot.

Before long, I notice he keeps looking in the rearview mirror, as if he's keeping tabs on something. Or someone. I turn in my seat to glance behind us, and when I spot the beat-up silver sedan on our tail, my stomach drops.

"He's been riding our bumper since we arrived on campus," Jason says. "Do you recognize him?"

I let out a frustrated sigh. "Yes. That's Gary Fisher—he's a local society blogger and gossipmonger. He often follows me around campus trying to get pictures to sell to the online tabloids."

Jason frowns. "Do people on campus bother you a lot?"

"There are usually a couple of photographers who try consistently to catch me coming and going from classes, but it's usually students who take the most photos. They try to sneak selfies with me in the background, thinking I won't notice. But I do."

I honestly don't know why anyone is interested in me. I'm not a Kardashian, not even close. I'm a nobody from Chicago who wants to stay that way. Yes, I inherited a lot of money from my paternal grandfather, but I've done nothing worthy of this level of attention.

I'm not famous. I haven't done anything noteworthy other than end up on those stupid lists of the wealthiest Americans under the age of twenty-five. Or under thirty. Or even under forty. No matter the list, Ian and I are both always at the top.

Personally, I think people are fascinated by wealth and the people who have it. Yes, I live a comfortable and privileged life, but I don't go around flashing my money and lording it over people. My grandfather founded one of the first telecommunications in the US. He was the genius who saw the potential in the technology. Ian and I just benefited from his ingenuity and success.

Jason spots an empty parking space, pulls in, and shuts off the engine. He quickly removes the black handgun from his ankle holster and slips it into a small metal cabinet fitted between the front seats. The cabinet is secured with a combination lock. "I hate having to leave this in the car, but it's better than getting arrested on campus for carrying."

"I don't think you'd ever need it on campus. It's a pretty peaceful place."

He nods as he turns in his seat to glance behind us. Gary Fisher is in his car, idling in the lane behind us.

"Stay in the car," Jason says just before he gets out.

He approaches Gary's car, and the two of them exchange rather heated words. When Gary speeds off, Jason comes around to my door and opens it. After I get out of the car, he grabs my backpack from behind my seat and slings it over his shoulder. "Where's your first class?"

I point across campus. "That way. It's about a ten-minute walk."

"Stick close to me at all times," he says as we set off.

I don't know what Jason said to Gary, but I doubt it scared

him off. Gary is tenacious. Sure enough, we're not even out of the parking lot before I hear him calling my name from somewhere behind us.

"Layla, wait! Layla! Where've you been? I just want to ask you a few questions. How did you feel witnessing your former bodyguard's death?"

"Keep walking," Jason mutters under his breath as he cups my elbow and propels me through the maze of parked cars toward the campus lawn.

I can hear Gary huffing as he jogs to catch up.

As soon as Gary reaches us, Jason drives him back a few feet. "I told you to get lost."

"Watch it, buddy!" Gary wheezes as he tries to catch his breath. "You can't push me around like that. It's a free country." He holds up a laminated badge that hangs on a lanyard around his neck. "Ever heard of freedom of the press?"

Jason laughs. "If you get within ten feet of her, you'll have to deal with me. Is that clear?"

Doing my best to ignore Gary, I walk quickly along the paved sidewalk path that leads to the science complex.

"Where are we headed first?" Jason asks.

"Anatomy class."

He makes a face. "That's a tough one."

I laugh, realizing he would have taken anatomy, too, as part of his medical training. "Yeah, but the professor makes it enjoyable."

"Why? Is he humorous?" Jason laughs at his own joke. "Get

it?" He pats his upper arm. "As in the humerus bone?"

I groan. "That joke's so old, it's not even funny. No, it's an enjoyable class because the professor is hot."

"Oh, great." Jason rolls his eyes. "Will your hot professor mind me sitting in on your class?"

I laugh. "The faculty here are used to me having someone with me. It's fine."

We enter the building where my class is held and find ourselves in the midst of a good-sized crowd of students waiting outside the lecture hall. Students mill around in the main hallway as they wait for Professor Kent to unlock the door and let us in. Some are sitting on the floor going over their notes. Others have earbuds in and are listening to music or videos on their phones. Fortunately, not many seem to have spotted me yet.

Jason stands close beside me.

"Layla, you're back!" cries a familiar voice.

I cringe when everyone in the hallway abruptly stops talking and turns to stare. A hush falls and suddenly it's deathly quiet. Their eyes widen when they see my face. Immediately, the camera phones come out, and people are snapping pics left and right. Jason steps in front of me and tries his best to block their view.

Charlene joins me. "I'm so glad you're back. I was afraid you'd have to drop your classes this term." She steps back and studies me. "Oh, Layla. Your poor face." She wraps me in a gentle hug. "I couldn't believe what I read in the papers. I'm so sorry."

Jason steps closer, as if to intercede, but I give him a reassuring smile. "It's okay. She's a friend."

You don't have any friends. Loser.

I like Charlene. She's older than I am, in her early thirties, and a single mom with two young kids. She was a stay-at-home mom when her husband died in a workplace shooting two years ago. She's using the life insurance money she received to go back to school to become a mental health therapist. Since we're both in the psychology program, we've had a number of classes together.

As Charlene looks me over, her soft round face is etched in motherly concern. "I'm sorry about Sean. That must have been awful to witness." Her eyes dart to Jason, then back to me. "Is everything okay?"

Loser. You're a pathetic loser.

"I'm fine," I say as I self-consciously raise my hand in an attempt to block my face from the sound of cameras snapping images in rapid-fire.

It looks like Gary caught up with us. "Layla, look over here!" he yells. "Hey, Layla! Come on, just one good shot of your face!"

I do my best to ignore him.

Charlene's curly black hair is pulled back in a bun, but a few loose corkscrew strands have fallen free to frame her face. Her light brown skin is heavily dotted with freckles. "I was so worried when you didn't show up for class the past two weeks."

"I was at home... recuperating. But I'm okay now. Really."

Charlene smiles apologetically at Jason as she squeezes in between us so that she's standing next to me along the wall. We stand shoulder to shoulder. She's close to six feet tall, nearly Jason's height, and I'm used to her looking down at me.

She nods subtly toward Jason. "Who's the new guy?" she whispers.

I smile, knowing that he's listening to every word. "That's Jason. He's my new bodyguard."

As she sneaks another peek at Jason, Charlene presses her hand to her chest. "That's so not fair. I want a bodyguard, too."

I notice Jason's pretending not to listen in on our conversation, but his smile gives him away. He's standing on the other side of me, leaning against the wall like the rest of us as he tries to blend in. He's doing a great job. He looks like any other college student—well, except maybe he's a lot hotter.

Out of the corner of my eye, I notice several phone cameras are still pointed in my direction as students try to sneak pictures of me. Most of those pics will end up on Instagram before class is even over, along with *#LaylaAlexander*, *#AmericanHeiress*, *#WhereHasSheBeenHiding*.

I know Gary's photos will end up online.

"Come on, Layla," Gary calls. "Your fans want to see what you look like. Just one good pic, I promise."

Yeah, show him your ugly face. You pathetic loser.

As Gary moves, so does Jason. He repositions himself so that he's essentially blocking the photographer. As I gaze up into his face, my heart flutters. He's clearly on high alert as he assesses everyone around us, his expression taut, his strong jaw clenched. He's a strikingly handsome guy with his dark hair and trim beard. And based on all the girls eyeing him, I'm not the only one who thinks so.

Two more students approach to welcome me back to class. These two I recognize as they sit right in front of me in the lecture hall, although we rarely do more than just say hello.

"Oh, my god, Layla. You poor thing," one of them says as she scans my face. I think her name is Andrea. "I can't believe those monsters did that to you."

The second one, a blonde whose name escapes me—I think it begins with an *S*. Sara? Sierra? Anyway, she eyes Jason curiously, then turns her gaze to me. "I'm glad you're back." Her gaze darts back to Jason. "Is that your new bodyguard? I read about Sean getting killed right in front of you. That must have been awful."

Before I can reply, a guy from our class approaches. He's big and blond, with a massively broad chest and thighs the size of tree trunks. He's dressed in jeans and a sports jersey. I know this guy—everyone does. His name is Reese.

"Hey, Layla," Reese says as he plants himself in front of me. I have to tip my head back to see his face. "You were gone so long, I was starting to think you'd dropped the class."

"Hi, Reese. I was out on medical leave." I'm not sure what else to say. I don't know this guy personally, but I know of him. Everybody knows who he is. Reese Hendricks. I think his father is some local big shot. Reese sits in the back of the room with his buddies, but he's never paid me any attention before now. In fact, I don't think he's ever spoken to me before.

He read about you in the news and looked up your net worth. You're a rich bitch!

Reese eyes Jason a moment, then turns his gaze back to me. "Would you like to grab coffee after class?"

My heart stutters in shock.

Is he asking me out?

Like on a date?

18

Layla Alexander

Reese's unexpected invitation has rendered me speechless. I'm saved from having to answer when our professor arrives and unlocks the door. He pushes it wide open, and it hits the wall with a loud clang.

"Good morning, guys," he says, sounding winded. He props the door open. "Sorry I'm late. Traffic was a bear this morning."

Everyone streams into the large lecture hall, shuffling shoulder to shoulder as we head to our assigned seats. Jason's right behind me, steering me through the crush of people.

I'm relieved I was saved from having to answer Reese, because I honestly didn't know what to say to him. I was completely tongue-tied. Part of me wants to say yes, and part of me wants to run in the opposite direction.

Make up your mind. I thought you wanted to go on a date.

I do.

Then why didn't you say yes? Finally, someone's dumb enough to ask you out. You should have said yes.

"Hey, Layla, I'll catch you after class, okay?" Reese says, waving at me as he heads for his seat at the back of the room.

Jason follows me, and when I slip into my seat, he looks down at the empty seat beside mine.

"It's all yours," I tell him. "This seat's reserved for my bodyguard."

He sits and hands me my backpack, which I set on the floor beside me and unzip it so I can retrieve my iPad and stylus for notetaking.

Charlene, who's seated to my left, keeps looking at me, then at Jason, then back to me.

She's using you, just like all the others.

No, she's not. We're friends.

You don't have any friends.

As our instructor turns on the overhead projector and gets ready to begin class, I notice Jason scanning the room, the rows of students, the multiple exits, the professor's lecture podium up in front. I wonder what he thinks about being back in school again.

Andrea and Sierra—that's her name!—who sit directly in front of me, keep sneaking glimpses. Way back in the last row, Reese and his buddies are talking in low voices, occasionally laughing, until the professor glares at them and they quiet down.

Charlene leans close. "I'm so glad you're back. I missed you."

"Thanks."

She's just sucking up to you.

I sigh as I power on my iPad and open up my notetaking app.

One of my biggest problems is I don't know who to trust. My whole life, kids have pretended to be my friend because of my notoriety, not because they really liked me. When I was young, my parents would throw these lavishly catered birthday parties for me and invite my entire class. There would be tons of food and cake and ice cream, chocolate fountains, pony rides, even magicians. Everyone who was invited showed up—not because they cared one iota about me, but because of the prestige it brought them at school to attend one of my parties. Even kids I didn't know, kids from other classes, would ask to be invited, or they'd simply tag along with friends. Everyone acted like they were my best friend at the parties, but when the festivities were over, they went back to ignoring me until my birthday rolled around the following year.

By the age of eight, I'd figured out what was going on, and I told my parents I didn't want any more birthday parties.

I was a painfully shy kid to begin with, and knowing that others just pretended to like me made it nearly impossible for me to trust anyone outside of my family. I remember wishing I was a nobody.

You *are* a nobody.

I honestly wish people didn't know who I am, or how much money is in my bank account. I'd love to be able to blend in anonymously with my peers. Instead, I'm far too visible, and for the wrong reasons. And if they knew the truth about me, it would be a thousand times worse.

They don't know I'm the girl who hears voices in her head.

They don't know I'm the girl who suffers from crushing anxiety and self-doubt.

And now they do know me as the girl whose bodyguard was shot dead right in front of her after he traded her to his drug dealer, who then sold her to a sex trafficking ring.

They know me for all the wrong reasons.

I wish I had a dollar for each time someone's ever asked if they could interview me for their vlog or take a selfie with me to post on sites— not that I need the money. It's the principle. I feel like a Kardashian, but without the fashion sense.

You wish you were a Kardashian. Idiot.

All I want is to be a normal college student. I want to have friends, go to parties, even go on dates. Is that too much to ask? I'm twenty-one years old, and I've never been on a date. Not once.

Charlene's the only one who's been nice to me and hasn't asked me for a single thing. In fact, I've offered her money repeatedly to help her with expenses until she graduates and gets a job, but she refuses to accept a single penny.

As the professor starts his lecture, I concentrate on what he's saying and take notes. It's hard to block out *her* constant chatter, the put-downs and the biting words, but I do my best. Occasionally, I glance over at Jason, who's reading an e-book on his phone. He seems oblivious to everything around us, but whenever I shift in my chair—cross or uncross my legs—his posture changes, and I catch him watching me out of the corner of my eye. I feel oddly comforted by his presence.

Andrea and Sierra spend as much time sneaking peeks back at Jason as they do listening to the lecture. In fact, I catch a number of female students eyeing him. I don't blame them. He's nice to look at.

Forty-five minutes later, the professor shuts off the projector and asks if anyone has questions.

"Meet for lunch?" Charlene asks me as she puts away her laptop. "The usual spot?"

"I'll be there." I have English class next, while she has calculus. We always meet up for lunch afterward at the same corner window table in the cafeteria.

As we're filing out of the classroom, Reese catches up with me. Jason's on my left. Reese moves in on my right, walking so close to me that his arm brushes my shoulder. He gives Jason a cursory glance over my head, then redirects his attention to me. "How about that coffee, Layla?"

Apparently, he hasn't forgotten.

My heart's pounding. This is my chance to say yes. It's just coffee, but that counts as a date, doesn't it? Especially when the guy asks. But I have English class in ten minutes, and I'm not the type to skip. "I'm sorry, but I can't. I have another class."

"No problem," he says easily. "How about a raincheck?" And before I can even answer him, he races off to join his friends.

I glance at Jason, who's watching Reese's retreating form. Then he snaps out of it and smiles at me. "Where to next?"

"English class."

Jason steers me toward the exit, and we walk outside into the sunshine.

I can't help smiling at the realization that someone just asked me out. It's a first.

"Here, I'll carry that," Jason says as he takes my backpack from me and slips it over his shoulder.

Too bad the guy who asked me out isn't the one I think I want.

19

Jason Miller

She told the guy no. Granted, she said no because she has another class in ten minutes, so she didn't actually have time to grab a coffee with the blond hulk. But still, she said no.

But what about next time? Assuming there is a next time. Assuming he asks her out again, which he probably will. I sure as hell would, if I were him. Hell, I'd ask her out if I was anyone other than myself.

I don't even know if she's interested in the guy. I guess this is something I'm going to have to get used to—guys asking her out. It's not like I'm allowed to have an opinion on the subject of Layla dating. She's an adult. If she wants to go out with someone, she can. I'll be the one tagging along as a reluctant wingman.

I'm her bodyguard, nothing more and nothing less. My job is to make sure she's safe and well at all times—and that's it. Being a third wheel on a date is just something I'll have to get used to. But if I'm being honest with myself, I admit the idea of Layla going out with someone bothers the hell out of me.

We have a professional relationship, damn it. Her parents *hired* me to protect their daughter, and as a professional, it's my job to carry out my duties with the utmost integrity. And that means I don't get to have feelings about Layla's personal life. If she wants to go out on a date, I'll have to sit there, grin, and bear it.

And that's a problem.

Because the thought of her going out with that blockhead makes me burn with jealousy. She's too damn good for him she's way out of his league. She's too beautiful, too sweet, too everything. He doesn't deserve her attention.

But I'm not allowed to feel jealousy. If I'm jealous, I'm doing my job wrong.

Layla seems lost in thought as we walk across campus to her next class. I scan the area, on the lookout for that photographer. There's no sign of him, but I catch countless people staring at us as we pass. They're not too subtle about taking pictures of Layla and whispering to one another as they type madly on their phones. I imagine those photos will be posted all over the Internet any second.

It's a nice day, a clear sky, and it's not too warm—which is a good thing as we're doing a lot of walking outside.

As we head to her next class, I can't help reminiscing about my own college experience. It's been a few years since I was in college. I went into the Army right out of high school, with the intention of becoming a combat medic. I watched a lot of war movies growing up, and I thought the real heroes were the guys who pulled the injured soldiers out of the fire and rubble and patched them up long enough to get them to a field hospital.

So I did basic training, then advanced training, and I served as a combat medic in Afghanistan. When I got out of the Army, I wanted to continue working as a medic, so I became a licensed paramedic and got a job back home in Chicago.

When I met Liam and Miguel at our favorite local watering hole, and we became friends, they talked me into joining McIntyre Security. At that point in my career, I was ready for a change. The PTSD I brought back with me after serving in Afghanistan was bad enough, but working as a paramedic wasn't any easier. It got so bad that I couldn't sleep some nights. I still suffer from insomnia. Some sights you just can't unsee, no matter how hard you try, or how much time has passed. Or how many therapists you've been to.

So I underwent even more training to learn how to be a bodyguard. Because of my medical background, Shane assigns me to clients who have significant medical issues, like Layla.

Layla's awfully quiet, and I wonder what's on her mind. She's probably thinking about the idiot who asked her out. I'm pretty sure we haven't seen the last of him.

Well, I have news for him. He won't be alone with her. Even if she agrees to a date—and that has yet to be determined—yours truly will be riding along with them. He won't have one single moment alone with her.

I'll make sure of it.

20

Layla Alexander

When I reach my English classroom, the door is open. I walk inside and take my usual seat in the back of the room. Students are milling around the rows of desks, chatting and laughing. I notice a girl sneaking a selfie with me in the background—I'm essentially photobombing her.

When she realizes I'm on to her, she shrugs as she gives me an innocent smile.

Jason takes the empty seat beside me.

He's so bored. I don't know how he can stand being around

you all the time.

Stop it.

If I were him, I'd want to kill myself.

"I said stop it!"

I realize I said that out loud when everyone in the room turns to stare at me. I can feel my face heating in embarrassment. I hate it when I slip up like that and talk back to her. The people around me think I'm nuts.

Jason lays his hand on my back. "It's okay," he whispers. "Ignore them."

I want desperately to put my earbuds in and listen to music to try to drown her out, but I can't because our instructor just walked in the room and class is about to start. Jason's watching me covertly, but I pretend not to notice. This is my life—going from one crisis to another, from drama to drama. It sucks, and he'll just have to get used to it.

I focus on what the instructor says and try to block out everything else—Jason's worried glances, students sneaking pictures, the monster in my head—all of it.

Pressure's building in my chest. My lungs feel tight, my skin prickly.

You're such a disappointment.

Near the end of class, I notice Jason consulting the app on his phone as he checks my blood sugar. He doesn't say anything to me, so I guess it's okay. When class is over, I slip my iPad into my backpack.

I have two more classes today—one a psychology class on early childhood development and the other chemistry. I'm taking four classes in all, and they meet on Mondays, Wednesdays, and Fridays. I only come to campus those three days.

But right now I get a short break because it's lunchtime, and I'm meeting Charlene.

21

Jason Miller

After Layla's English class, we head for the cafeteria in the student union to meet her friend for lunch. I like Charlene. She's got a good, solid mom vibe about her, and I think she's good for Layla. I don't get the feeling she's after anything. Those other two girls who were fawning over Layla in her anatomy class seemed a bit suspect to me. And don't get me started on the big blond guy. He strikes me as an entitled ass, and I think he's just looking for arm candy.

As I follow Layla into the cafeteria, she heads straight for the deli counter, getting in line behind several people. As I wait with her, I notice a lot of people stealing glances at her, trying not to be obvious that they're staring. This poor girl can't go anywhere without getting stared at. It sure takes some getting used to. I've never had a client who had so little privacy.

On impulse, I lay my hand on the back of her neck and gently squeeze. She's so tense, her muscles bound taut. I massage the back of her neck, trying to loosen those tense muscles, until she rolls her head back and groans with pleasure.

"That feels so good," she murmurs.

We're both enjoying this a little too much. It started out innocently enough, but when she groaned like that, my dick responded in a very inappropriate way.

Instantly, I release her, and when my fingers brush accidentally against her ponytail, electricity snakes up my arm to the base of my skull, and I shiver.

I'm pretty sure I'm going to hell for that.

"So, what are you getting?" I ask, hoping to redirect my thoughts. I'm still learning her likes and dislikes. I know she likes strawberries and sparkling water.

She rattles off a well-practiced answer. "A grilled chicken wrap on a low-carb tortilla with cheese and veggies, with a raspberry vinaigrette dressing. And a bottle of unsweetened tea. I brought my own packet of Stevia."

"Good choices."

"What about you?"

I glance around at the well-stocked café. They've got everything from burgers to pizza to sushi. "I'll probably grab a burger and fries. And a water."

I'm reminded to check her blood sugar level. I grab my phone and take a look at the monitoring app. The level's heading downward, but it's nothing to worry about, especially since she's about to eat.

I catch sight of a guy staring at her from across the cafeteria. He looks a bit starstruck, like he caught sight of a celebrity. *Yeah, buddy, I get it. She's a knock-out. Move on.*

Layla's a complicated client, that's for sure. I've got guys staring at her because she's gorgeous. I've got people snapping pics of her left and right because of her notoriety. And then there's Reese. I could tell from Layla's body language that she really didn't know how to answer the guy. Was it because she wasn't interested and didn't know how to turn him down? Or was it because she was interested, but she didn't know how to say yes?

Layla seems pretty sheltered, and she appeared to be a bit shell-shocked when Reese asked her out for coffee. Given her history, I wouldn't be surprised if she's never dated before. And that makes my protective instincts jack up to a whole new level. Reese strikes me as a frat boy with a big ego, and if that's the case, he's barking up the wrong tree.

After Layla grabs a tray and gets her chicken wrap, I carry the tray over to the burger station and grab a double burger and some fries for myself. We hit the refrigerated beverage cases and grab our drinks.

While we're standing in line at the check-out, Layla spots Charlene entering the building. The two wave at each other, and Charlene goes off to grab her food. When the cashier rings up our purchase, I reach for my wallet to pay for our lunches, but Layla beats me to it.

"I'll get it," she says as she hands the cashier her student ID card. "I keep money on my student cash card," Layla explains. "So I don't have to use a credit card." She leans close to whisper. "I don't want to risk having a credit card stolen."

I wonder what kind of limit is on her credit card. I'm sure it's astronomical.

I don't say anything as the cashier checks us out. I can't have her paying for my meals. If anything, I should be the one paying. I can always expense the charges. But she shouldn't be paying for *me*. It doesn't feel right.

I follow Layla to a table for four by a window overlooking a flower garden. We've barely gotten seated when Charlene joins us. She takes the chair across from Layla, closest to the window. Layla has the window seat, and I sit next to her.

"So, Jason," Charlene says, addressing me directly for the first time. "You're a bodyguard." She winks at Layla, who's grinning as she sips her tea.

"I am," I say. "And you're a college student."

Charlene nods as if to say touché. "So glad we got that cleared up. How are you liking UChicago?"

"From what I've seen so far, it's impressive." I stick a fry in my mouth and chew. "What's your major?"

"Psychology. I plan to be a mental health counselor."

"Jason's a former Army combat medic," Layla says.

Charlene's eyes widen. "Wow. Combat? Real combat?"

I nod. "One tour in Afghanistan."

She winces. "That must have been a stressful job."

"It was, but also very rewarding." I catch sight of Reese at the check-out paying for his food. When he's done, he heads our way, carrying a tray with a mountain of food.

Wonderful. Here we go again.

"Hey, Layla," Reese says as he stops at our table.

Layla's face lights up with a shy smile. "Hi, Reese."

"Is it okay if I join you guys?" He sets his tray on the table, pulls out the empty chair directly across from me, and sits.

"Sure," Layla says after the fact. She fiddles nervously with a napkin, her gaze going to Charlene and then to me.

I'm having trouble reading her. She seems nervous, but I'm not sure if it's nervous in a good way or in a bad way. I think we need to establish some code words.

"So," Reese says to me. "You must be the new guard dog."

Hell, he knows exactly who I am. It's simple math—with Sean gone, I'm clearly his replacement. "Yes, I'm Layla's guard dog."

Reese laughs, then takes a bite out of a slice of pepperoni pizza. "So you're not her boyfriend, then," he says with way too much satisfaction.

His comment bugs the hell out of me, but it's accurate, so I can't argue the point. "That's correct."

He grins smugly. "I just wanted to be sure." Then he redirects his attention back to Layla. "So, Layla. It's too bad we didn't get a chance to grab coffee this morning. How about dinner tonight instead?"

Layla's jaw practically drops, and she looks to me, but she doesn't say anything. I'm not sure what she's looking for. Permission? Advice? Then she turns back to Reese. "Um, I'm sorry, but I don't think I can. I've got a lot of studying to do this week."

"Surely you can take a few hours off for dinner. You've got to eat, right? Come on. I'll take you somewhere really nice."

Layla stares down at her food, then suddenly her gaze snaps toward the window, and she stares out at the flowers. No doubt she's distracted by the voice.

"Come on, Layla—" Reese says. He loses his train of thought when it's apparent Layla's not listening to him. His gaze snaps to me, his blue eyes blazing, as if it's my fault she's tuned him out.

Too bad, pal. "You heard her, Reese. She said no."

"Who asked you?" he snaps. "I was talking to Layla. And for your information, she didn't say no. She said she didn't think she had time. There's a big difference."

Layla's attention returns to us, and she looks like she wants to crawl under the table. Probably because we're sitting here talking about her like she's not even here.

With a scowl, Reese drops his half-eaten slice of pizza onto his plate, wipes his hands on a napkin, and shoots to his feet.

"I've got to run to class now."

I glance at Layla, who's back to staring out the window. She's completely checked out. Charlene's watching her closely.

Reese picks up his tray. "I'll see you around, Layla."

I monitor Reese's retreat, but my main concern is for Layla. I lay my hand gently on her shoulder. "Layla? You okay?"

No response.

I lean forward a bit so I can see her expression. Her eyes are glittering with unshed tears, and I wonder what the voice is saying to her. I nudge her gently. "Come on, honey, talk to me."

Her gaze suddenly snaps to mine. "What?" She looks from me to Charlene, then to Reese's empty chair. "He's gone?" She sounds more than a little relieved.

I nod. "Yeah, he's gone."

She glances at her phone screen to check the time. "I've got to get to my next class." She grabs her backpack off the floor and stands. She ate barely a third of her wrap.

"What about your lunch? You need to eat."

"No time." Then she looks at Charlene. "I'm sorry, but I've got to run. I'll see you later in chemistry."

"Is everything okay?" Charlene asks.

But Layla's already walking away, carrying our tray back to the cafeteria to throw away the trash. I grab my burger and follow her, taking big bites to finish it off. I need the calories.

"Wait," I say to Layla just as she's about to return her tray, along with her mostly uneaten lunch. She hardly touched her wrap. I snag it off the tray before she can throw it away and hold it out to her. "Eat."

She frowns. "I'm going to be late to class."

I check the time. "You're not going to be late. Eat some more, *please*. A few more bites, at least. You need the protein."

She huffs. "Fine." Then she opens up the wrap and picks out the pieces of grilled chicken and shoves them in her mouth, chewing furiously.

It's all I can do to keep from smiling.

I'm not sure what happened to her back at the table, but I need to know. Was it Reese who set her off?

When she's eaten all the chicken and finished her tea, I set what's left of her wrap on a tray on the conveyor belt and take her backpack from her, throwing it over my shoulder. "Let's go."

She follows me out of the cafeteria, and once we're out on the sidewalk, she takes off toward her next class.

"So, what happened back there at the table?"

She shrugs. "Nothing."

"Layla, wait." I grab her arm and pull her to a stop. "Tell me what happened. Was it Reese or the voice?"

"The voice."

"What'd she say?"

She looks away. "It's nothing."

I know Layla well enough to know that when she says it's *nothing*, it's probably *something*. "Tell me what she said."

Layla turns pained eyes on me, and I watch them fill with

tears. The words come out of her in a bitter rush. "She said he wants to fuck me so he can brag to his friends. She said he's not really interested in me. No one is. I'm too defective for anyone to waste time on. I'm just a *trophy fuck*." Then she pulls away and resumes walking.

Ignoring the hollowness I feel in my chest, I rush after her. When I catch up, I lean in and say something I have absolutely no business saying. "She's got it all wrong, Layla. You're amazing. Reese would be damn lucky to go out with you, and he knows it."

Her expression transforms instantly from devastated to hopeful, and that makes my chest hurt even more. I need to help this girl, even if it makes me miserable. "Do you like Reese? Do you want to go out with him?"

Stifling a smile, she shrugs. "I hardly know him, but he seems nice. I wanted to say yes, but I chickened out, especially when *she* started in on me."

Fuck.

This is going to suck.

"If you like the guy, then tell him yes." *I can't believe I just said that.*

Her shoulders drop. "It's probably too late."

"Trust me, it's not too late. He stormed off because he was pissed at *me*, not at you. If you talk to the guy—hell, just smile at him—he'll ask you again. I guarantee it."

She smiles. "You really think so?"

Reluctantly, I nod. "I know so." If my client wants to go out on a date with this guy, I have no choice but to help make it happen.

 Even if it kills me.

22

Layla Alexander

As I walk into my next class, my heart is pounding, not because of our hurried dash across campus, and not because a virtual stranger asked me out to dinner, but because of something Jason said.

He said I was amazing.

He only said that because he works for your parents. He's sucking up.

You don't know that. Maybe he meant it.

It's job security. And for the record, he's wrong. You're just a trophy fuck, and you can't even do that right. You've never

fucked anyone.

Shut up.

Deny it all you want, but you know it's true.

Did he really say that, or is it just wishful thinking on my part? God, wouldn't it be incredible if someone liked me for *me*? Not for my money or my face. Not because of who I am, but just because I'm *me*? Because someone thought I was interesting or fun to be with.

Ha. That's never going to happen.

You don't know that.

Jason could have anyone he wanted. Look at him. He's hot as hell. And you're a fat, ugly, pathetic loser.

Shut up.

It's the truth, and you know it.

It's not.

My mind is racing, and my psychology class is all one big blur. I can't focus on anything. We're studying the developmental phases of toddlers, but I can't stop thinking about what else Jason said—that Reese would be lucky to go out with me.

He didn't mean it.

I ignore her.

He thinks you're a pathetic child.

When class ends, I pack up my iPad and stylus, slip them into my backpack, and head to my next class for the day, which is chemistry. On the way, I stick my earbuds in and select one of my favorite playlists. *She* won't shut up, and I need a distraction. Jason tries to initiate conversation as he walks me to my next class, but I don't feel like talking. I can't help thinking maybe she's right about me and it is all just wishful thinking on my part.

When I walk into my classroom, I immediately spot Charlene sitting in her seat. I sit next to her, and Jason sits on my other side. The instructor walks in right after us, and I scramble to get ready to take notes.

Charlene leans close and whispers, "So, about Reese? What d'you think?"

My face heats as I flatten my lips to keep from smiling. Honestly, I'm not sure what I think about Reese—I hardly know him. Yes, he's good looking, but that's all I really know. I guess I'm flattered that he asked me out, not once but twice. "I'm not sure."

Charlene's lips curve up. "Are you seriously considering his invitation?"

I shrug, but before I can say anything more, the instructor turns to face the class and begins lecturing.

I steal a glance at Jason, but he's focused on his phone. It looks like he's reading again. I like a guy who reads. For a moment, I consider the improbable possibility of Jason asking me out. Of course that would never happen. It can't. I imagine it would be against his company's rules. And I'm sure my parents would throw a fit and possibly fire him.

The thought of losing Jason is unacceptable. He's only been with me a short time, but I've never had a better bodyguard. He's actually nice to me and fun to be with. It feels like we're just hanging out, and not like he's paid to protect me.

But he is paid to protect you. He wouldn't spend one second with you if he didn't have to.

She loves reminding me that someone like Jason is out of my league. I know she's right, but I don't need my face rubbed in it.

When class is over, I say goodbye to Charlene. "I'll see you Wednesday."

She gives me a hug, and then we part ways.

"So, that was your last class for the day?" Jason asks as we step outside the building.

"We can go home now."

The sky has turned overcast, and the clouds are an ominous shade of gray. We pick up our pace when we hear thunder rolling in the distance. It looks like we're leaving just in time. Halfway to the car, a light rain starts without warning.

"Crap, no umbrella," Jason mutters. He slings my backpack over his shoulder and takes my hand, pulling me along with him as he jogs toward the parking lot. "Stick close to me."

"It's just a little water," I say, laughing. I really don't mind the rain. "I won't melt."

I move in close to Jason, my body pressed against his. As his scent and body heat envelop me, my knees go weak. He smells incredible, a mix of cologne and laundry detergent, soap, and something else. Something tantalizing that heats me up from head to toe. Something that draws me closer to him.

"Hang on tight," he says as he picks up the pace, and we're practically running to the car.

When we reach the Challenger Jason opens my door for me, and I jump inside. He sets my backpack on the floor behind me, then runs around to the driver's side and jumps in.

"Remind me to bring an umbrella next time," he says as he runs his fingers through his wet hair.

I reach up to touch my own hair, which is wet as well.

Before starting the engine, he unlocks the gun safe, retrieves his handgun, and tucks it into his ankle holster. "Much better."

I relax back against my seat and watch the rain run down the windshield in rivulets. Thunder cracks loudly from close by, and I jump. It takes me a moment to realize we're not moving yet. Jason's just sitting there behind the wheel. "Is something wrong?"

He pulls out his phone and checks my glucose monitor. Then he leans back in his seat and sighs. "So, what do you think? How did your first day back to campus go?"

"It was okay. I'm glad to be back in my classes."

"What do you think about Reese? Are you interested?"

I sigh. "He's not really interested in me. He just wants to date a local celebrity."

Jason shifts in his seat to face me. "I asked if *you* were interested in *him*."

I shrug. "I don't even know him."

"Do you want to get to know him?"

I'm surprised at the questions. "Are you encouraging me to go out with a perfect stranger?"

He laughs. "No. But if it's something you want, we can make it happen. I'd have to go with you, of course."

"Oh, I'm sure he'd love that."

Jason grins. "Think of me as your wingman."

I toss him a sharp glance. "This isn't a rom-com." But it does seem like Jason's going out of his way to encourage me to go out with Reese, and that hurts. I guess it's proof that he doesn't have any interest in me beyond that of his job.

He sighs heavily. "What I mean is, if you want to go out with the guy, then I'll support you. I just want you to be happy, Layla. If going out with Reese will make you happy, then, well, I'll do whatever it takes to make that happen."

I turn to face forward and buckle my seatbelt. "Can we go home now, please?"

Jason finally starts the engine, and we head home. For some reason, it bothers me terribly that he's so quick to say he'll make this date happen. I almost wish he'd try to talk me out of it.

Why would he do that?

I don't know. Maybe because—

Oh, please. Get real.

Neither one of us says much on the drive home. As soon as Jason parks the car, I hop out, grab my backpack, and rush inside through the back door.

"Hello, Layla," Margaret says as I step into the kitchen. "Would you like something—"

But I don't stop to hear the rest of what she has to say. I need to be alone. My chest is tight and hurting, and I don't know why. A really good-looking guy asked me out today, and I should be happy about it. But for some reason, it only makes me sad.

Because he's not the one you want.

I'm already through the kitchen when I hear Margaret say, "What's wrong with Layla? Did something happen?"

I can barely hear Jason's answer.

"She's all right. She's just a little overwhelmed."

A little overwhelmed? He has no idea! Suddenly, I'm on the verge of tears.

I don't hear another word they say because I race down the hall and up the stairs to escape into my bedroom before anyone sees me crying.

* * *

I don't know why I'm in such a bad mood.

Yes, you do.

Shut up.

I can't believe you seriously think anyone would want to date

you.

Reese does. He asked me.

I told you, you're just a trophy fuck. He scores big points if he's seen dating the Chicago heiress.

I walk into my closet and change into workout clothes—knit shorts and a tank top—and then I head downstairs to the workout room. I'm going to run *her*—and this crappy mood—out of my system.

With my earbuds in place, and one of my favorite workout playlists playing, I hop on one of the treadmills and slowly crank up the speed until I'm running at a good clip, my feet pounding on the black rubber deck. I run like the hounds of hell are chasing me, because right now that's how it feels. I run like I'm Jane Eyre out on the moors, fleeing Mr. Rochester, trying in vain to outrun my feelings for the man I can't have.

Jason thinks I'm upset because some guy asked me out. I'm not. What's really getting to me is that Jason asked if I *wanted* to date the guy. He even offered to help make it happen if that's what I wanted.

It's not.

Reese isn't the one you want.

She's right.

You can't have the one you want.

No kidding.

Besides, he'd never be interested in you.

Again, she's not wrong. Since when has the monster started making sense?

"How about you shut up and let me run?" Sometimes, when I'm alone and no one can hear my crazy, like now, I respond to her out loud. It all feels more satisfying that way.

When a hand settles on my shoulder, I jump, my heart rocketing up into my throat. I stumble off the treadmill, yanking off the safety cord in the process, which automatically shuts off the machine. Firm hands steady me as I rip out my earbuds and turn, coming face-to-face with Jason, who's also dressed in workout clothes—a pair of tight-fitting shorts, a black tank top, and black running shoes. One glimpse at his rock-hard thighs makes me flush all over.

"I'm sorry I startled you," he says as he releases me.

"It's okay." Part of my hair has fallen down from my ponytail. Feeling self-conscious, I shove it out of my face. I probably look like a hot mess.

"Mind if I join you?" he asks.

I try not to stare at his body as I struggle to catch my breath. He's so... fit. Like every inch of him is firm and chiseled and sculpted. My pulse starts racing. "Where did you come from?"

He shrugs apologetically. "I'm sorry. I thought you knew I was here. You told me to shut up and let you run."

"Jeez, I wasn't talking to you. I didn't even see you come in."

"Then who were you—*oh*." He pauses when he realizes I was talking to the voice in my head.

"Yeah, when I'm alone—or think I'm alone—I sometimes talk back to her."

"So..." He gestures to the treadmill beside mine. "Is it okay if I join you?"

"Sure. Wait—how did you know I was down here?"

"When I heard you leave your room, I followed. I guess you didn't notice."

"Sorry, I was preoccupied. I came down here because exercise helps me cope." I climb back onto the treadmill and reattach the safety clip to my top.

I start running again, gradually working my way back up to my top speed. Jason easily keeps pace with me, and I'm pretty sure he could run a lot harder if he wanted to. *The showoff.*

After about twenty minutes on the treadmill, he hops off and walks over to the free weights, picks up a set of barbells, and starts doing arm curls. Now he really is showing off. Holy cow, those biceps. I stare at his reflection in the mirrored wall as his muscles flex in stark relief beneath his taut skin. Those big weights must be heavy, as he's straining and grunting with each lift.

Stop drooling. You're embarrassing yourself.

I force my gaze away from Jason and run another twenty minutes, until I'm hot and sweaty and still just as agitated as I was before. I came down here to get away from him, and he followed me. Watching him lift weights isn't helping.

"I'm going back upstairs to do homework," I say, hopping off the treadmill. "I'll see you at dinner."

Jason wipes his sweaty face on a towel. "I'll walk with you." I'm tempted to tell him not to bother, but I don't want to be rude. As we climb the stairs, there's a heavy silence between us, and I'm not sure how to break it. Why am I making this so awkward?

"See you later," I say when I reach my room. I step inside and start to pull the door shut.

"Layla, wait." Jason wedges his foot inside the door.

I turn back, my pulse in my throat. "Yes?"

He looks conflicted. "You can tell me anything. You know that, right? If something's bothering you, we can talk about it."

I sigh. "I'm fine, Jason."

He frowns, clearly not buying my answer. "Okay. I'll see you at dinner."

He closes my door, leaving me alone with my thoughts. I need a distraction, so I take a shower to wash all the sweat off of me. When I'm done, I pull on a robe and sit down to check my blood sugar level. I feel wiped out, exhausted. It's more than just a post-workout fatigue.

Sure enough, my blood sugar level is plummeting, which isn't a surprise after a physical workout. I grab a box of apple juice, my phone and earbuds, and curl up in my armchair by the hearth.

I select my playlist of sad songs because that's how I feel… melancholy.

Forget him. He's off-limits.

I know.

23

Jason Miller

After Layla disappears into her bedroom, I stand outside her door debating what to do. Obviously, something's bothering her, but I haven't figured out how to read her yet. She's twenty-one—no longer a teenager, but just barely a woman, and she's led a very sheltered life. I don't know when to push her and when to give her space. I don't know her well enough to know if today's mood shift is typical for her and I should just accept it, or if it's an indication that she's struggling with something.

I decide to give her some space for the moment. Maybe

she's had enough of me for today and just needs a break. I head to my own room to relax for a while. Dinner is served at six, and it's only four, so we have a couple of hours to kill. I make myself comfortable on the sofa in my room and watch some educational videos on auditory hallucinations.

The more I learn about what it's like to have these kinds of voices in your head, the more I hurt for Layla and what she's going through. God, she's stronger than I ever imagined. Despite what she endures on a daily basis, she still manages to do well in her classes. She manages her diabetes very well, and she keeps moving forward.

A few minutes before six, I wash up and get ready for dinner. Then I stop at Layla's door and knock. When she opens the door, her dark eyes are bloodshot.

"You've been crying," I say.

She shrugs. "It's nothing."

It pains me to see her looking so defeated. There has to be something I can do to help her. On impulse, I reach out and brush her soft cheek. Even that slight contact sends a shiver of awareness up my arm. When her eyes widen in startled surprise, I drop my hand. "What's wrong? You can talk to me, you know. That's why I'm here—to help you."

Immediately, I know I said the wrong thing because her lips flatten, and her eyes tear up again.

Jesus, why do I keep screwing up with her?

"Layla? What'd I say?"

She pushes past me and heads for the stairs. "Nothing. It's

time for dinner."

Sighing, I scrub my hands over my face before following her. I always feel like I'm two steps behind her when what I need to do is get out in front.

* * *

After finishing a gourmet meal of filet mignon with roasted vegetables, salad, and homemade rolls with herbed butter, Layla stands and lays her linen napkin on the table. She gives everyone a small smile. "If you'll excuse me, I have a lot of homework to do." And then she leaves the room.

She was quiet throughout the meal. I didn't miss the concerned glances her parents gave her and each other. Oh, sure, Layla smiled when necessary. She laughed at the appropriate times and answered her parents' numerous questions about her first day back on campus. But she clearly wasn't her usual bubbly self. She was disconnected and often seemed distracted, her gaze wandering off as she stared across the room at nothing.

I rise to follow her, but Ruth lifts her hand, stopping me.

"Jason, please wait." She looks concerned, as does Martin, who's sitting at the opposite end of the table.

Ruth waits until Layla is safely out of hearing before she says to me, "Sit a moment, will you?"

I do as she asks since I can hardly ignore her request.

Ruth glances at her husband, then at me. "Did something happen at school today? Layla seemed uncharacteristically subdued just now." She meets her husband's stern gaze. "Is there something we should know about?"

I sigh. "Nothing significant—I mean, nothing regarding her security. A local photographer followed us onto campus, but I chased him off. A number of students took pictures of Layla, but she seemed to take that in stride. One of her classmates asked her out for coffee, and she declined. Later, he asked her out to dinner, and again she said no." I shrug. "That's about it. But I agree with you. Something's bothering her."

The parents share a long look, the two of them communicating silently, as if they each know what the other is thinking.

Ruth continues. "Someone asked her out on a date?"

I nod. "A student in her anatomy class."

"Layla attracts a lot of attention from men," Ruth says. "She's a beautiful young woman. And then there's her wealth to consider—that's an attraction in its own right. She's constantly getting asked out—or even worse, propositioned. She has always said no because she's afraid to take a risk. She doesn't know who to trust." Ruth's gaze shifts from her husband back to me. "It all goes back to trust, Jason. Many people have tried to take advantage of her over the years, either socially or financially. And her lack of confidence in her own judgment is exacerbated by the voice, which tells her everyone is out to use her."

Martin sets down his wineglass. "Who asked her out?"

"Reese Hendricks. If you want, I can run a background check on him."

Martin shakes his head. "That won't be necessary. I know Reese. I play golf with his father. From what I know, he's a decent young man from a good family."

"Like most young women her age," Ruth says, "Layla wants to go on dates—it's something she's never done before. She wants to experience romance, love, the usual things girls dream of. Because of her challenges, it's not easy for her. Perhaps she does want to take this young man up on his invitation, but she's afraid to take a chance." She sighs. "Maybe you could encourage her to say yes. You'll go along with her on the date, of course. That goes without saying. She can never be left alone with someone who hasn't been thoroughly vetted."

Even as I'm nodding, I'm fighting a sense of dread. I knew this might happen. I'm going to be the third wheel on Layla's dates. With any other client, it wouldn't be a problem. I've actually accompanied numerous female clients on social outings—dates, even. But this is different. This is Layla, and my feelings for her are complicated.

"Certainly," I finally say, knowing I have to say *something*. And I sure as hell can't say what I really want to say, which is *I'm not really comfortable with the idea of Layla dating.*

Fuck.

I am so screwed.

Ruth nods. "This will be an important milestone for Layla."

"My wife and I try to give our daughter as much freedom as we think she can handle," Martin says. "It's never been our goal to keep her a prisoner in her own home. We want her to experience life. We want her to feel as much like a normal girl her age as possible."

"It's a fine line," Ruth says. She looks conflicted as she glances at her husband, then at me. "We want you to encourage her to take acceptable risks. We trust that you'll keep her safe."

I rise from the table. "Understood. If you'll excuse me." I nod to the parents and take my leave.

After returning to my room and changing into sweats and a T-shirt, I tune into Netflix. I need some mindless entertainment to get my mind off the idea of Layla going out with Reese. I'm still flipping through the options, looking for something to watch, when I hear a soft knock on my door.

I mute the TV. "Yes?"

The door opens, and Layla pokes her head inside the room. "Can I come in?"

"Of course." I wave her in.

She steps inside and closes the door behind her. Then she just stands there, looking unsure.

"Is something wrong?" I ask.

She shakes her head. "No. I just—I could use some company." She gestures toward her room. "It's getting a little too loud over there, if you know what I mean."

I nod, realizing she's referring to the voice. Finally, she's coming to me for help. We're making progress. "Do you wanna watch something with me?" I nod to the TV.

She smiles as she crosses the room and joins me on the

sofa. "What are you watching?"

"Nothing yet. Have you got any suggestions?"

Her eyes light up. "How about *Supernatural*?"

"Sounds good. Which season?"

"I've binged them all at least twice. Surprise me."

Layla sticks a spare pillow behind her back and gets comfortable beside me, propping her feet up on the coffee table next to mine. She's wearing a pair of light gray socks with smiling avocados on them.

I pull up a random episode of *Supernatural* and we settle in to watch it.

Every once in a while, I sneak a peek at her. I don't understand her mood swings. She's been distant with me most of the day, and now she wants to hang out. Maybe I'll never understand her, and maybe that's okay. I'm just grateful she's here with me now. After what I've read about how vicious and unrelenting the voices can be, I'm willing to give her a hell of a lot of leeway. Whatever she needs—whatever I can do to make life a little easier for her—I'll do it.

One TV episode melds into two, and then into three. The next time I glance over at her, she's nodding off. It's late, and she's obviously tired. I should send her back to her room so she can get some sleep.

But first, I check her glucose monitor—it's fine.

When I turn to face her, her eyes are closed, her head leaning back against the cushions. She looks so peaceful I hate to disturb her.

I allow myself a moment to look at her. God, she's exquisite. I don't blame Reese for asking her out. If I were a student in her class, or anyone besides her bodyguard, I sure as hell would too.

Ruth's words come back to me. *"Layla wants to go on dates—it's something she's never done before. She wants to experience romance, love, the usual things girls dream of."*

It's hard to believe she's never been on a date before. I'm sure it's not due to a lack of suitors. I imagine guys ask her out left and right. I've only been on campus with her one day, and already someone's asked her out twice.

On impulse, I reach out to touch her cheek, but I pull my hand back at the last second. I have no business touching her. That's crossing a line. I made a vow to her parents to protect her—to earn her trust—and I won't ever break that vow.

I sit quietly for a while, just taking in her extraordinary beauty. It breaks my heart that her life is filled with such difficulties. Because of her diabetes, everything she eats and drinks is scrutinized. Her glucose levels could crash dangerously low if she's not careful. Her waking moments are haunted by a voice that feeds on her insecurities and is determined to tear her down.

My gaze locks onto the faint bruises that linger on her face and throat. When I think of what those bastards did to her, I seethe inside. I want to hit something.

It's getting pretty late, and no matter how much I enjoy having her here with me, she needs to be in bed. I don't think her parents would appreciate finding her in my room this late, no matter how innocent. No matter how platonic.

And it is platonic—regardless of what I feel for this girl. Regardless of what I want. Or even what she might want.

I'm her protector.

And that's all I can ever be.

With a soft moan, Layla turns toward me. We're just inches apart now, almost face-to-face. I feel her warm breath on my skin, and it sends shivers down my spine. When my dick begins to respond, I move back, regret swamping me.

"Layla?" I shake her gently. "Bedtime, honey. It's late."

Her dark lashes flutter open, and she smiles sleepily up at me. In that moment, she's just a girl, and I'm just a guy. My heart stutters, and my chest tightens as my breath catches in my throat.

Reality comes crashing back, and I sit back to put distance between us.

"What time is it?" she murmurs sleepily.

"Almost midnight."

"Oh, sorry. I guess I fell asleep."

"It's okay. But you'd better get to bed."

She straightens and lowers her feet to the floor.

"I'm curious," I say as she rises. "Why did you want to hang out in my room tonight? I mean, I'm glad you did—don't get me wrong. But you ignored me all afternoon and evening. What changed?"

"I didn't want to be alone. There aren't many people I can

relax around—my parents, my brother and Tyler, and now you. You're like family."

Oh, great. She sees me as another brother.

But this is an important step for her—for us as a team. "I'm glad you can relax around me. It means a lot."

As she smiles, I find myself staring at her mouth. It's a good thing I'm still sitting, because those lush pink lips make me weak in the knees. "Come on. I'll walk you to your room."

After I return to my own room, I wash up, turn off the light, and climb into bed. I try to think about anything other than Layla, but I'm failing miserably. My head is spinning with impossible scenarios.

There's no way in hell I can allow myself to fall for this girl.

But the problem is, I'm afraid it's already happening, and I don't know how to stop it.

And to top it off, I'm going to have to encourage her to go out on a date with another man.

24

Layla Alexander

Today is Tuesday, and that means I don't have to go to campus. It's my day to stay home and do homework. Back when Sean was my bodyguard, I could go all day on Tuesdays and Thursdays without ever having to see him. I'd stay in those days so there wasn't anything he needed to do with me, or for me.

This morning after breakfast, I head for the sunroom to read *Jane Eyre* in preparation to write a paper on symbolism for my English class.

The sunroom is undoubtedly my favorite room in the entire house. It faces south, so it gets full sun pretty much all day. The exterior walls are floor-to-ceiling glass, and to take advantage of all this sunlight, I've filled the room over the years with plants of all shapes and sizes—from potted trees that tower overhead to lush ferns and brightly-colored tropical flowers. The sound of water splashing in the three-tiered stone water fountain distracts me from *her*.

This room is essentially a greenhouse with a warm, balmy climate all year around. It's my happy place. This is where I come when life gets to be too much.

This morning, I have the room to myself so I stretch out on the comfy lounger and start reading. But I'm not alone for long.

Jason walks in and whistles. "Whoa," he says as his gaze sweeps the room. "Impressive." Then he looks at me. "Margaret told me I'd probably find you here." He heads for the water fountain and peers inside. "What, no coins?"

I laugh. "No, sadly it's not a magic fountain. Believe me, I wish it was."

Jason shoves his hands into his front pockets as he turns to me. "Any plans today?"

"Nope. I'm just going to read, and then I'm going to start writing my English paper."

He nods. "If you don't think you'll need me for the next hour or two, I thought I'd take the opportunity to run some errands."

"Go right ahead."

"Thanks. Call if you need me. I won't be far away."

"Where are you going? Unless it's something personal. I don't want to intrude on your privacy."

"You're not intruding. I'm just gonna stop by my apartment to collect my mail and pick up a few things I need. Maybe do a little shopping while I'm out." He looks down at his worn, faded jeans and T-shirt. "I could probably use some new clothes."

"You look great—I mean, you don't need to dress up for me." Suddenly, I'm fascinated by the idea of his private life. I'd love to see his apartment. "I could do my homework later. Would you mind if I tagged along?"

He doesn't want you tagging along like an annoying brat.

"You're welcome to come," he says. "You'll probably be bored out of your mind, though."

"I'd love to see your apartment."

He motions toward the door. "Let's go."

Before we leave, Jason runs up to his room to get his gun. Then we leave the house through the rear door.

He digs his keys out of his front pocket. "I hope you don't mind, but I need to fill up the gas tank."

"Sure." I'm trying to act nonchalant, but the truth is I'm excited to be going with him to run errands. It's such a small thing, but it gives us a chance to hang out like friends would. And I love riding in the Challenger. It's such a guy car.

We stop at the nearest gas station, and I watch from inside the car as he pumps gas. I realize I know very little about his personal life. Does he have a girlfriend? Or good grief, is he married? What about his family? Do they live nearby?

He's probably married, idiot.

No, he's not. He would have told me.

Why would he tell you anything? Look at him. Of course he's married.

After filling the tank, we're off again.

"You're not married, are you?" The question pops out of my mouth, and my cheeks flush. I'm horrified at the idea, because if he's married but living with me—practically babysitting me—that's got to be awful for his wife. And for him.

He laughs as he pulls out into traffic. "No. I'm not married."

"Do you have a girlfriend?"

"Nope. I'm single. I'm not even seeing anyone right now. It's kind of hard to date with my schedule."

It's your fault he has no personal life.

I don't know what to say to that, because *she's* right.

"That's terrible."

He grins. "It's okay. I knew what I was getting into when I accepted a full-time assignment. It's fine, Layla. I'm exactly where I want to be."

He gives me a smile that seems utterly genuine. The thought pops into my head that if we were *together*, then he wouldn't have to choose between his work and his private life.

That's stupid. You idiot.

We arrive at Jason's apartment building—an impressive

structure made of glass and steel, located on Lake Shore Drive and overlooking Lake Michigan. He pulls into an underground garage and parks in a numbered slot.

"Is this a reserved parking spot?" I ask.

He nods. "It's one of the perks of working for McIntyre Security. My boss owns the building."

We take an elevator up to the forty-sixth floor, then I follow Jason out of the car. We turn left and walk down the hallway to the last unit on the right. He unlocks the door and pushes it open, motioning for me to enter. "Home sweet home," he says.

I step into the living room and kitchen combo. It's sparsely furnished in masculine colors, but neat and tidy. "It's nice."

He laughs. "Compared to where you live, this is a shoebox."

He's laughing at you.

He is not.

He is. Idiot. You're so stupid.

"Layla?"

As I turn to face him, I realize he's been talking to me. "I'm sorry, what?"

He smiles. "I asked if you wanted something to drink."

"Oh, no, I'm fine. Thanks. Can I have a tour?"

"Sure, but there's not much to see." Grinning, he points down the hallway. "There's just two bedrooms and a bathroom. You can pretty much see everything from here."

"Well, it's nice." I turn to look at the brown corduroy sofa and matching recliner. The furniture is obviously old and well lived in. The coffee table is a bit scuffed. "It looks very comfortable."

"You're being nice, but thanks." He heads for the kitchen, motioning for me to follow him. It's a small galley kitchen with just enough room for a table and two chairs. He opens the refrigerator and pulls out a chilled bottle of water. "You sure you don't want anything to drink?" He screws off the cap and takes a long swig.

"Well, since you mentioned it, I am kind of thirsty."

He pulls a second bottle of water from the fridge and hands it to me. "Come on. I'll give you the nickel tour."

It takes two minutes for him to show me his bedroom, which is also tidy, and the small bathroom right across the hall. The second bedroom is cluttered with everything from workout equipment to cardboard boxes.

He shrugs. "I told you, there's not much to see." He points down the hallway. "I'm just going to grab a few things from my bedroom and the kitchen, and then we can go."

I nod and follow him to his bedroom. I try not to stare at the huge king-size bed with its dark blue comforter and matching sheets and pillows. This is where he sleeps. A thought occurs to me. I wonder if he sleeps naked when he's here in his apartment. Then I wonder if he sleeps naked back at my house. *Good grief.* I saw quite a bit of his bare torso the day he answered his bedroom door without a shirt on, and it only makes me wonder what the rest of him looks like.

He grabs some things from his dresser and closet and drops them into a tote bag. Then he heads for the kitchen and opens the pantry door. After dropping a few more items into the bag, he says, "That's it. You ready?"

I nod.

"Do you mind if we make a stop on our way back to the house? I really need to get some new clothes." He glances down at the distressed jeans he's wearing and his faded T-shirt. "I feel a bit underdressed. I was thinking about stopping at Water Tower Place."

My eyes light up. I love that place, and I hardly ever go. But then I realize I'm wearing old jeans, a long-sleeve T-shirt, and no make-up. The bruises are visible. Water Tower Place is an upscale shopping mall. "I'm not really dressed for it."

He holds up a finger as if to say just a minute and then rushes off, disappearing into his bedroom. He returns a moment later with a bright blue Chicago Cubs baseball cap, which he places on my head. "Remember how well one of these worked the last time?" He tucks some loose strands of my hair behind my ears and pulls the brim down low over my eyes. "No one will recognize you."

I catch my reflection in a mirror hanging on the wall and smile because he's right. "Okay."

Jason locks his door, and then we head for the elevator. Once inside, he presses the button marked LOBBY. "I've got to stop and pick up my mail."

I'm smiling as we exit the elevator into a spacious, well-lit lobby. There are over a dozen people milling around, chatting by a coffee bar or relaxing on chairs and sofas scattered around the space. No one bothers to look our way as we head down a short hallway. Jason stops at a door marked MAILROOM, opens it, and I follow him inside a small room filled with locked boxes.

I stand beside him as he collects a small bundle of envelopes from his mailbox. He quickly flips through the envelopes, throwing half of them into a recycling bin.

"Junk mail," he says.

As we leave the mailroom and head for the stairwell that leads down to the parking garage, I feel like I'm wearing a disguise. I could go anywhere in the city, and no one would recognize me. I'm just a girl, out with a guy. *Nothing to see here, folks.* I'm enjoying this way more than I should.

It's not a date, you idiot.

I know, but it kind of feels like one.

Don't be stupid.

Jason deposits his stuff into the trunk of his car. "Would you like to walk downtown? We wouldn't have to worry about finding parking. It's not far."

When I gaze at my reflection in the car window, I'm reassured that the baseball cap does a good job of hiding my face. And I can't remember the last time I walked around downtown Chicago, amidst the crowds of tourists and locals. "Sure. Let's walk."

After locking up the car, we walk toward the shopping district on North Michigan Avenue. The sidewalk is crowded with shoppers, mostly tourists. When a group of rowdy teenagers heads our way, Jason pulls me out of the way.

He ends up putting his arm around me and holding me close. "Don't want you getting trampled."

Being this close to him sends my pulse racing. I can feel the heat of his body and I can smell his scent, mixed with cologne. Suddenly I'm warm all over and certain parts of my body are tingling. For a moment, I think this is definitely what it's like to go on a date.

It's not a date, you idiot. Stop kidding yourself. He would never go out with a loser like you.

But *she's* wrong. This is sort of like what a date would be, isn't it? Going out, going shopping. Walking together, side by side. And it'll be lunch time soon, and Jason will insist that we stop and get something to eat. He'll have to, so my sugar level doesn't drop too low.

25

Layla Alexander

"So, where to?" I ask Jason as we reach the shopping district.

Both sides of the street are filled with towering shopping malls and lots of huge name-brand stores. The streets are jammed bumper to bumper with cars and buses. The sidewalks are teeming with people, and on nearly every block there are panhandlers sitting out with their buckets, asking for money. A few of them play musical instruments or show off some talent in hopes of garnering donations.

"Under Armour," Jason says, naming a store I've never

been to. "And then a men's clothing store. I need socks and underwear, jeans that aren't ripped, and a suit and tie in case I need to escort you somewhere with a dress code."

Grinning, I swat his arm. "Don't be silly. I never go anywhere fancy."

"Hey, you Alexanders are a pretty big deal in Chicago. I should upgrade my look."

"My parents are a big deal, yes. But I'm not. I never attend any society functions with them."

Jason stops in front of a brightly-lit, modern store on North Michigan. "This will do."

I have to tip my head back to see the impressive store sign above. *Under Armour.* I peek through the glass storefront to see an army of physically fit male mannequins wearing all manner of men's underwear and sportswear. *Whoa.* I didn't know eye candy would be involved.

I feel the warm weight of Jason's hand on my back as he opens the door and coaxes me inside. "Come on. I promise I'll be quick."

"Take your time," I tell him, my eyes wide as I take it all in. "I'm not in any rush."

The store is bustling with shoppers, mostly men, who peruse the displays of sweatpants, T-shirts, running outfits, sneakers, hoodies, and all kinds of gear that athletic people would want. If the sheer number of shoppers is anything to go by, this is a pretty popular place.

As soon as we're inside the store, Jason drops his hand

from my back, and I feel a pang of disappointment. I like it when he touches me. I know it's not anything romantic. He's just being friendly, that's all, and I could always use another friend.

You don't have any friends.

Yes, I do. Stop it.

He taps me on the shoulder. "Layla?"

"Hmm? Sorry, what?"

"I asked if you'd help me pick some things out."

I know he's just being nice. He's a grown man; he doesn't need help shopping. One of the first things I noticed about Jason is that he has great style. No matter what he's wearing, he looks good in it. His body is a lean, muscular work of art, like a Grecian statue. And his taut skin is like a canvas decorated with dark ink.

I see the way women look at him, like he's a piece of cheesecake and they want to devour him. We've only been in here a few minutes, and already I've seen a number of women eyeing him.

Yeah, I know. He's hot.

Too bad you're not.

"I need some basics," he tells me.

I follow him to a display of men's briefs. Well, they're sort of like boxers, but they fit more tightly, at least on the mannequins. He rummages around on a display table until he finds the style and size he wants. He selects a package of black underwear.

I glance up at the mannequin that's wearing the same underwear and feel heat surging up my neck to my face, because now I have a pretty good idea what Jason's got on beneath his jeans. And if he looks anything like these mannequins do beneath his clothing, then *wow*.

Forget it. You'll never find out.

When he pulls a pair of gray sweatpants off a rack, I can't help but chuckle.

"What's so funny?" He seems amused by my reaction.

Blushing, I stifle a laugh. "It's nothing."

He wraps his arm around my neck and pulls me close. "Come on, Layla, spill it. What's so funny about a pair of sweatpants?"

I'm still laughing. "Men in gray sweatpants—it's a popular meme on social media, that's all. I told you, it's nothing."

But I can tell from the look on his face that he knows exactly what I'm talking about. Grinning, he rolls his eyes at me, and now I'm blushing for sure.

While Jason tries on a pair of black running shoes, I watch a really attractive blonde woman trying on a pair of running shoes as well. She's paying more attention to Jason than to where she's going, and she walks right into a display of shoeboxes, sending half a dozen of them tumbling to the ground.

I turn away, pressing my lips together to keep from smiling. I don't blame her one bit; he is nice to look at.

After Jason buys what he needs here, including the shoes,

we walk over to Water Tower Place to find a men's clothing store. There, he buys a pair of jeans, some T-shirts, a pair of black slacks and a matching jacket, a white button-down shirt, and a black tie.

He also buys a pair of men's shiny black loafers. "Now I'm ready for any occasion that might arise," he says. He winks at me.

While we're here, I can't resist stopping at the American Girl doll store. "I was crazy about these dolls when I was young," I tell him.

We walk through the store looking at all the displays, at the dolls and furniture and accessories. He points out a doll with long black hair, dark eyes, and light-brown skin. "This one looks like you."

I smile. "I have the same exact doll. When I was a kid, I desperately wanted a doll that looked like me. Most of the dolls I saw at the store were blonde or had brown hair or red. I couldn't find any that looked like me."

"I know you're adopted," he says. "Do you know what your ethnicity is?"

I shake my head. "Not exactly. We know almost nothing about my birth parents—just that they were in high school when my birth mother got pregnant with me. When they found out I was diabetic, they put me up for adoption. I guess they weren't up to dealing with my health issues. I remember my mom said something about my birth father being a foreign exchange student, but I don't know where he was from.

I think he was from one of the Middle Eastern or North African countries. My birth mother was in foster care at the time she got pregnant, and I don't think she had a good support system. I don't blame them for giving me up. They were just kids themselves, and I'm sure they were overwhelmed and scared. I know what that feels like. I'm sure they did what they thought was best for all of us."

He nods. "That couldn't have been an easy decision."

By the time we're done shopping and back out on the sidewalk, it's half past noon. I catch Jason checking my blood sugar levels on his phone. I do feel a bit shaky and clammy, which means my sugar is low.

"Lunch time," Jason says as he tucks his phone back into his pocket. "What sounds good?"

"How about Moroccan? I know a great place not far from here. Ian's taken me there many times. We'll pass it on our way back to your apartment building."

He motions for me to proceed. "Lead the way."

We walk about five blocks to the restaurant. Jason sticks close to me when the pedestrian traffic is heavy. When a large crowd comes barreling toward us, he pulls me out of their path and tucks me beneath his arm.

"Here it is," I say, stopping in front of an old brick townhouse that's been converted to a restaurant.

We walk up the front steps, and Jason opens the door for me. I smile as I step inside and smell the delicious aroma of roasted meat and veggies.

"Just the two of you?" asks the smiling young man standing behind the host's podium. He's tall, with pale skin, curly red hair, and freckles.

"Yes, two," Jason says. "Thanks"

The host eyes me curiously, practically staring. "Excuse me, but are you Layla Alexander?"

Ugly. He thinks you're ugly.

I guess the baseball cap didn't help as much as I thought it would.

The guy grins. "I've never seen you in public before. On social media, yeah, all the time. But never in public." He dips down to see me better beneath the ball cap. "I hate to ask, but would you mind if I take a picture with you? My friends will never believe this."

Jason steps in front of me. "How about getting us a table? D'you mind?"

The host winces apologetically as he grabs two menus and heads into the dining room. "Sorry. Right this way."

The dining room is small and cozy, with just a dozen tables. There are potted trees—probably fake—throughout the room. Moroccan paintings and textiles hang on the walls, and brightly-colored rugs adorn the old oak floors. Over each table hangs an antique light fixture.

The host lays our menus on the table. "Someone will be right out to take your orders."

Jason pulls out a chair for me, and I sit. Then he sits across from me. "The ambiance is amazing," he says as he looks around the room.

"Ian and I like to come here. He likes to tease me and say I'm probably a half-Moroccan princess."

Jason laughs as he opens his menu.

"What's so funny?" I ask.

"It's just that, when I first saw you, I thought you looked like a Disney princess, so I don't think Ian was that far off."

Now it's my turn to laugh.

You idiot. He's laughing *at* you.

He is not. Stop it.

You are so gullible.

By the time our server comes to our table—a tall, dark-haired young man—Jason has decided what he wants. I already know what I want. After placing our food orders, we drink mango-flavored sparkling water while we wait for our food.

I'm amazed at how easy it is to talk to him. We ramble from one topic of conversation to another without any awkward pauses.

He asks me about school, about my major. "So, why psychology?"

"I guess because I'm fascinated by the complexities of the human brain. I want to better understand it, so maybe I can better understand why I hear *her*." I tap on my skull. "Maybe someday I will."

"Based on several memoirs I've read, some people who hear

voices think they articulate their own fears and insecurities."

As I sip my water, I nod. "She definitely preys on mine."

He gives me a gentle smile. "When I look at you—at how intelligent you are, how compassionate, how *beautiful*—it's hard for me to see what you have to be insecure about."

He's lying. He thinks you're pathetic. A joke.

I swallow against the sudden painful lump in my throat because I'm so afraid she's right. "Looks can be deceiving."

Fortunately, I'm spared talking about this because our server arrives with our food.

"This looks wonderful," Jason says as he tries his delicately-spiced chicken and vegetable dish. He groans. "Oh, god, that's good."

I smile, glad he likes it.

Jason picks up his bottle of sparkling water and holds it close to his lips. "There's something I've been wanting to ask you," he says before taking a sip.

My face heats, and I smile. "Yes?" Today has been an amazing day, just spending time with him. It's been fun and relaxing. I think this is what it must be like to experience life with someone special by your side.

"I wanted to ask you about Reese Hendricks."

My smile falls as my stomach drops like a stone. "What about him?"

"I was just wondering if you like him."

I shrug. "I hardly know the guy."

"I know, but I mean, are you interested in getting to know

him better?"

"I don't know." *Why is he asking me about Reese?* "I told him no."

"Maybe you should reconsider."

"What? Why?" My happiness evaporates instantly. I was having such a good time with Jason, and I thought he felt the same. I thought we were connecting. *But now he's encouraging me to date someone else?* "I thought you didn't like him."

Jason shrugs. "Like you, I hardly know the guy. He and I got off on the wrong foot, and maybe I was too hasty. I should give him another chance. If you think you'd like to go out with him, tell him you changed your mind. I'm sure he'd be thrilled to hear that."

How could I have been so stupid?

Because you're an idiot.

I don't know what to say. I'd love to go out on a date, yes, but not with Reese.

With who, then? With Jason? Please, don't be so stupid.

I say the first thing that pops into my head. "He seems nice."

Jason frowns. "Yeah, he does. I was just thinking that—if you wanted to, I mean—you could go out with him. Give him a chance. Get to know him better."

You idiot. You're not girlfriend material. You're a paycheck. That's all.

I have nothing to say to that because *she's* right. My stomach tightens, and my food settles like rocks in my belly. Pain knifes my heart, and the ache is agonizing. Have I been making a fool of myself this whole time, thinking Jason and I were becoming friends, when really I'm clinging to him, hoping for a friendship and wishing desperately for more?

I really am pathetic.

I told you so. Now stop it. You're embarrassing yourself—and him.

My eyes start to burn, and I know I'm a second away from making a fool of myself. I lay my fork on the table. When I feel my lips start to tremble—a surefire sign I'm about to start crying—I pick up my bottle of water and take a long sip.

"Excuse me." I shoot to my feet. "Restroom." That's all I can manage as I bolt from the dining room and down the hallway.

My pulse is racing as I reach the bathroom. It's a small room with a single toilet and a white porcelain sink mounted on the wall beneath a small gold-framed mirror. Fortunately, it's empty. I step inside, lock the door behind me, and lean against it.

Tears stream down my hot cheeks. "How could I have been so stupid?"

For you, that's pretty easy.

Shut up!

The pain I'm feeling is crushing—it's akin to stabbing slivers of jagged glass into my skin. I have no one to blame but myself. Jason's just doing his job. It's not his fault I'm crushing

Cut yourself. Cut your skin. Cut out the pain. Do it. Do it.

Her words terrify me.

Do it. Cut yourself. You'll feel better. You know you will.

The urge to do what she says is so strong, it scares me. My hand shakes as I pull my phone out of my pocket. I know I should call for Jason, but I can't bring myself to do it. I don't want him to see me like this. Instead, I call my brother.

Ian is laughing as he answers the phone. "Hey, sis. Sorry, we were just—um, never mind. What's up?"

"I—" My throat closes up on me. I can't bear to say the words out loud.

"Layla?" His tone grows serious. "Are you okay?"

"No." My answer is hardly more than a shaky breath.

"Where are you? Where's Jason?"

But I can't stop crying long enough to answer him.

"Never mind. I've got you on GPS." He rattles off the name of the restaurant, and then I hear a car engine roar to life. "Where are you, exactly? Are you safe?"

"I'm in the bathroom," I whisper.

"Where's Jason?"

"I left him at our table."

"Stay put. I'm on my way. I'll be there in six minutes. Don't do anything, you hear me? Don't *touch* anything."

"Okay." I know he's referring to anything *sharp*.

"Promise me, Layla."

My voice breaks on a sob. "I promise."

There's a knock on the bathroom door. "Layla?"

It's Jason. He's coming to do his job.

What do you expect? You're just a job to him. A stupid, pathetic job.

Shame envelops me, and I sink to the floor and lean against the door. *Hurry, Ian, please.*

Jason knocks a little more forcefully the second time, and then he tries the knob. But it's locked. "Layla, answer me." He sounds angry.

But I can't answer him, because I can't stop crying. *I'm such an idiot.*

You're an idiot. You're an idiot. You're an idiot.

I hear nothing but the insidious echo of her voice in my head.

26

Jason Miller

I can hear her crying through the locked door, and that's actually a good thing. I can handle an emotional client. I know for a fact that the knife from her place setting is still on the table, and to my knowledge she doesn't have anything sharp with her.

I soften my voice. "Layla, honey? Please open the door."

No answer.

I try the knob once more, but it's pointless. I could easily kick this old door in, but I'm afraid I might hurt her in the process. So I pull a lock-pick set out of my jacket pocket and have the knob unlocked in ten seconds. The only problem is, the door still won't budge. She must be blocking it.

"Layla, please." I'm not above begging her. Right now, it's paramount that I get into this room so I can make sure she's all right. I don't think she can hurt herself in there, but I can't take that chance. Hell, if she tried, she could hurt herself with anything, even a hair clip.

Fuck!

I press my weight against the door. "Sweetheart, please let me in. Whatever I said, I'm sorry. Please talk to me." I'm not entirely sure what I did wrong, but I know with absolute certainty that it was something *I said* that set her off. But all I did was ask her about going out with Reese. "Is this about Reese?"

I manage to nudge the door open an inch, just enough that I can peer into the room and catch her reflection in the mirror over the sink. Her eyes are red, her cheeks wet from crying. The pain she's feeling radiates from her dark eyes, and the sight of it breaks my heart.

This is all my fucking fault.

I can't see much below her neck, so I can't tell if she's hurt herself. "Layla? Are you hurt?" *Please, god, let her say no.*

Time slows to a crawl as I try to ease the door open more. I just need a foot or so of clearance so I can slip into the room and assess her condition firsthand. If I have to, I'll force the door open.

Suddenly, there's a hand on my shoulder, accompanied by a familiar voice. "Jason, it's okay. I've got this."

I turn to see Ian standing behind me, Tyler at his side. Ian's expression is taut. Tyler looks like he wants to kill something—most likely me.

Ian knows Layla a hell of a lot better than I do, so I step back. He presses his face into the opening. "Hey, sis," he says calmly. "I'm here. Let me in."

Immediately, the opening widens. Ian slips into the room and closes the door behind him.

Tyler grabs my arm. "What the fuck happened?" he growls. He's livid.

I meet his accusing gaze head-on. "Honestly, Tyler, I'm not sure. We were at our table eating lunch, everything was fine, and then she bolted for the bathroom and locked herself in."

His dark eyes narrow on me. "Well, obviously *something* happened."

Frustration eats at me. "I'm racking my brain, Tyler. We were talking about Reese—"

Tyler frowns. "Who?"

"He's a guy in her class who asked her out. She said no, but I suggested she reconsider. He's a good-looking guy. I thought maybe she'd be interested in him. But I don't see how that would set her off."

"Wait—you were trying to talk her into going out with another guy?"

"Well, yeah. Ruth said—"

"Forget it. I've heard enough." Tyler shakes his head at me like I'm a complete numbskull. "Don't you know anything about women? Hell, even I get it." He moves closer to the door to listen to what's being said on the other side.

Ian is talking quietly to Layla. A few moments later, we hear the faucet running. When the door finally opens, Ian appears first, looking a bit harried. "She's okay." His gaze goes to Tyler first, and the two of them share a long, poignant look. Then he looks hard at me. "I'm taking my sister home." He says this with absolute certainty, as if he's daring me to contradict him.

I nod. What else can I do? If Ian takes her home, Tyler will be with them. If she's not safe with a former homicide detective, then she's not safe with anyone. Hell, she's probably safer with them than she is with me at this point, because apparently I'm clueless when it comes to women. "Okay. I'll follow."

But then I remember my car is back at my apartment building, and chances are Ian and Tyler have a car close by. They'll have a huge head start on me.

Shit.

Layla walks out of the bathroom huddled against Ian, who has his arm securely around her as he walks her down the hallway.

I move to follow, but Tyler stops me with a firm hand on my shoulder. "He means *our* place," he clarifies. "Not the parents' house." And then he follows after them.

As I watch them walk away, I notice blood on the sleeve of Layla's hoodie. Damn it, she did hurt herself.

As they disappear out the front door, I immediately feel the void left behind from Layla's absence, like there's suddenly a gaping hole in my chest. How did she become such a big presence in my life so quickly? She's a complicated girl, one minute smiling and laughing, and the next minute she's suffering a level of emotional pain that I have no experience with.

I hand our server more than enough cash to cover our bill and a tip and head for the exit. Right now, I just want to be with Layla. It stung when I realized she'd called her brother for help rather than me. I guess I haven't earned that level of trust with her yet.

But that's something I'll rectify, no matter what it takes.

* * *

I pull up in front of Ian and Tyler's townhouse and park in the driveway behind Tyler's black BMW. Ian's bright blue Porsche is parked under a makeshift carport, as they've turned the old carriage house, which used to serve as a garage, into the offices for their new private investigation business.

I race up the steps to the front door and knock. The door opens almost immediately, and Tyler steps back to let me in.

"How is she?" I ask.

"She's okay. She's resting right now, with Ian."

I glance around the foyer, trying to get my bearings. There's a living room to the left of the front hall and a smaller room to the right—something that looks like an old-fashioned parlor. Straight ahead is a staircase, and beyond that is the kitchen. "Where is she?"

"Before I take you to her, let me remind you that Ian's been her lifeline since childhood. She trusts him."

"Are you saying she doesn't trust me?"

"She hasn't known you that long. Layla tries hard to keep the more painful aspects of her life private. She's not going to spill her guts to you and let you know how much she's hurting."

"But it's my job—"

"Your job is to keep her physically safe. She holds her emotions pretty close. I think Ian's the only one she lets see her as she truly is."

I scrub my hands over my face and blow out a long breath. I hear what he's saying, and I get it. Ian has a long track record with Layla, and I'm new to her life. But damn it, I want that level of trust with her. I meet Tyler's dark gaze. "Can I see her?"

"They're up on the roof, in the greenhouse. Ian told me to send you up."

With a grateful nod, I head for the stairs, taking them two at a time as I rush up to the roof.

27

Layla Alexander

A lot of people are out on the lake this afternoon. As far as the eye can see, countless boats skim across the glassy water's surface beneath a pale blue sky. Up here in the greenhouse, three floors above the ground and surrounded by lush ferns and potted trees, we're in our own magical world.

Ian loves his greenhouse—it's his escape when the world gets to be too much. And at the moment, it's mine too.

I take comfort in my brother's arm wrapped around my shoulders, and I lean into him.

"D'you want to talk about it?" he asks quietly. His head is pressed close to mine.

"Not really." Sniffling, I press a tissue against my nose. I've been crying since we left the restaurant.

"Come on, Layla. Tell me what upset you."

I swallow past a painful lump in my throat. "He said I should go out with Reese."

"Who's Reese?"

"A guy in my class who asked me out."

"And Jason said you should go out with him?" Ian sounds skeptical.

"Yes."

"Do you want to?"

"Not really. I mean, he seems nice, and I'm flattered. But no, I don't want to go out with *him*. I don't even know him."

Ian's quiet for a moment, as if he's trying to read between the lines. "Is there someone you *do* want to go out with?"

"Maybe." It's hard for me to admit even that little bit.

"Is it someone from school?"

"No."

"Is it someone I know?"

I almost crack a smile. It's like we're playing a game of Twenty Questions. "Yes."

"Is it Jason?"

I don't respond, and that's enough of an answer for Ian.

He groans softly. "Oh, Layla."

"It's stupid, I know!" I try to pull away, but he tightens his hold.

"It's not stupid. It's just—it's impossible."

I sigh. "I know. I'm just a kid to him."

"It's not that." He sighs, too. "As your bodyguard, he can't get personally involved with you. And Mom and Dad would never stand for it. In fact, I'm sure Dad has already warned him off you. He did the same with Tyler when we first started dating."

"Yeah, but Tyler ignored the warning, right? He continued to see you anyway."

He grins as he pulls me close again. "Yeah, but Tyler was just a guy I'd met—he wasn't my *bodyguard*. That's a whole new level of complicated."

"But I'm an adult."

Ian chuckles. "Tell that to Mom and Dad."

"Would it be considered unethical if Jason liked me?"

"Yes."

And therein lies the rub. I haven't known Jason very long, but I think I know him well enough to know that he'd cut off his own arm before he willingly did something unethical. "So it's pointless, then."

"I'm afraid so, sis. I'm sorry."

At the sound of a quiet knock on the greenhouse door, I pull away from Ian and wipe my damp cheeks. I'm sure my eyes are red and puffy, but there's nothing I can do about that now.

Ian lays his hand on my knee. "Is it okay if Jason comes in?"

I shrug. "I can't hide from him forever." Not if he's going to remain my bodyguard. And losing him isn't an option.

"Come on in, Jason," Ian calls.

The door opens, and Jason walks in. His eyes are immediately on me. "Hi, Layla."

I shift my gaze back out toward the lake. "Hi."

After giving me a quick hug, Ian stands. "I think I'll go downstairs and help Tyler with—whatever. You guys talk." And then he disappears out the door, leaving Jason and me alone.

Jason approaches the bench where I'm sitting. "Is it okay if I join you?" He points at the spot Ian just vacated. "Can I sit?"

When I shrug, he sits beside me and stares out at the water across Lake Shore Drive. "This is one helluva view, isn't it?"

I nod. "Ian bought this place because of the view."

Slowly, Jason reaches for my wrist and holds it up so he can examine the smear of blood on my sleeve. "How did you hurt yourself? You didn't have a knife, did you?"

"No." I pull my wrist free. "I scratched myself."

"With what?"

"My fingernails."

He sighs. "Can I see?"

I pull up my left sleeve, and he gently holds my arm as he inspects the scratches on the inside of my wrist. The bloody marks are mostly dried. He doesn't say anything about the old scars there, the ones that have faded to fine white lines and nicks.

"Can you tell me why you did it?" he asks. His voice is gentle, and it doesn't feel judgmental. It's more curious than anything, like he really wants to understand.

He'll never understand you. You're a nutjob. You're crazy.

"Because sometimes the pain of scratching or cutting drowns out the other pain I'm feeling here." I press my hand over my heart.

"Did it work?"

"No. It just made me feel worse because I knew my family would be disappointed in me."

"I don't think they're ever disappointed in you, Layla." He slides his hand down to mine and links our fingers together. "They just worry about you. Will you tell me why you felt such pain?"

I shake my head. "I'd rather not get into it."

"Layla, please. If I'm going to be your bodyguard, I need you to trust me with everything that bothers you."

"It doesn't matter anymore."

"Of course it matters."

"No, it doesn't. Anyway, I've decided to go out with Reese."

"What?" He sounds surprised. "Are you sure? I thought it was the idea of going out with Reese that set you off."

"No, it wasn't that." Jason has no clue about how I feel. "Besides, it's irrelevant now. Yes, I'll go out with Reese. I'll tell him when I see him in class tomorrow."

Jason's brow furrows. "You don't have to if you don't want to. No one's pressuring you to do it."

"I want to."

No you don't.

"He seems like a really nice guy," I say.

He's a stranger.

You're just a trophy to him. Arm candy. That's all.

"Yes, I imagine he is," Jason says guardedly. He turns on the bench to face me and takes both of my hands in his. He waits until I'm looking him in the eyes before he says, "How do I become the person you call first? How do I become your safe place?"

My heart squeezes painfully. Doesn't he know that's what I want him to be? I want him to be the one I trust most in the world. I want that with all my heart. Is it possible to meet someone and know right away that they're the one?

"I failed you today," he says.

His sincerity hurts so badly I have to look away. "It wasn't your fault."

He looks me in the eye for a long moment, then faces forward and slips his arm across my shoulders and tugs me close, just like Ian did. "I'm sorry, Layla, for whatever I did to upset you. I don't ever want to hurt you."

But he's not my brother. That's not what I want from him. I lean my head against his shoulder, grateful that I have at least this much with him. "It wasn't your fault. You didn't hurt me. I hurt myself." And that's true on multiple levels—both physically and emotionally. I was stupid to think Jason would ever be interested in me.

Yes, you're stupid. You idiot.

I fight to ignore *her* and just relax against Jason. I should enjoy these moments with him when I have the chance. "So, I guess we're going out to dinner with Reese," I say, attempting to sound upbeat. I just wish I could feel excited about the prospect.

"Looks like it," he replies. He sounds about as excited as I do, which isn't saying a lot.

Maybe going out with Reese is exactly what I need—to focus on someone beside Jason. I need to get over him one way or another.

28

Jason Miller

When we get back to the house, Layla disappears into her bedroom to do homework. At least that's what she tells me. Honestly, I'm not surprised she wants her space. Things have been strained between us all afternoon, ever since the incident at the restaurant. I'm glad Ian could come so quickly to intervene, but it still bothers me that Layla wouldn't let *me* be the one to help her. I'm perfectly capable of being who she needs.

This is the first time I've ever had a client who I felt real friendship for. She's not just a job. She's someone I've grown to care about in a very short period of time. I don't just want to keep her *safe*; I want her to be *happy*.

I sure hope Ruth is right about Layla wanting to date. As much as it kills me to think of Layla going out with this guy, if it will make her happy, then so be it.

Now it's up to me to figure out how in the hell I'm going to sit there and watch this guy fawning over Layla. Because if he so much as *touches* her, or heaven forbid if he tries to *kiss* her—and why the hell wouldn't he?—I don't know how I'll cope.

For dinner that evening, it's just the two of us, so we eat in the kitchen. Her parents are at a professional meeting. We eat in relative silence, and Layla picks at her food. She didn't eat much of her lunch, and now it looks like she's not going to eat much for dinner. I'm betting her sugar level is already bordering on low.

I pull out my phone and check her glucose monitor. "Please try to eat more."

She shrugs. "I feel fine."

"Your glucose level is seventy. I'd like to see it higher."

She stabs a piece of roasted chicken with her fork and stuffs it in her mouth and chews. "Happy now?" she says, sounding like a petulant teenager.

I'm finding it hard not to laugh. "A little."

After we eat, she heads back upstairs to her room. She says she has homework to do, and I believe her, but I also think she's avoiding me. I give her some time alone, but after a couple of hours I grow restless. I want to see her—I need to make sure she's okay.

I head to her door and knock.

"Come in," she says.

I walk in and find her sitting at her desk, typing away on her computer keyboard. She's in her pajamas already—a pair of pink plaid flannel bottoms and a skimpy white top. When I catch a hint of cleavage, my body reacts instantly. I force myself to look away.

I transfer my gaze to her computer screen. It looks like she's writing her essay on *Jane Eyre*. "How's the paper coming?"

"Good. I'm just about done with the rough draft that's due Friday."

"Are you ready for school tomorrow?"

She nods. "I guess I'll be seeing Reese again tomorrow."

"Oh, right." My stomach churns at the thought. "You don't have to talk to him if you don't want to. I just thought maybe—"

"It's okay. I do. He seems like a good guy."

"Yeah, he does." I have to bite my tongue to keep from disagreeing. I think he's an entitled prick, but that's just me.

Absently, I wander over to her bookcase and skim all the DVDs. "Look at all these. Now who's old school?"

"Ian gave me his DVD collection when he moved out. He streams everything now. So do I, but I keep these because they belonged to him. I'm sentimental."

I pull a copy of *Guardians of the Galaxy* off the shelf. "This is a good one. I love the soundtrack."

"Do you want to watch it?" she asks, her eyes lighting up.

"Sounds good, yeah." I like the movie, but I love spending time with her more. "When? You mean tonight?"

"Why not? I'm done here." Layla hits a few keystrokes, then powers down her laptop. She moves to the sofa and picks up the TV remote to call up the movie and starts the film. When the catchy seventies music starts up, she smiles and pats the seat beside her.

As the movie's opening sequence begins, Layla puts her feet up on the coffee table, and I follow suit. It's nice to be able to relax with her. I'm hoping the awkwardness from earlier this afternoon is behind us.

When there's a lull in the movie's action, I reach over and squeeze her hand. "If you do go out with Reese, I'll be coming with you. I want to make sure you understand that. You won't be alone with him." *Not ever, if I have my way.* God, just the thought of her alone with him makes me queasy.

Even as she nods, the corners of her mouth turn down. I find myself staring at soft lips that draw me in like a moth to a flame. My gaze climbs to meet hers, and as her dark eyes lock onto mine, I feel a surge of heat throughout my body, and my heart beats double-time. I turn back to face the screen, and it's several minutes later that I realize I never let go of her hand.

We're holding hands.

Shit.

When I sneak a peek out of the corner of my eye, I see she's smiling.

"Sorry." I release her hand and give it a friendly pat. I don't want to make too big of a deal out of this.

She just keeps smiling. "It's okay."

My body reacts to her proximity in a very inconvenient and unprofessional way. I try to focus on the movie in the hopes that my body stands down. When it doesn't, I have to shift in my seat to hide my body's rather obvious reaction.

This can't fucking happen.

My body isn't allowed to react to hers. Not to her touch, not to a look from her, not from a word—nothing.

By the time the movie nears the end, she's yawning. It's late, and she should be in bed. I quietly check her sugar level.

God, I wish she was just some random girl, and I was just some random guy, and we met at a party, and I asked for her name and—

Stop it, you idiot. It can't fucking happen.

* * *

After I leave Layla's room and head back to my own, I'm way too restless and worked up to go to sleep. I have a serious problem where Layla's concerned. When I look at her, I don't just see a client. I see an incredible young woman who occupies a hell of a lot of my mental bandwidth. She's smart, she's funny, and she's so damn humble. And my god is she beautiful. Sometimes I find myself simply staring at her, unable to look away. With her money and looks, it's a wonder she's not a vain, self-centered debutante. But she's not. If anything, she's too modest. She has no idea of her appeal.

And of course her vulnerabilities heighten my desire to protect her. I really don't know how I'm going to handle Layla going out on a date with that blockhead Reese or with any other guy. He has no clue what she's been through.

And yes, she's emotionally complicated. I'm still shaken by what happened today at lunch. Everything was going fine until suddenly it wasn't, and she ended up locked in a public bathroom, where she *hurt* herself. She fucking hurt herself on *my watch*. And it was Ian she called for help.

Ian.

Not me.

Damn it, I wanted it to be me.

After a quick shower, I put on underwear and slide between the cool sheets. And then I lie there wide awake for what feels like hours.

I was hoping I could get my mind off Layla, but I can't. I can't stop thinking about the fact she's probably going to say yes to Reese tomorrow. And of course that leads to the inevitable questions and concerns.

What if they hit it off?

What if she ends up liking him and they take their relationship to the next step?

It's entirely possible that she could, at one point, want to have sex with him. How the fuck am I going to function after that?

With a sense of dread, I realize the truth—I won't be able to. If she becomes involved with someone, I'll have to ask to be reassigned. And that thought's depressing as hell.

I'm still awake an hour later when I hear something that sets my senses on alert. It's coming from next door.

I hear it again—a cry, followed by a whimper.

I'm out of my bed in a heartbeat, taking time only to pull on a pair of sweatpants before I race out of my room. I don't bother to knock on her door. I barge right in. The room is dark, and it takes me a second to make out her form on the bed, huddled beneath the covers. "Layla?"

She's thrashing, and her limbs are tangled up in the bedding.

I sit on the side of the bed and gently grip her shoulders. "Layla? Wake up, honey."

She wakes with a start and shoots up into a sitting position. Her eyes are wide with fright, and she glances around as if disoriented. "Where are they?"

"Where's who? There's no one here." I coax her to face me. "Layla? You're safe."

She looks around the room as if she doesn't quite believe me, but finally the tension in her body eases, and she turns her head to face me. "I dreamed about the ball gag." She circles her wrists. "And the handcuffs." She lifts haunted eyes to meet mine. "Those men were here in my room."

"That's not possible. The ones who are still alive are in jail awaiting trial. They're never getting bail."

Her entire body shudders, and she lies back down.

There's no way I can leave her like this, not when she's scared and shaking. Making a quick decision, I lie down beside her, on top of the bedding, and press my body against hers. I wrap my arms around her and pull her close. "It's okay. You're safe. I'll stay with you."

She melts into me, as if seeking warmth and security. Gradually, the shaking eases until it stops completely, and I lie awake in the dark, wondering how I'm going to survive this. She sighs quietly, and then her body relaxes back into sleep.

I want her.

But I can't have her.

Instead, I'm supposed to hand her over to some fucking jackass who doesn't deserve her, who doesn't even *know* her. And it's fucking killing me.

I lie here with her, holding her close, to protect her from the world that is sometimes too much for her.

* * *

The next morning, shortly after we arrive on campus, Reese is waiting for Layla on the front steps of the building where her anatomy class is held. As we approach, he leans back against the red brick wall, trying to look *oh, so casual* and cool. Dressed in ripped jeans, a burgundy UChicago hoodie, and high tops, he looks like he just came from a fashion shoot. And I'm sure that's not a coincidence.

"Hi, Layla," he says as he pushes away from the wall and walks toward her.

She slows her steps. "Hi, Reese."

He jogs down the last couple steps to meet us. He's standing one step above, so he towers over her like a giant. He gives me a brief, calculating look before he turns his attention to her. "How's it going?"

"Fine," she says, craning her head up to see him.

"Come on, I'll walk you to class." And then he gives me a pointed look that says *get lost*.

Layla looks to me, a mix of wariness and indecision written on her face.

Reluctantly, I nod. "It's okay. I'll be right behind you."

Reese motions for Layla to proceed him, and when she does, he moves between us in an attempt to block me from following. Behind her back, he shoots me a glare. "I'll take it from here, pal."

Over my dead body.

I follow them, never more than a few feet behind.

"How about dinner tonight?" he asks her. "I'd like to take you someplace really nice."

I can't hear her response, but when he puts his arm around her and pulls her close, I can guess.

She said yes.

My stomach drops like a stone.

Once we're in the classroom, Reese leaves her to go sit at

the back of the room with his buddies, in their assigned seats. I sit on Layla's right, and Charlene sits on her left. I listen in on the girls chatting before the professor starts lecturing.

"He's taking me to Tavern on Rush," Layla tells her friend.

At least he has good taste in food.

When class is over, Reese waits for Layla outside the door. "What's your address, babe? I'll pick you up at seven."

"Actually, no," I say, only too happy to butt in. "She'll meet you at the restaurant."

He scowls at me. "I wasn't asking you."

"Sorry, but no one comes to her house."

Reese shrugs. "Fine, whatever." Then he smiles at Layla. "I'll see you tonight." Before parting, he gives her a peck on the cheek.

As I watch Reese walk away, I wonder how the hell I'm going to make it through the evening.

29

Layla Alexander

I'm a nervous wreck by the time we get home from campus. I can't stop thinking about my dinner date this evening. I'm nervous and excited, but also more than a little scared. I'm not sure I'm ready for this. Reese doesn't know anything about my health issues, and I'm not ready to share that information with someone I've just met.

When we get home, my sugar level is pretty low, so Jason makes me eat a snack to tide me over until dinner. After that, to kill time, I go up to my room and work on homework.

I'm finding it hard to concentrate when I'm so nervous

about tonight. But that's not the only thing occupying my mind. All day I've been remembering what it felt like to wake up in the middle of the night to the feel of a warm male body pressed against my back. At first, I nearly screamed in panic, but I quickly realized it was Jason.

I don't remember much of the nightmare I had last night, but I sure do remember Jason coming into my room and comforting me. He must have fallen asleep in my bed. With his arm wrapped around me, I felt safer than I have in ages. I was able to fall back to sleep. But when my alarm woke me in the morning, he was gone. I know I didn't dream him up. He was really there in my bed.

I don't know why I said yes to having dinner with Reese. Honestly, I'd rather just stay home and have dinner with Jason and my parents. But I already said yes, and it's just dinner. It's too late to back out without things getting awkward. How long can one dinner take, anyway? An hour? Two hours max? And then I'll be home again. Maybe I'll be able to talk Jason into watching another movie with me tonight.

"Hello, sweetheart," Mom says as she walks into the sunroom. She's obviously just arrived home from work, because she's dressed in a dark teal suit with a cream tailored blouse. "Margaret tells me you have a dinner date tonight with a boy from school."

I laugh. "He's a senior, Mom, which means he's probably twenty-two. He's hardly a boy."

She smiles as she takes the seat across from mine. "I'm

sorry. You're right. Where are you and your gentleman friend going for dinner?"

"To Tavern on Rush."

She looks pleased. "Very nice. What time are you meeting him?"

"Seven."

She nods with a satisfied smile. "I hope you have a lovely evening." Then she stands. "If you don't mind, I'll go get out of this suit and into something more comfortable." She walks over to me and brushes my cheek with her fingers. "I'll miss you at supper tonight, but I'm glad you're going out. It'll be fun, I'm sure. I can't wait to hear all about it when you get home."

At five-thirty, I go up to my room to get dressed and spend twenty minutes debating what to wear. Something chic, but not too dressy. I don't want to call attention to myself, but I don't want to be underdressed either. In the end, I decide on a black ribbed knit dress with long sleeves and a turtleneck collar. The dress reaches mid-thigh; beneath it I wear a pair of black leggings and short black boots. It's classy, but not over the top. And you can't go wrong with a little black dress, even if it has long sleeves and a high collar.

The long sleeves are necessary to hide the still-healing scratches and the old scars on my arms. I definitely wouldn't want to have to explain any of those to my date.

To complete the outfit, I put on some large gold hoop earrings and a gold chain necklace with a heart-shaped locket. I decide to leave my hair down. I think it makes me look more sophisticated.

All dressed, I stand in front of the large gilded mirror in my closet and smile. *Not bad.*

You look like a prostitute.

I laugh. *I do not.*

It's actually not that bad.

Oh, my god, you said something nice? I'm shocked.

Don't let it go to your head. You're still just a trophy fuck.

I'm not having sex with Reese. We're just having dinner.

That's what you think. He wants to get you drunk, take you home with him, and screw your brains out.

I laugh again. "That's definitely not happening. Apparently, you haven't met my bodyguard."

Idiot.

But before I hear anything more, I'm distracted by the knock on my bedroom door.

"Time to go," I say as I head for the door and open it.

Jason's standing in the hallway dressed in his new black suit and tie. *Wow. He looks…*

Hot.

Gorgeous.

Intimidating.

Handsome.

And you still look like a prostitute.

"Shut up."

Jason grins at me. "I take it that wasn't directed at me."

"No, sorry." I motion for him to come in. "Just give me a sec. I need to brush my teeth."

While I'm in my bathroom doing just that, Jason walks up behind me with his phone in his hand. I'm sure he's checking my glucose monitor. "Watch what you eat tonight," he says as he looks at the reading. "You're already running a bit high. Make good choices."

I laugh. "Yes, *dad*."

He shakes his head. "I'm definitely not your father."

And then I recall that he spent at least half of last night spooning me in my bed, and the reminder causes heat to creep up my neck to my cheeks. Suddenly, I feel flushed.

On our way out, I stop in the dining room to say goodbye to my parents, who are eating dinner. I hug and kiss them both.

"Have fun, sweetheart," Mom says. She's smiling, but I detect her eyes are suspiciously glittery, as if she's on the brink of tears.

My dad locks his gaze on Jason. "Make sure she's home by nine."

"Dad!" I roll my eyes.

"Stay out as long as you like," Mom says. "Just be home by eleven. That's reasonable, right?"

I laugh at them both. "Don't worry, I'll be fine."

Jason follows me out, and we leave through the rear kitchen door to the parking area. He unlocks my door and gazes down at me, his dark expression hard to read. His jaws are clenched tightly, and a muscle tics in his cheek. He looks… unhappy. Bordering on angry.

As he slides into the driver's seat and starts the engine, he grips the steering wheel and asks, "Ready?"

"As ready as I'll ever be." I clasp my hands to keep them from shaking.

"You don't have to do this if you don't want to. You're allowed to change your mind at any time. Just say the word."

"No, it's okay. I want this." I want to get this over with. At least I'll be able to say I've been on a date.

He puts the car in reverse and backs out of the parking spot. "You look stunning, by the way. Reese is a lucky man. Just remember that. Never settle for just anyone."

I'm still smiling as we pull out onto my street and head for downtown.

When we arrive at the restaurant, Jason finds off-street parking nearby, and we walk the two blocks to the restaurant. We're ten minutes early, but Reese is already there, waiting on the front stoop.

When he spots me, Reese smiles widely and walks down the steps to meet me on the sidewalk. "Wow, you look amazing." He pulls me into his arms and gives me a hug. When he releases me, he looks over the top of my head at Jason, who's standing a couple of feet behind me. "You can go now. We'll call if we need you."

I'm shocked by how Reese speaks to Jason, dismissing him as if he's a servant. When I turn to look at Jason, he takes a step back and nods. "Have a good dinner," he says to Reese. Then he meets my gaze. "I'll be close by if you need anything." When he winks at me, I bite back a grin.

Reese takes my hand and leads me up the steps to the restaurant's entrance. Inside, he greets the hostess. "Hendricks. We have a reservation."

I know this place is super popular and it's hard to get a table on short notice. Somebody must have pulled some strings to get a reservation.

While we're waiting for the hostess to take us to our table, I sneak a peek at my date. He's wearing black dress slacks and a white shirt, no jacket. But he does have a tie on. I must admit, he looks very handsome. His blond hair is neatly styled, and he's freshly shaved. Standing this close to him, I detect a whiff of expensive cologne. Compared to most of the other men standing in the waiting area, Reese dwarfs them with his broad shoulders and muscular body.

The hostess grabs our menus and escorts us to a table for two near the edge of the dining room. The round table is covered in a white brocade tablecloth. There are two crystal wineglasses and coffee mugs already in place, as well as an ornate gold candelabra holding five tall white tapers.

As we sit, our escort lights the candles. "While you're looking over your menus, your server will come to take your drink orders."

"Thank you," I say.

"I already know what I'm having," Reese says as he lays his menu on the table and leans back in his chair. "The biggest steak they have and a baked potato." He pats his firm, flat belly. "I'm starving."

I try to be inconspicuous as I glance around the dining room looking for Jason. To my surprise, he's standing not far from us, leaning against a wall and trying to blend in. I don't think Reese has spotted him.

I divert my gaze to my menu and study the offerings, trying not to give Jason's location away. Somehow, I don't think Reese would be as amused as I am that Jason's close enough to hear our every word.

"So," Reese says. "I'm glad you changed your mind about going out with me. I've had my eye on you for a while now."

I smile at him, but don't know what to say to that.

"I read the stories in the news, about your previous bodyguard and the sex trafficking ring. That must have really sucked."

My heart slams into my ribs at the mention of Sean and that awful day. My pulse starts racing and all I can do is nod. "It was awful." *Please, let's not talk about this.*

"Is it true that your bodyguard was gunned down right in front of you? Did anyone do CPR?"

I stare at my menu. "Can we not talk about this, please?" This isn't at all what I expected. He's no better than the photographers who hound me, wanting information and comments for their news stories.

"Well, it was pretty big news," he says. "Still is. I'm sure you get asked about it all the time."

"What's your major, Reese?" I ask him. I'm reaching for any topic other than what happened to me.

"I'm pre-med. Cardiology. I'll take over my dad's practice one day. Dr. Hendricks? You've probably heard of him. He's a big shot around here."

Everyone's staring at you.

No, they're not.

Yes, they are. They're staring. And laughing behind your back. They think you're a joke.

Stop it.

I try hard to block her out, but she keeps on and on, the words jumbling together.

I catch Reese watching me curiously. I smile at him, then return my attention to the menu. I'm trying so hard to act normal. To not bring attention to myself. *I can do this.* I can be like any other girl out on a date.

When our server comes to take our orders, Reese orders the biggest steak on the menu, a baked potato, and a bottle of red wine. *An entire bottle.* I order a grilled salmon filet with steamed veggies and a bottle of imported sparkling water.

When our drinks arrive, I nervously uncap my bottle of water and take a sip.

Reese shakes his head and laughs. "I spent a freaking fortune on a bottle of expensive wine, and you're drinking water?

How old are you, Layla? Five?"

The ridicule in his tone sends a shaft of pain right through me. My heart starts pounding, and my cheeks burn. "I'm not five."

He's laughing at you. They all are. Because you're a joke. A stupid joke.

"Then drink up." Reese pours wine into my empty glass and hands it to me. Then he picks up his own glass and offers a toast. "To us. To the first of what I'm sure will be many dates."

My stomach knots as I stare at my wineglass. Alcohol doesn't mix well with my psych medication, and to make things worse, it can have a weird effect on blood sugar. That, combined with a meal, will send my glucose levels up quickly.

Everyone's staring at you. You should be ashamed.

God, why won't she just shut up for once?

I glance across the room toward the window, which overlooks a quiet little courtyard that offers customers bench seating outdoors. The tiny, clear fairy lights strung from the tree limbs are magical. I wish I was out there instead of in here.

"Layla?"

This is the worst date ever.

I shouldn't have come.

"Layla, look at me. Are you even listening?"

Everyone's staring at you.

My pulse is pounding, and my skin crawls. I can feel the

weight of everyone's stare.

I can't do this. I thought I could, but I can't.

"Layla!" I hear a loud snapping sound. "Hey, space cadet! Pay attention, will you?"

Startled, I turn back to face Reese.

He's leaning close, practically in my face. He snaps his fingers just inches from my nose. "Hello? Earth to Layla." He laughs. "Is there anyone in there?"

A heartbeat later, a furious Jason is looming over Reese, his expression dark and tight. "Get out," he says through gritted teeth, his voice nearly a growl. "Either you get the fuck out of this restaurant right now, or I will throw you out."

Reese looks taken aback as he glances first at Jason, then at me. "What the hell?"

Jason grabs hold of the back of Reese's shirt collar and tugs, nearly toppling his chair. "Right now. Out. I won't tell you again."

"Fine!" His face beet red, Reese shoots to his feet, causing his chair to scrape back loudly. He points at me. "What the hell is your problem?" And then he redirects his finger toward Jason and scowls. "And you? You're just the fucking hired help. Go find someone else to piss on." And then he stalks out of the restaurant without a backward glance.

I lift my gaze to look at Jason, who's staring at the door Reese just walked through. He's wound tight, his jaw clenched hard, his nostrils flaring, and for a minute I'm afraid he's going to go after Reese. He even takes a couple of steps toward the door.

"Jason?"

He freezes in his tracks, then turns back to me. Instantly, his expression softens as he looks me over. "Are you okay?"

As I look toward the exit, I nod. I'm half-afraid Reese will change his mind and come back.

Our server arrives then and sets our plates on the table. "Can I get you anything else?" he asks me. He avoids looking at Reese's vacant seat and the angry male standing behind it.

"No, thank you," I murmur.

As the server walks away, Jason looks at me, then at Reese's plate, which holds a twenty-ounce steak and a huge baked potato, and then my plate. He meets my gaze and grins. "These meals are too good to let go to waste." He grips the back of Reese's chair. "May I join you for dinner?"

The suffocating weight of a horrible evening evaporates. "Please do."

Jason sits and flags down our server to ask for a bottle of sparkling water. When it arrives, he pops off the top and lifts his bottle. "How about a new toast? To a delicious meal and good company."

For the first time all evening, I have a real reason to smile. "The very best."

30

Jason Miller

I wanted to strangle Reese the moment he snapped his fingers in Layla's face. *No one* snaps their fingers at Layla— she's not a fucking dog. I was seething as I stormed over to their table, and it took everything I had in me to refrain from body slamming him to the floor and beating him senseless. The gall of that presumptuous, entitled prick! How dare he treat her like that?

But we got the last laugh. After Reese runs off with his tail tucked between his legs, I take his vacated seat, and Layla and I proceed to eat a fantastic meal together.

"I'm sorry, Layla." I reach across the table for her hand and hold it in mine. "I never should have encouraged you to go out with him. This is on me."

"It's not your fault." She laughs shakily. "At least now I can say I've been out on a date."

"A shitty one. You deserve so much better. You deserve someone who treats you like a queen."

Blushing, she takes a bite of her salmon.

"How is it?" I point to her meal.

"It's wonderful. How's your steak?"

"Perfect. Medium rare, just how I like it. I have to admit, the blond hulk has good taste in food. Too bad he's a fucking moron."

She laughs.

The color has returned to her cheeks, and she looks happy and relaxed. I'm kicking myself for ever suggesting that she go out with Reese. I understand why Ruth thought it might be a good idea, and that I should encourage her to say yes, but the outcome just wasn't worth it.

Layla can't go out with just any random schmuck who asks her. She needs someone who knows her well, really understands her, and accepts her. She needs someone to love her unconditionally, because she's perfect just the way she is. Reese clearly isn't that person. I don't know if there's anyone good enough for her.

"Remind me to thank Reese," I say as I polish off the last bite of my steak.

"I'll be sure to do that. If he's still talking to me, that is."

"No loss if he's not. He's an asshole."

While Layla is programming the carb count of her meal into her device, I pay our bill. Then we leave the restaurant. It's only eight-thirty, still pretty early. We linger on the sidewalk out in front of the restaurant, neither of us seeming in a big hurry to go home.

"Since we're out, is there anything else you want to do?" I ask her. "We might as well make an evening of it. You don't have school tomorrow."

She grins. "How about some dessert? There's an ice cream shop just a block over that sells really good low-carb ice cream."

"Sounds good to me. Lead the way."

As we walk along the crowded sidewalk, she drifts closer and closer to me until we're walking shoulder-to-shoulder. Her boot catches on a crack in the pavement and she stumbles. I grab her hand to steady her, linking our fingers together.

As we continue walking, neither one of us seems in a hurry to let go. So, we walk hand-in-hand, like any other couple out on the street. I know this isn't a great idea, but is it really going to kill anyone if we hold hands? Friends hold hands, right? And we're definitely friends.

When we reach the ice cream shop, we climb the steps to the entrance. I open the door for her and hold it as she steps inside and gets in line behind another couple. We each order two scoops of low-carb ice cream. Chocolate for me, and strawberry for her.

"Let's walk down to the bridge to look at the river," she says to me when we step outside to eat our ice cream. "It's so pretty at night when the lights flicker on the surface of the water."

We stroll down N. Michigan Avenue, eating our ice cream, until we get to the bridge over the Chicago River. We stop at the railing and look out over the water and at the little strip of restaurants that line both banks of the river. A leisurely parade of tourist boats, small powerboats, and kayakers pass underneath the bridge. The intersection is crowded with pedestrians. An older African-American man playing a jazz saxophone has gathered quite a crowd in the square.

It's not long before I notice the group of girls standing not more than ten feet away from us who are staring at Layla, whispering among themselves. A couple of them try to be subtle about taking pictures. I don't think Layla has noticed. I hate that her privacy is constantly being trampled upon by curious strangers. They may not mean her harm, but they're causing harm by imposing on her life.

I shift casually so that I'm standing behind Layla. I stretch my arms out, one on each side of her, and grasp the railing in front of us. I've essentially boxed her in so she's not so visible to passers-by.

When she tilts her head back and smiles up at me, my breath catches and I find myself fighting a powerful urge to lean down and kiss her. And I can tell from the glint in her eyes that she's thinking the same thing.

Instead, I give her an apologetic smile. "It's getting late. We should probably start walking back to the car."

Her smile falls. "But it's only ten."

"How about we watch a movie when we get home? You can pick."

"Deal."

Layla's pretty quiet on the way back to the house. She seems lost in her own thoughts. I wish I could ask what's on her mind, but I feel like I'd be prying too much. And it's hardly fair if I ask her what she's thinking about when I can't give her the same courtesy.

When we arrive back at the house, Ruth and Martin are seated at the kitchen table with Margaret. The three of them look up at us expectantly.

"Well?" Ruth says with a smile. "How did it go?"

Layla beams. "I had a wonderful evening. The dinner was amazing, and then we got ice cream and walked down to the river to watch the boats." She stops to hug her mom. "If you'll excuse me, I'm going to change. Jason and I are going to watch a movie." And then she races out of the room.

I move to follow her, but Ruth stops me. "How did it go, really? It sounds like she had a good time."

I hate to be the bearer of bad news. "Reese acted like an ass and humiliated Layla in the restaurant. I ran him off."

Ruth frowns. "But I don't understand. She was in such a

good mood just now. She seemed happy."

Oh, shit. Now it's confession time. "We couldn't let two great meals go to waste, so we stayed and ate dinner together. Then we got ice cream and went for a walk. It was the least I could do to try to salvage her evening."

"I see," Ruth says. Her smile falls as she glances at her husband.

Martin looks me in the eye, but he doesn't say anything.

Shit. The last thing I need is for the parents to think I did something inappropriate with their daughter. I protected her, damn it. I'll always do that.

Ruth nods to me. "Thank you, Jason."

And with that comment, I know I'm dismissed.

Great. I head upstairs to change out of my suit. I'm in my closet pulling on a pair of sweatpants when I hear a knock at my door. Quickly, I grab a T-shirt and pull it on before I answer it.

Layla's father is standing at my door. "Can we talk?" he asks.

I nod. "Here? Or somewhere else?"

"Here is fine." He walks into my room and closes the door behind him.

I'm immediately on alert. If he's here to criticize me for having dinner with Layla—

"Jason," he begins.

He's pacing, which isn't a good sign.

What if he fires me?

My chest seizes up tight and my heart pounds. I can't lose this assignment. I can't contemplate someone else taking my place, someone else being responsible for Layla's safety.

Immediately, I go on the defensive. "I did the right thing tonight, Martin. You didn't see Layla's face when he called her a space cadet. It damn near broke her heart. Yes, I ran him off, and I'd do it again. He treated her like shit, and I won't stand for that. I know you made me promise—"

"Jason."

I stop my tirade and suck in a breath. Whatever's coming is coming. I might as well brace for it. "Yes, sir?"

"Slow down, son." He crosses the room to stand in front of the hearth and gazes up at an oil painting hanging over the mantle. It's a portrait of a young boy and a German Shepard dog. "This is me when I was four, and that's Goliath. He was my best friend. I loved him dearly. He died the year I graduated from high school. Broke my heart." Martin turns to face me. "In many ways, you remind me of Goliath."

His dog? That doesn't sound good.

Martin laughs. "I meant that as a compliment, believe me. Goliath was the truest friend I ever had, and he was a real protector. Like you are." He meets my gaze. "Jason, when we first hired you, Ruth and I extracted a promise from you."

"You did, sir, and I assure you I have never once behaved inappropriately with Layla. I—"

He lifts his hand to cut me off. "Relax, son. We know that."

"Then what—"

"My wife and I have noticed a change in our daughter since you signed on to her protection detail. We've seen her *happy*. We've seen her smile and laugh. I'm not exaggerating when I say we don't see her do those things very often."

I watch him warily, unsure where this is going. Is he about to sack me, or give me a medal?

"Ruth and I have been talking, and we've decided to rescind that promise you made us."

My brains slams to a halt. "I don't understand."

His lips quirk up in a small smile. "I'll just spell it out, shall I? Ruth and I have come to the realization that you're the best thing that's ever happened to our daughter. You make her smile and laugh—and those are things we cherish. And unless we're greatly mistaken, you seem to enjoy spending time with Layla. You're a good man, Jason. And that's why we're releasing you from your vow."

Stunned, I stand there and stare at him, which only makes his grin bigger. "I'm not sure I follow."

"Let me be very clear," he says. "So there's no misunderstanding. If you were to decide that you wanted to date our daughter, you'd have our blessing. Is that clear enough?"

"Yes, sir. Perfectly clear."

Martin nods, seemingly satisfied. "All right then. Enjoy your evening." And he departs from my room, leaving me in a state of shock.

Surely, I didn't hear that right. My heart starts thundering as his words sink in.

Date our daughter. You'd have our blessing.

Holy shit.

My mind is reeling as I make a pit stop in the bathroom to wash up. I splash on a bit of cologne—not too much. Girls like that. Then I leave my room and knock on Layla's door.

My pulse is racing. Everything's different now.

"Come in!" she calls.

When I open the door, I spot Layla seated on the sofa with the remote control in her hand. For a moment, I'm speechless as I stare at her. Her parents released me from my promise. That doesn't mean my boss would be okay with the idea of me dating my client, but it doesn't say anything in our employee handbook specifically banning me from doing that.

"Jason? Are you okay?"

"Yeah, sure." I close the door behind me. "I'm fine."

* * *

As I stand there staring at her, I don't see a client. I see a beautiful young woman who takes my breath away. One who's no longer off-limits to me. I'm completely at a loss as to how to proceed.

Do I tell her?

Hey, fun fact—your parents said they'd be fine with it if we started dating. What d'you say?

What if she doesn't want that with me? What if I'm just a bodyguard to her, and she's not looking for anything more? Would that make *me* the presumptuous, entitled prick? And how do I find out if she's interested without putting her on the spot?

Everything just got really complicated really quickly.

She eyes me warily. "Are you sure everything's all right?"

"Absolutely."

Smiling, she points to the switch on the wall. "Would you mind turning off the light?"

I turn off the chandelier and join her on the sofa. Suddenly, just sitting next to her takes on a whole new meaning. A wall—a barrier—between us is suddenly gone, and my body is lit up like a bonfire.

She puts her feet up on the coffee table, and I smile when I see she's wearing socks with panda bear faces on them. She starts shuffling through the movies on demand. "What do you want to watch?"

"It's your turn to pick," I remind her.

She looks pensive. "I'm trying to think of something a guy would like."

"Anything you choose is fine, really." And it's the truth. I probably don't have the attention span right now to concentrate on a movie. I'm preoccupied by the fact that she's right here beside me and her parents have untied my hands.

"How about the new King Kong movie?" she suggests.

"That sounds great." Seriously, we could watch anything, and I'd be happy.

As the movie starts rolling, I check her blood sugar level, and it is good, just like she said.

"You're in a good mood," I say. "You're not upset over what happened with Reese this evening?"

She shakes her head. "Not really. I didn't want to go out with him in the first place. I just wanted to go on a *date*." She shrugs. "Now I have."

"You should have told me you didn't want to go out with him. I never would have encouraged you to go if I knew you didn't want to."

"It's all right." As she settles back on the sofa, her arm lightly brushes mine, and she glances up at me with those big, beautiful eyes. "I'm glad you were with me tonight. Thanks for what you did."

"You don't need to thank me. I—"

"Please don't say you were just doing your job."

"I wasn't going to say that."

"Then what were you going to say?"

For a moment, I can't take my eyes off of her. *She's no longer off-limits*. At least as far as her parents are concerned. But she's still my client. We don't exactly have regulations against dating our clients—hell, my boss married a client—but I'm not sure how he'd feel about this.

"Jason?"

"Sorry, what?"

"What were you going to say?"

Oh, hell. I don't even remember what we were talking about. "Um…oh, right. I was going to say that I would do anything to make you happy."

At my stark admission, her eyes widen. "Really?"

I chuckle. "Yes, really."

I can tell the moment she gets nervous because she starts biting her bottom lip. "Because you're such a dedicated bodyguard?" she asks.

"I am a dedicated bodyguard, yes. But no. That's not why I'd do anything to make you happy. Bodyguards are obligated to keep their clients *safe*, not happy."

"But you want me to be happy?"

I nod. Then I use my thumb to gently tug her bottom lip from between her teeth. "Don't bite your lip. You'll hurt yourself."

Her cheeks deepen in color as she flushes. I suspect she's even holding her breath. In anticipation maybe?

But she's no ordinary girl, and so I can't assume anything. I need to know for sure.

I reach out with my index finger and tuck her hair behind her ear. "I can't handle the idea of you getting hurt." That's the honest truth.

The movie has started, and neither one of us is paying any attention to it. Layla's eyes search mine, and there's a small frown turning down the corners of her lips. She looks increasingly worried.

"Hey," I say softly. "What's wrong?"

When her eyes fill with tears, my heart contracts painfully. *Damn it*. This isn't going how I'd hoped.

A single tear spills from her bottom eyelid and rolls down

her cheek. I catch it with the pad of my thumb. "It's okay. Don't cry."

She swallows hard. And then abruptly she looks away, her brow furrowing. "Stop it," she hisses. Her voice cracks. "For god's sake, just stop."

I realize she's not talking to me. She's talking back to the voice. I turn her face to mine. "What's she telling you?"

Layla shakes her head. "I can't."

"You can't tell me?"

"That's right."

"I think you should tell me because I'm pretty sure she's wrong."

She laughs, the sound watery as she's holding back tears.

"Tell me, Layla."

Her eyes are stark with pain. "She says you think I'm pathetic. That you're laughing at me."

Pain stabs me in the chest, and I have to fight myself not to reach out and take her in my arms. I lean close, pressing my forehead to hers. "She's wrong, Layla. She's dead wrong. I don't think you're pathetic. I think you're extraordinary. I think you're the smartest, kindest, most beautiful girl I've ever known."

Her breath catches on a sob, and she stares at me in utter confusion.

I realize I'm not being fair to her. She has no idea how our circumstances have changed. "Layla?" I hold out my palm, and she stares at it. "Would you like to go out on a date with me Friday night?"

Her eyes widen so quickly it's almost comical. "What?"

I smile, still holding out my hand. "Will you go out with me?"

She's staring at me like she doesn't trust her own ears. "Do you mean on a date-date? Like a real date?"

I bite back a smile, because I need to take this seriously. "Yes, a real date."

"But my parents—"

"Actually, they'd be fine with it."

"What are you talking about?"

"After dinner, your dad told me that he and your mom would be fine if we started dating."

Her eyes widen. "Are you serious?"

When I nod, she ever so slowly places her hand in mine. I curl my fingers around hers and draw her hand to my lips to kiss it.

Abruptly, she looks away and shakes her head. "No. Stop. He is not."

"I'm not what?" I ask her.

"Lying to me."

"No, honey. I'm not lying to you. It about killed me tonight when I drove you to a restaurant so you could meet another man for dinner. I wanted to punch him in the face. Reese did me a favor when he disrespected you, because he gave me an excuse to chase him off." I squeeze her hand. "Jealousy was eating me alive."

She still looks skeptical, cautious, probably because the monster is feeding her loads of bullshit.

"Layla?"

"Hmm?"

"Can I kiss you?"

The breath leaves her lungs in a rush, and she actually starts shaking. *Yes.* Her lips form the word, but no sound comes out.

"Was that a yes?"

She nods.

"Because I really need to be sure. I need you to say the word."

"Yes," she says, this time in a clear voice. "I want you to kiss me."

31

Layla Alexander

Time stands still as my gaze locks on Jason's mouth. He has beautiful lips, and right now the corners are tilting up. He's smiling. *At me.* I have to seriously question whether or not I'm hallucinating.

Yes, you're hallucinating. None of this is real. He'd never want to kiss you in real life.

Maybe he does.

Don't be an idiot.

And then he leans close, moving slowly, until his mouth presses against mine, so gently at first I barely feel the subtle pressure, just a light warmth against my lips, followed by a puff of air.

Is this really happening?

And then he pulls back and studies me, as if he's expecting me to wig out on him.

You're just a trophy fuck.

I am not.

You are so damn gullible! You idiot.

I look away. "Stop it!"

"Hey." Jason's voice is gentle as he locks onto my gaze. "Who do you trust? Me or her?"

"You," I answer without hesitation.

"Then don't listen to her. Listen to *me*."

I wish it was that easy.

Jason leans in again, this time his lips settling more fully on mine. He releases my hand and slides his fingers into my hair, holding me loosely as he deepens the kiss.

I'm struck by the realization that this is my first real kiss. Yes, horrible people did horrible things to me, but this—this is my first *real* kiss. I want to focus on happy memories and not the bad ones.

I want to lose myself in the heat and scent of him. He smells so good. Partly it's his cologne, and partly it's the smell of fresh laundry, but mostly it's just *him*. His scent heats my body and makes my belly quiver.

Jason's hand drifts up to the back of my neck. I never imagined anything could feel this good. Tingles of pleasure race up and down my spine, and my entire body reacts. My breasts feel heavy. My belly clenches hotly, as does the aching spot between my legs.

He pulls back a bit and brushes his thumb over my bottom lip. "I've wanted to kiss you so badly."

"Me too."

His smile is beautiful, the way his eyes light up and their corners crinkle. And then he licks his bottom lip and moves in for another kiss. This one is different. It's hotter and a bit hungry. His lips begin to move, sliding cautiously against mine, and when I feel the tip of his tongue stroke my lips, tasting me, the breath leaves my lungs in a hot rush.

Jason's fingers gently grip the back of my neck, and he holds me close for a kiss. I'm not afraid of *this*. I'm not afraid of *him*, and the realization is liberating. My hands move of their own accord, skimming up his arms, and then across his firm, broad shoulders, and then higher still until I'm cupping his face. His trim beard feels strange against my palms, softer than I expected.

With a harsh groan, he shivers at my touch, and I realize he's just as shaken as I am.

He wants this, too.

Heat sweeps through me, and my body aches. All of me longs for something *more*. For the things I've only read about in romance novels, but never experienced myself.

When a whimper escapes me, Jason's hand tightens on the

back of my neck, and with a groan, he nudges my lips apart. I gasp when his tongue touches mine, velvety soft as it strokes me gently. I suck in a breath.

He pauses a moment. "Doing okay?" he murmurs against my lips.

I nod, but don't dare try to speak. I'm not sure I could put a coherent sentence together at the moment.

Jason slowly pulls back, smiling as he touches my bottom lip. He swallows hard and then sighs. "I'm trying really hard to take things slowly."

I shake my head. "I'm fine. You don't need to slow down because of me."

His smile deepens into a grin. "Oh, honey." He brushes my cheek. "You have no idea—" But he stops there, as if he's already said too much. He leans against the back of the sofa and pulls me close, his arm sliding around me. "Maybe we should watch the movie now."

Wait! What happened to the kissing? I liked the kissing. "Why?"

He actually laughs. "Because we need to slow down."

"Maybe I don't want to."

He links our fingers together and kisses the back of my hand. "Well, maybe I do."

"What does that mean?"

"It means I need to put the brakes on."

"For me or for you?"

"For both of us. I want too much, and you're not ready."

"I'm twenty-one, Jason. I'm an adult."

"Yes, but you've never dated before. In fact, you've probably never kissed anyone before today."

"Everyone has to start somewhere."

He laughs. "I'm just now processing the fact that your parents gave me their blessing. I'm not sure I'm ready to tempt fate." He cups my face in his hands. "You are the most beautiful, most courageous woman I've ever met, and frankly I'm in awe of you." His dark eyes search mine. "But Rome wasn't built in a day. We need to take this slowly. There's too much at stake here for me to risk screwing it up. So, baby steps, okay?"

"All right." On impulse, I reach out to touch his cheek, but my hand freezes halfway.

"It's okay, you can touch me. Trust me, you can do anything you want."

After I brush my fingers over his beard, my fingertips travel up the edge of his cheek, up to his temple. And then I trace the dark slash of his eyebrow, and the bridge of his nose. Jason closes his eyes and lets out a heavy breath.

Taking his reaction as a positive sign, I run my fingers through his hair.

His entire body shivers, and I'm amazed that I have that kind of impact on him. Feeling emboldened, I lean close and press *my* lips to his.

His eyes flash open in surprise, and there's no mistaking the fire I see in their depths.

"Sweetheart, you are playing with fire," he warns, his voice suddenly rough.

"It's all right. You won't burn me."

"You're so sure of me?"

"Absolutely."

Grinning, he brushes my hair back from my face. "You are going to be the death of me. I only have so much restraint."

I feel heady with a mixture of power and relief. The way he's talking to me—the way he's opening up to me. This is a first. I've never had such an intimate conversation with a man before.

I lean forward and kiss him. His lips part immediately, and he nudges mine to open as well. My nerves are tingling from my scalp to my toes.

His hand in my hair feels exquisite.

You whore!

I flinch, then pull away.

"What's wrong?" he asks.

You're a whore. A slut.

Jason pulls me back into his arms. "It's okay," he murmurs as he rubs my back. "Tell me what she said."

"She called me a whore."

His expression is a mix of sadness and resignation. I can tell he's realizing just how messed up I am. I'll never be a normal girl. "You should go," I tell him. I nod toward the door. "I'm not fit company right now."

He reaches for my hand. "That's even more reason for me

to stay."

I try to tug my hand free, but he tightens his hold. "Who do you trust? Me or the voice?" he asks again. It's our mantra.

"You."

"All right, then. I'm right, and she's wrong. It's that simple." He puts his arm around me. I lean my head against his shoulder and relax into him and we hold hands as we watch the rest of the movie.

Baby steps.

32

Jason Miller

Thursday is a quiet day. Other than taking Layla to her weekly appointment with Dr. Hartigan in the morning, we stay home and hang out. She does homework at her computer desk in her bedroom while I lie on the sofa in her room and read. When she's done with her schoolwork for the day, we spend some time in the workout room and then watch a movie.

Friday morning, I drive Layla to campus after breakfast. Gary the photographer is lying in wait for us just off the campus grounds, and he follows us in. Just like the last time, he shadows my car until I find a parking spot.

Before we exit the car, I lock my handgun in the safe. My ankle holster feels empty without it. I glance over at Layla, who looks a bit pale.

"It'll be okay, I promise," I say as I lay a reassuring hand on her leg. She's anxious about seeing Reese. I have to admit, I'm not excited about the prospect either.

"I dread seeing him again."

I reach for her hand and kiss the back of it. "If he says anything obnoxious, ignore him. Let me deal with him."

Gary Fisher is lying in wait for Layla just outside the car, his camera poised and ready. It's a shame I'm not permitted to carry on campus. I think if I waved a gun in his face, he'd have second thoughts about harassing Layla.

"I'll get out first," I tell her. "You stay in the car until I come around and open your door."

The moment Layla steps out of the vehicle, Gary is snapping picture after picture. I'm tempted to grab his camera and smash it on the pavement, but then I'd end up in court.

"Don't you have anything better to do?" I ask him as I position myself between his camera and Layla.

"Come on, man," Gary says. "Just let me get a few good shots, and then I'll leave her alone. Her pics are as hot as she is. I'm just tryin' to make a living."

Infuriated, I block him as he tries to step around me. "Maybe you could make a living some other way, one that doesn't involve stalking innocent young women."

"She's not just any young woman. She's a public figure."

"She's a college student, pal. That's not newsworthy."

"Yeah, but the bruises on her face are. They're fading, but I can still see 'em. The public wants to see them, too. And they want details on the shooting of her previous bodyguard." Gary tries to slip around me, but I drive him back with a shove. "Come on, Layla," Gary says, taunting her. "Just answer a few questions. Is it true that you were involved with your previous bodyguard? Is that why he was killed? Was it a crime of passion? Or jealousy?"

Gasping, Layla fists the back of my shirt.

"Get the fuck back," I growl as I threaten to take a step toward Gary.

"Ignore him, Jason," Layla says. "He's not worth it. Let's go to class."

I stand down, knowing she's right. If I go off on him, he's just going to be even more intent on getting a story out of her. I lock the car and take Layla's hand. Keeping her by my side, I walk her across campus.

Gary follows, taking more pictures, but he stays a good twenty feet back. Smart guy.

When we reach the campus sidewalk, Layla tries to tug her hand free. "People will wonder if they see us holding hands."

"Let them wonder." I stop to face her, my tone softening. "Do you not want people to know we're dating? Is that it? It's okay if you don't."

Her eyes widen. "Of course not. I don't want to keep it a

secret. But if the public finds out we're dating, they'll start hounding you, too."

I pull her close and plant my lips on hers. As we kiss, I can hear Gary's startled reaction and the rapid-fire clicking of his camera as he takes a series of shots. "Oh, my god!" Gary says. "Are you two together? Like romantically? Since when?"

"Well, now they know," I say, grinning as I pull back from her.

She smiles up at me. "You're in for it now."

"Let them do their worst."

When we're almost at her first classroom, I slow us down. "Are you ready for this?" I'm not entirely sure I'm ready. If Reese mouths off to Layla one more time, I just may lose it.

"I don't really have a choice. I can't miss my class."

I open the door and usher Layla into the building. "If he says anything obnoxious, I'll handle him."

As usual, the students loiter in the hallway while they wait for the professor to unlock the lecture hall door. Charlene is already here, and when she spots Layla, she smiles and waves us over.

I follow as Layla heads for her friend, but before she reaches her destination, Reese emerges from the crowd and plants himself directly in front of Layla, blocking her way. He looms over her, his hands on his hips.

As Layla comes to an abrupt stop, I move in front of her, easing her back. I glare at Reese. "Don't even think about it."

"I just want to talk to her, that's all."

"You said enough the other night at the restaurant. She doesn't want to talk to you."

"Come on, it was just a joke." Reese peers around me and smiles at Layla. "Hey, baby, we need to talk. It was just a misunderstanding. Your guard dog overreacted."

I hear Layla snicker behind me. *Guard dog.* She likes that.

Layla steps out from behind me and faces Reese. "No, we don't need to talk. Let's just forget it happened, okay?"

Reese scowls. "No, it's not okay." Then his expression softens. "Hey, baby, come on. It was just a big misunderstanding, and this jerk" —he points to me— "overreacted. Let's start over."

"That's enough, Reese," I say, pressing my hand to his chest and driving him back. "Leave her alone. You were an ass to her at the restaurant. She's not interested in a do-over."

Reese sneers at me. "How about you let her speak for herself?"

"Jason's right," she says. "I'm not interested."

The big blond hulk sneers at me. "Oh, I'll bet you're loving this, aren't you? You make me out to be the problem, when *she's* a certifiable nutjob."

Layla gasps.

I grab Reese by the collar of his hoodie and shove him into a wall. My grip on his clothing is nearly cutting off his air. "Not another word, you hear me? You don't look at her, you don't speak to her. And if you try, I will make you regret it, is that clear?"

Reese's face turns beet red before I release him. Grimacing, he staggers back and shoves a finger in my direction. "You're the one who's going to regret it. Nobody speaks to me this way, douche bag."

Four big guys step up behind Reese, and for a minute, I'm wondering if I'm going to have to fight all five of them right here in this hallway.

But before anyone can make a move, the professor arrives and unlocks the classroom door. "Good morning, everyone," the man says as he steps aside to let students file into the room.

I shadow Layla into the classroom and follow her and Charlene to our seats. Reese heads straight to the back of the room to sit with his buddies. Five against one? I doubt any of them are trained fighters, but they're big motherfuckers, and all combined, they probably outweigh me by at least two hundred pounds. I could take them, but it wouldn't be pretty. Somebody would get hurt. Hopefully it won't come to that because I really don't want Layla to see me fighting.

While the professor lectures about the structure of the kidneys, I read on my phone. This author talks about how and when the nature of her voices changed from antagonistic to more congenial. She talks about how her voices gradually morphed from criticizing her to cooperating with her, even encouraging her. That's what I hope for Layla.

After I pause to check her glucose level, I go back to reading. Monitoring her sugar levels has become second nature to me now. I do it without even thinking. She also checks throughout the day, and between the two of us, we manage to stay pretty well on top of it.

When class ends, the students file out of the room. Reese and his friends are some of the first ones out the door. I notice Layla lingering a while as she chats with Charlene. They're confirming their standing plans to meet up for lunch in the cafeteria.

The chatting goes on a little longer than usual, cutting into her time to get to her next class. I think Layla's procrastinating. I think she's afraid to walk out of this classroom—afraid that Reese will be waiting to ambush her in the hallway and cause more trouble.

Damn, I wish I could carry on campus. But I sure as hell can't pull a gun on a student. That would get me banned from campus in a heartbeat, and possibly put in jail, and then I'd be screwed.

Finally, the girls go their separate ways. Our mad dash across campus to her next class—English lit—is uneventful. There, she turns in the rough draft of her paper on *Jane Eyre* and takes a pop quiz on the assigned reading. Knowing her, she'll ace the quiz.

Then it's off to lunch. We meet Charlene at the cafeteria. Layla gets her usual grilled chicken wrap and tea. I grab a couple slices of pizza and a bottle of water. We meet Charlene at the usual table.

Charlene asks Layla to catch her up on all the drama that

happened outside the anatomy classroom.

After Layla tells the story, Charlene scans the crowded cafeteria. "I don't see him anywhere."

"Good," Layla says as she takes a sip of her tea.

We eat in peace, then the girls separate again, Charlene heading to her next class, while Layla heads to her psychology class.

Layla and I are halfway across campus when Reese and his friends make an appearance.

Shit.

I was afraid of this.

I'd love to make a go at them—hell, even all five of them—but I can't. Not with Layla here. I can't do my job and protect her if I'm involved in a brawl. And that's exactly what it would be.

The five hulks start walking toward us across the lawn, fanning out in an arc. Reese is in the middle, with two friends on each side.

I release Layla's hand and gently push her in the direction of the nearest building. "I want you to go into that building, find an administrative office where you'll be safe, and call your brother to come get you. Got it?"

She looks frantic. "Jason, no! I'm not leaving you."

"Layla, I mean it," I growl as I point at the nearest building. "We don't have time to debate this." And then I'm completely out of options, because the first of the five goons rushes me.

Layla screams when I shove her out of the path of this

mountain barreling down on me.

Fuck.

I really don't want Layla to see this.

Like all McIntyre Security bodyguards, I'm well versed in martial arts—Jiu Jitsu, kickboxing, MMA. But my personal favorite is Krav Maga. It's swift and brutal, and it does the job.

The first guy who comes at me has the momentum of a freight train—a serious miscalculation on his part. At the last second, I duck, pivot, and slam my elbow into his abdomen, knocking the breath out of him. He drops to the ground like a stone, coughing as he struggles to catch his breath.

Somewhere to my right, Layla screams.

Automatically, I turn to search for her. Three more of them rush me at once, catching me off guard. Two of them grab my arms and pin them behind my back. As I struggle to break free, the third guy slams his fist into my face, once, twice, three times. Blood rushes from my nose and lips. I can feel my left eye throbbing as it starts to swell.

Layla's sobbing now, crying my name. I kick out at the guy who's using my face as a punching bag, dislocating his kneecap. He goes down hard. I use my feet to knock the two holding me to the ground, and a couple of well-placed kicks ensures they won't be getting up any time soon. They'll both be pissing blood for days.

With his four buddies on the ground, Reese comes running at me, his face screwed up in anger, his chest heaving as he sucks in air. He's all brute force with no finesse as he swings at me. I sidestep him, pivot, and use my foot to send him crashing to the ground hard enough to knock the wind out of him.

I hear multiple sirens then. Campus police are on their way.

Fuck.

Layla runs to me, throwing herself into my arms. "It's okay," I tell her as I hold her shaking body.

"You're bleeding," she cries.

Here come three cops running this way. Five guys are lying on the ground, either half unconscious or struggling to breathe, and I'm the only one standing. It looks like I'm about to be arrested.

An older woman dressed in a navy-blue suit, who saw the entire thing, approaches. "I'm Dr. Porter, chair of the biology department. Can I be of assistance?"

"Yes." I pull out my phone and send off an emergency text to both Ian and Tyler. "Please take care of Layla until her brother arrives."

My phone chimes as they both reply, saying they're on their way.

The woman nods as she holds her hand out to Layla. "Come with me, dear." Then to me, she says, "Tell her brother to come to the biology office. I'll keep the young lady with me until he arrives."

I nod as I send Ian and Tyler a second text with further instructions. Once that's taken care of, I step closer to Layla, laying my hands on her shoulders. "Honey, I'm sorry. Ian's coming. You'll be okay."

Layla's visibly shaken as the professor leads her away.

The officers reach us a moment later, and they quickly assess the situation, call for emergency medical teams, and cuff me. There are plenty of bystanders, including Dr. Porter, who saw what happened. They'll be giving statements—hopefully ones that exonerate me. I didn't start this; they did. I just ended it.

In the meanwhile, I'll be sitting in the campus police station, worrying about Layla. I just hope they'll let me make a phone call. Looks like I'm gonna need some help.

And I hope I don't get fired in the process.

33

Layla Alexander

"Your name is Layla, right?" the woman says as she leads me to one of the science buildings. "I'm Dr. Porter."

She opens the door for me, but before I go inside, I glance back at Jason just in time to see a police officer handcuffing him. Jason turns his head in my direction, and our gazes lock. Pain tears through me at the sight of his bloody face. His nose is bleeding, as is his bottom lip. And it's all because of me.

"Come with me, dear," the woman says as she shuffles me inside. The heavy door closes behind us with a loud clang. "I saw what happened just now. Those young men rushed him, and your friend was just defending himself. Once the police get to the bottom of it, I'm sure everything will be fine."

We walk down a short hallway until we come to an office. She ushers me inside, then through an inner door to her private office. "You can wait with me here until your brother comes. Ian? Is that his name? Your friend texted him."

"Yes." It's all I can manage at the moment. I keep picturing Jason's bloody face. And I don't think I'll ever be able to forget the sight of those guys holding Jason while the third one punched him, over and over. Reese is a monster. His friends are, too.

"Have a seat, Layla," the professor says as she points to a chair beside her desk. "You look like you're about to collapse. Can I get you something? Water or coffee? Anything?"

I shake my head. "Thank you, but no." My phone buzzes with an incoming message from Ian.

Ian: we're coming

Of course by *we* he's including Tyler. Tyler and Ian are attached at the hips these days. Wherever you see one, you see the other. I'm so happy for them.

I glance at the woman who's now seated behind the desk. She has short silver hair and pretty blue eyes. Her round face is softly wrinkled. She's a complete stranger to me, but she has an air of confidence about her that's comforting. I do as she says and sit, but I'm still in chaos mode.

I can't believe Reese and his friends attacked Jason like

that. It was cowardly and underhanded, five against one. And even outnumbered, Jason had the upper hand. "Are the police going to arrest Jason?" I ask.

"I assume you're referring to the young man who very efficiently incapacitated five rather large opponents?"

As I nod, I picture the way Jason looked as he delivered striking blows and kicks that knocked those guys on their asses. He was like a machine, all coordinated power and swift action. It's like he didn't even think about what he was doing—his body just acted. But not before one of them got a few powerful blows in.

"I imagine he's on his way to the police station right now," she says. "But don't worry. There were plenty of witnesses who will attest to the fact that those five students started the fight, including me. Your friend reacted in self-defense."

He's going to get fired, and it's your fault. You idiot.

No, he won't.

Of course he will. He's already been arrested. He's going to jail.

Stop!

Do you think your parents will keep him around after this? If you do, you're even crazier than I thought. Idiot.

Shut up!

It's all your fault.

"Layla?"

I hope you're happy.

I wrap my arms around my torso and try to stop shaking.

What if she's right? What if he gets arrested and my parents fire him?

"Layla? Is everything all right?"

I don't want another bodyguard. I want Jason. It's not fair. None of this is his fault. He was just trying to protect me.

I told you, it's your fault. He probably hates you now. You've probably destroyed his career.

My stomach churns at the thought that Jason might blame me. I would understand if he did.

I grab my earbuds from my backpack, shove them in my ears, and turn on some music. Closing my eyes, I try to block everything out and focus on the lyrics to the songs. It helps me drown *her* out.

I don't know how much time has passed when I feel a gentle hand on my knee. When I open my eyes, I see Ian crouching beside my chair. Tyler's right behind him, talking on his phone.

"Hey, sis." Ian gently removes my earbuds. "Are you okay?"

"Ian." My voice breaks, but I manage to maintain my composure. I throw my arms around my brother, and he wraps me in a bear hug.

"Hey, everything's going to be okay," he says. "Tyler's on the phone right now with Jason's boss." My brother glances across the desk at Dr. Porter. "Thanks for watching out for my sister."

The woman nods. "It was no problem. I'm happy to help."

Ian turns back to me. "Can you tell me what happened?"

My voice shakes. "We were walking across campus when five guys ambushed Jason. One of them punched him several times in the face. You should have seen him, Ian. He knocked them all to the ground. He was incredible. Did you know he could fight like that?"

Ian smiles. "Yeah, I knew he could do that."

"We have to help him."

Tyler ends his call. "Troy Spencer is on his way to the police station. So is Shane. They'll take care of Jason."

"Who's Troy?" I ask.

"Shane McIntyre's attorney," Ian says. "And now Jason's." He rises to his feet, then pulls me to mine. "There's nothing we can do for Jason right now. Let's get you home."

"Do Mom and Dad know?" I ask.

Ian nods. "I told them. Dad's in court all afternoon, but Mom's taking off early. She'll meet us at home."

"Do you think they'll fire him?"

Ian winces. "I'm not sure. It's possible."

"We're dating." I blurt the words out.

Ian's green eyes widen in surprise. "Are you serious? Do Mom and Dad know?"

I nod. "Jason said Mom and Dad gave him their blessing. I haven't had a chance to tell you."

Tyler rolls his eyes. "Why does he get it so easy?"

From what I heard, Dad wasn't so understanding when he discovered Tyler and Ian were dating. He actually threatened to end Tyler's career over it.

Ian laughs. "Come on, let's get Layla home."

34

Jason Miller

I'm seated in front of the campus police chief's desk, while he, Shane, and the company attorney, Troy Spencer, are conversing out in the hallway. I can see them through a glass wall, but I can't make out what's being said.

When the campus police brought me in, I was permitted to make a phone call. I called Shane, and he set everything in motion. Shane and Troy showed up within a half-hour. Now Troy is negotiating with the police chief—at least that's what it looks like to me.

Troy and Shane are both dressed in dark suits with white

dress shirts and ties. Troy makes a striking figure in his Armani suit, with his lean build and dark hair and eyes. He and Shane stand shoulder to shoulder as they make their case to the chief. The two of them make a formidable pair.

I barely know Troy, but I do know that when there's trouble, he's the one who gets called in to fix it. He has a reputation for getting things done. I know he's bailed Shane out of more than a few scrapes. Tyler too. And then there was the time that Tyler actually had Shane arrested—but that's another story.

The fact that I'm no longer handcuffed says a lot.

Earlier, before Shane and Troy arrived, I heard the words *assault and battery* being tossed around, but I haven't been arrested yet. There were at least a half-dozen witnesses to the scuffle; hopefully their statements will make it clear that Reese and his buddies were the aggressors, not me. I was just defending myself and protecting my client.

Troy has a lot to say to the chief, and Shane's looking on, seemingly at ease. No one has told me anything about how Layla's doing. I just hope Ian's with her. She's going to need support right now from the people she trusts, namely her family.

I watch as the police chief nods at something Troy says. Then the three men come back into the office. Shane and Troy stand on either side of me.

The chief takes a seat behind his desk. "Mr. Miller, witness statements corroborate your assertion that those five men attacked you, and that you were simply defending yourself. All of them were assessed on site, and none seemed to have suffered any significant injuries. They were brought in for questioning, though, and it looks like charges will be brought against them. As for you, you're free to go. We'll be in touch if we need anything."

I stand, anxious to get out of here and find Layla. "Thank you, sir." Then I turn to Shane and Troy. "Thanks, guys."

"It's no trouble at all," Troy says as we shake hands. He checks his watch. "If you'll excuse me, I'm due in court in an hour. Let me know if you need anything more." Troy nods to Shane. "We'll talk later."

Shane nods. "Thanks, Troy."

The chief returns my personal items to me—my phone, my car keys, and my wallet.

Shane claps a hand on my back as he walks me out the door. "Thanks for not critically injuring five members of the student body. I appreciate your restraint."

"I can't say I didn't want to. It was tempting. Those assholes scared the shit out of Layla."

"I'm sure they did. Still, I appreciate you holding back."

I check my phone for messages and find one from Ian. "Looks like Ian and Tyler took Layla home. Her mom is on her way home, too." I wince. "Do you think they'll fire me?"

Shane shrugs. "There's no telling."

"I'm sorry, Shane, for putting you in this position."

He squeezes my shoulder. "No need to apologize. I would

have done the same thing if I were in your shoes." He sighs. "The only thing Ruth and Martin care about is Layla's safety and happiness. I doubt they're going to be upset that you got into a fight with some hot-headed college kids. The only way to know for sure is to head home and face the music. But I don't think you have anything to worry about. You were just doing your job."

Shane and I leave the police station, but before we exit the building, I stop him. "There's something you need to know about."

"What's that?"

"Martin and Ruth have given me permission to date their daughter."

Shane's eyes widen in surprise, but he doesn't say anything.

"I wanted you to know, in case that's a problem for you. For the company, I mean."

Shane contemplates the situation, then shakes his head. "I did not see that coming." He sighs. "It certainly complicates things for you, but if her parents are okay with it, then I won't stand in your way. Like I said, their daughter's safety and happiness is what they care about."

As we step out of the building, Gary's there, along with another photographer I've never seen before, both of them snapping pics of me.

"Hey, Jason!" Gary says. "Were you arrested? Are you being charged with anything? Where's Layla? What does she think about the fight?"

"Congratulations," Shane says as he claps his hand on my back. "Now you're famous, too."

When I glare at Gary, he steps back. Still, he dogs me all the way to my car.

"Who started the fight? Was Layla there when it happened? Did you lose your job?"

I ignore the barrage of questions as I get in my car.

"Come on, Jason," he pleads as he raps on my car window. "Just one comment. One statement. Anything."

"No comment."

The only thing I care about right now is getting home to Layla. I just hope she isn't too traumatized by what happened today.

* * *

I park in my usual spot, next to Layla's Fiat. On the other side of her car is Ian's Porsche. Damn, that's a sweet vehicle. And on the other side of the Porsche is Ruth's black BMW. It looks like the whole family is here, except for Martin. I don't see his car.

Something tells me he's the one I should be most worried about.

I walk in through the rear door. André and Claire are in the kitchen, prepping ingredients for this evening's dinner. I hope I'll still be around to eat it. They both take one look at me and flinch.

"You don't look so good, Jason," André says.

I touch my bottom lip, which is swollen and throbbing. "I've had better days."

When Margaret walks into the kitchen, she gives me a guarded smile. "Hello, Jason. I'm glad you're back. Everyone's in the living room. They're expecting you."

As I head that way, I'm not sure what to expect. A welcoming party, or a firing squad?

I pause outside the living room and take a deep breath, attempting to prepare myself for anything. When I walk into the room, the conversation ceases immediately, and the room goes silent. Layla is sitting on the sofa next to her mother, who has her arm wrapped securely around her daughter. Layla's eyes are red. Clearly, she's been crying. Ian and Tyler are seated on another sofa.

With a cry, Layla jumps to her feet and runs right to me. She literally throws herself into my arms, wrapping trembling arms around my neck as she presses her face into the crook of my shoulder.

"Are you all right?" she whispers.

"I'm fine, honey." I simply hold her for a while, rubbing her back and relishing the feel of her in my arms. I'm relieved to see she's okay.

I glance across the room at Ruth, not knowing what to expect. Anger? Disappointment? No. I get none of that. She actually looks… pleased. That surprises me. When she meets my gaze, she smiles.

I let out a heavy breath, relieved beyond belief that the Alexanders aren't going to immediately show me to the door.

I gently peel Layla off me so I can hold her at arms' length and look her over. "Are you okay?"

She nods. "You're not under arrest?"

"They let me go. There were plenty of witnesses who attested to the fact that Reese and his friends started it, and I was only defending myself."

Despite the fact we have an audience, I pull Layla back into my arms and hold her securely, my hand cupping the back of her head. I kiss her forehead, and then she rests her cheek on my chest.

Ruth stands and walks over to us, her expression impossible to read. My heart pounds as I wait to hear what she has to say.

When she reaches my side, Ruth places her hand on my shoulder. "I'm glad you and Layla are okay. That's all that matters."

"Ruth, I—"

She shakes her head. "It's fine, Jason. You don't need to justify your actions to us. Martin and I trust that you made the right call—that you put Layla's welfare first."

I nod. "I did."

She smiles as she pats my shoulder. "Well, then. That's all that matters." Ruth turns to her son and Tyler. "Won't you two handsome gentlemen join us for dinner? It would be lovely to have the entire family together. Martin should be home in about an hour." She turns her attention back to me and Layla. "We have so much to be grateful for this evening."

* * *

Dinner is indeed a celebratory event. A very expensive bottle of wine is passed around the table, but Layla and I stick to drinking sparkling water.

"I'm proud of you, son," Martin says to me as he raises a glass in my direction. "You look a little worse for wear, but you handled those thugs with restraint."

I rub a hand over my mouth. "I'm sure I've looked better."

"From what I hear, it sounds like you handled yourself quite well, one against five no less. I hope you're not too badly injured."

"No, sir," I say. "I'm fine. Just a few minor cuts."

"I take back anything good I might have said about Reese Hendricks." Martin shakes his head dismissively. "I've spoken to Troy Spencer, and he's confident there's nothing for us to be worried about. You were simply doing your job—protecting my daughter. No one was seriously hurt, but you made your point. It's a win as far as I'm concerned."

"Thank you, sir," I say, fully aware that, as a judge, he probably knows what he's talking about.

After dinner, Layla and I excuse ourselves to go upstairs. I really want to talk to her alone so I can make sure she's doing as well as she seems. I follow her into her bedroom and close the door behind us. Instantly, she tears up.

I pull her close. "It's okay." I just hold her for a good while, breathing in her scent and feeling grateful that she handled everything so well. "You didn't hurt yourself?"

"No. Professor Porter was there in the room with me the whole time. The voice was horrible, though, so I used my earbuds to try to block her out. And then Ian and Tyler showed up and brought me home."

I release her and skim my fingers down her arms. "I'm glad you didn't hurt yourself."

"I'm trying not to."

"I'm proud of you for how you handled today. I know it wasn't easy." I take her hand and lead her to the sofa.

She reaches out to touch my face gently, her fingers gliding lightly over my cheeks and forehead. "It was awful seeing that guy hit you. You're going to have a black eye. And your nose is swollen. I hope it's not broken." She shudders. "You were incredible. You knocked those guys to the ground in *seconds*."

"I was afraid it would scare you to see me do that."

"It didn't scare me. I was so proud of you." She's looking at me like I performed some kind of miracle.

"It wasn't much of a fair fight," I admit. "I'm trained in martial arts, and obviously they aren't." I cup her face in my hands and gaze into her dark eyes. I see a lot of things there—mainly joy and relief. What I don't see is fear, and I'm grateful for that.

She stands and grabs my hand. "Come to the bathroom so we can wash the blood off your face."

I did wash up in the bathroom at the police station, but I

guess I didn't get it all. As I stare at my reflection in the bathroom mirror, Layla gets out a washcloth and wets it.

"Here," she says. "Let me."

I lean against the counter and let her wash my face. She dabs gently at my skin. "It's okay," I say, laughing. "I won't break." Still, her gentle attention is soothing after such a stressful afternoon.

When she's done, she pats my face dry with a hand towel. "As good as new," she says.

I turn and look at my reflection once more. My bottom lip is a bit swollen, but it's already healing. I touch my nose, moving the cartilage back and forth. It's just a bit tender. I've had worse. "I don't think it's broken." I lean forward and kiss her forehead. "Thank you, nurse. You did a fine job."

Layla smiles.

"I told my boss we're dating. He seemed okay with it."

"I talked to my mom, and she said she's happy for us."

I laugh. "I was worried I might get fired. Of course, the night's still young."

"No one's going to fire you. I won't let them." Suddenly, Layla looks away, and I can tell she's distracted by the voice.

"Hey," I say as I pull her back to me. "Don't listen to her. Whatever she said, she's *wrong*." I cup her face in my hands. "Who do you trust?"

She smiles. "You. But what she said is true. It's my fault you were hurt. If it weren't for me, that never would have happened."

"Come here." I lead her out of the bathroom, back to the sofa in her room, and we sit. I find myself staring at her lips, so soft and pink and kissable. So damn tempting. But I force myself to put the brakes on. Even though we're officially dating, she's not ready for a serious relationship.

It's ironic that Layla has all the money in the world, but the simple things she wants can't be bought. "What do you want, Layla? If you could have anything, what would it be?"

She's silent a moment as she contemplates my question. "What I want most is to be normal, like any other girl my age. I want to have a boyfriend. I want to move out and be independent. I love my parents to death, but I want a chance to be on my own, to prove that I can take care of myself."

"Do you think you're ready for that? It's a big step."

She chuckles. "I wouldn't be completely alone, would I?" She reaches up and touches my face. "If I moved out on my own, you would come with me, right? And not just as my bodyguard. We could share a place."

"I have an apartment in a nice, secure building. If you really want to move out, and your parents are okay with it, we could move into my place."

Her eyes widen as my suggestion sinks in. "Are you serious?"

"Why not? But your parents would have to agree. And we could start with a trial run. We could stay at my place for a weekend and see how it goes. I think your parents would feel better about the whole idea if we did it in stages."

"Oh, my god, yes!" She grabs hold of my shirt and pulls me close, planting one on my cheek. "Let's do it."

35

Layla Alexander

My mind reels at the thought of spending an entire weekend with Jason at his apartment. I jump to my feet. "I'm going to ask them right now." I can barely contain my excitement. This is something I've dreamed of for a long time.

Jason walks downstairs with me to the living room, where we find my parents enjoying glasses of wine. We sit side-by-side on the love seat across from my parents.

"Mom, Dad," I say, "There's something I want to tell you. I mean ask you."

Mom sets her wineglass on the coffee table. "What's that, sweetheart?"

The words pour out of me in a nervous rush. "It's not that I'm unhappy here at home, because I'm not. I love you guys. And I love living here. I love this house. But there comes a time in everyone's life when they feel ready—" My pulse takes off and my throat closes up on me.

Jason rubs my back, offering silent support. His quiet, steady presence gives me the courage to keep going.

They'll never agree to this.

You don't know that.

You can't be trusted on your own.

Oh, stop it.

I laugh nervously when I realize my parents are watching me. "Sorry. What I wanted to say is I've been thinking about moving out on my own—well, not completely on my own, but with my bodyguard, of course. Before you say anything, I would just like to remind you that a lot of people my age have already moved out of their parents' homes. A lot of students live on campus or in apartments. I'd just be doing what so many others my age already do."

"I see," my father says in a neutral tone. "Apparently, you've given this some thought."

"I have." When Mom still hasn't said anything, I keep blabbering on. "Jason suggested we do a trial weekend at his apartment. That is, if you guys are okay with the idea."

"And where is that?" my mom asks.

"He lives in an apartment building on Lake Shore Drive. It's not far from Ian's townhouse."

"The building is fully secure," Jason says. "With private underground parking and on-site security twenty-four-seven. And there are two bedrooms."

My face heats at the mention of bedrooms, because now I realize that the sleeping arrangement is probably the uppermost question on everyone's mind. I honestly hadn't thought that far ahead.

Now your parents are picturing you sleeping with Jason. I told you, you're a whore.

Oh, my god, shut up.

Mom and Dad stare at each other, doing their silent communication thing. It's crazy how they practically read minds.

"Well," my mom says in a careful and thoughtful tone. "I can see how a young woman your age would be eager to pursue independence and venture out on her own."

"Ian moved out when he was eighteen," I remind my parents. "And he lived *alone*. At least I'll have a bodyguard."

"Yes, but Ian's a boy," my father says, stating the obvious.

"That's sexist, Dad."

"Yes, but it's true," he counters.

I catch Jason grinning. My parents don't look thrilled about my idea, but at least they haven't come right out and said no. I'm pretty sure if they did, Jason would rescind his offer.

They're still doing their silent communication act.

My dad addresses Jason. "And you're okay with this arrangement?"

"Yes, sir," Jason answers without hesitation.

"Please let me do this," I plead. "Jason said he'd only agree if you guys do."

"Very well," my dad finally says after a last long look at my mom. "A trial run." He raises his index finger. "*One* weekend, and then we'll reassess. And not this weekend. Let's wait at least a week and let poor Jason recover from the events of today."

Jason squeezes my hand. "Sounds fair."

"Deal!" I say to my dad. And then I throw my arms around Jason, and he hugs me back.

* * *

"Are you sure you're ready for this?" Jason asks as he watches me pack my suitcase. "It's only for a weekend. Do you really need to bring that much stuff?"

"You never know what you'll need. I'd rather bring too much than not enough."

It's been a week since my parents agreed to let me do a trial run at Jason's apartment for the weekend. I'm even more excited than I was before because I've had a chance to think about it. We'll be living together in his apartment, just like any other couple. We're officially dating now, although it's been pretty platonic. Jason thinks I'm not ready for more. I disagree.

What better way for our relationship to progress than living together? Just the two of us, with no chaperones. We'll have his place to ourselves. It's going to be fantastic.

"Yes, I'm ready," I tell him. "Why? Have you changed your mind?"

He smiles. "No, I haven't changed my mind. I just want to make sure you haven't."

"Absolutely not. I'm looking forward to this. It'll just be the two of us—no staff. Just us."

He laughs. "Right. There will be no one to do your laundry for you, no one to cook for you. Or buy groceries. You'll have to slum it like the rest of us peasants."

"But that's just it. I *want* to do those things for myself. I want to prove that I can take care of myself."

You're going to crash and burn.

No, I won't. I can do this.

I give it twenty-four hours before you run back home in tears.

That's not going to happen.

I make a mental checklist of everything I've packed for the weekend—clothes, pajamas, toiletries, laptop, tablet, phone, multiple chargers, and my meds. I'll switch out my insulin pump before we leave and pack an extra one in case I need it before I get back. I even pack some apple juice boxes and a few other snacks in case I have a sugar low. I think I've thought of everything.

I place everything I need into a large rolling suitcase and

set it outside my bedroom door. Jason steps out of his room with his duffle bag slung over his shoulder. "Ready to go?"

Grinning, I nod. "Ready as I'll ever be."

After we take our things to his car, we go back inside to say goodbye to my parents.

My dad has a stoic expression on his face as he hugs me tightly and whispers, "Have fun and be safe, young lady. Call if you need anything."

The smile on my mom's face is belied by the tears glittering in her eyes. When she hugs me goodbye for the longest time, I'm afraid she's not going to let me go. "I know you need to do this," she says. "We get it. We really do. Just remember your dad and I will always be here for you."

"It's just for the weekend, Mom," I remind her. But we both know this is the first step on a life-long journey. First a weekend, and then hopefully soon after that we'll move to Jason's apartment full-time.

My parents surprise me when they each hug Jason as well.

It's surreal as we head out to the car. Jason opens my door, and I climb inside.

My parents are standing at the back door, and they wave as we pull out of the parking area and head down the alley.

It's dark now and the rain falls in a light drizzle. The windshield wipers sweep lazily across the glass, pushing the water droplets aside. The dark pavement ahead of us is shiny wet, and the oncoming car lights flicker through the rain.

I'm simultaneously nervous and excited. I've never done

anything remotely like this in my life. I never had a sleepover with anyone. I never went to camp. Other than hospitalizations and trips with my family, this will be the first time I've slept away from home.

Jason pulls into an underground parking garage, parks, and turns off the engine. "I don't have many supplies in my apartment right now. We'll have to go grocery shopping."

"Sure, that's fine." I try to sound nonchalant, but the truth is I've never been to a grocery store. Margaret and André do all the household shopping.

Bringing our luggage with us, we take the elevator up to Jason's floor. It's a long ride up. The car glides to a smooth stop, and the doors open. I step out into the hallway.

"To the left," Jason reminds me. "Last unit on the right."

Oh, yes. Now I remember. When we arrive at his door, he hands me the key. I'm so nervous, my hands are shaking, but I manage to unlock the door and push it open.

As soon as we step inside, Jason starts turning on lights. "Let's get some fresh air in here." He slides open a glass patio door and immediately a breeze sweeps into the room, bringing with it the faint scent of lake water.

I join him at the door and look out at Lake Michigan. "What a wonderful view."

"That's why I picked this unit."

A moment later, there's a light knock on the door.

"I'll get it," Jason says. He opens the door, and a cute brunette with blue eyes and dimples sticks her head inside and smiles.

"Hi, I'm Erin. You must be Layla. Welcome to the building."

36

Layla Alexander

The girl at the door smiles at me, her blue eyes crinkling at the corners. She points down the hall. "I live with my boyfriend in the last apartment on the left."

She's just sucking up to you.

No, she's not.

Yes, she is. You're the poor little rich girl. Of course she wants to befriend you.

I do my best to ignore the voice and act normal. "Thanks. I'm glad to be here."

"Come on in, Erin," Jason says as he waves her inside. He leans out the open doorway and glances down the hall. "Where's Mack?"

"He's coming," the brunette says. "He ran into Liam and Miguel on their way out, and they got to talking."

Erin looks to be about my age. Her straight dark hair is cut in a sleek chin-length bob, and her eyes are a startling blue. I see faint freckles dotting the bridge of her nose and cheeks.

"Erin's a good friend," Jason explains. "Her boyfriend, Mack Donovan, works for the same security company I do. In fact, almost everyone on this floor works for McIntyre Security."

"And I work at Clancy's," Erin says. "You know, the bookstore downtown."

My face lights up at the mention of books. "I love that place."

"You should come visit us there sometime. I work for Beth—you know, Shane's wife." She points up toward the ceiling. "They live upstairs in the penthouse apartment. Beth owns the bookstore."

"Layla hasn't met Shane and Beth yet," Jason says.

Erin grins. "We definitely need to rectify that." She winks at me. "Beth is dying to meet you. She's Tyler's sister. You two are practically family now. And by the way, don't be surprised if you get a lot of drop-in visitors this weekend. Everyone's anxious to meet you."

"Meet me? Really?" I'm confused as to why anyone would even know I was here, let alone want to meet me.

Because you're a freak. They're curious.

Jason shrugs. "Word gets around fast. This building is full of McIntyre Security employees, and I might have told a couple of friends."

"There you are," says an unfamiliar deep male voice from behind me. I turn to see a huge man standing in the open doorway. He has dark hair and eyes, and he's so tall he fills the doorway. He practically has to duck to come inside. "Hey, babe," he says to Erin as he joins her.

Erin slips her arm around the big man's waist and leans into him. "This is Mack. Honey, this is Layla Alexander, Ian's sister."

Mack nods to me in greeting. "Nice to meet you, Layla." Then he looks to Jason. "Welcome back, buddy. We've missed you around here."

"Thanks. It's nice to be back. We're just here for the weekend."

There's a commotion in the hall, and we look to the open doorway as two guys pop their heads in, both of them grinning. One of them I know—Miguel Rodriguez. But the other one, ash-blond hair and brown eyes, I've never seen before.

"Heard you were back, man," the blond says to Jason. He's talking to Jason, but his curious gaze is mostly on me.

"Hey, Layla," Miguel says, waving. "It's good to see you." He nods to the blond beside him. "This is Liam."

"Liam McIntyre," Jason clarifies. "My boss's youngest brother."

"And the most handsome," Liam says as he winks at me. "Welcome to the building."

Erin glances down at our bags. "Come on, guys. We should let them get settled in." She herds them all out into the hallway. "Let's get together soon, Layla, okay? We girls are seriously outnumbered in this building. I could use an ally."

"I'd love that." It would be nice to have a female friend to talk to. And since she works in a bookstore, I like her already.

Once we're alone, Jason closes the apartment door and pulls me into his arms. "I hope you didn't mind the welcoming committee."

"Of course not. I didn't realize you had so many friends here."

"Most of the people I know from work live in this building. That has its ups and downs. There's always someone around if you want company, but if you want to be alone, you're probably going to get a lot of folks knocking on your door whether you like it or not." He kisses my forehead. "Ready to unpack?"

Jason hauls our luggage down the hall, stopping first at his bedroom. He tosses his duffle bag onto his king-size bed. Then he wheels my suitcase to the smaller bedroom at the end of the hall—to the *guest* bedroom.

He doesn't want you in his bedroom.

He's just being considerate by giving me my own space.

You're so gullible. Such an idiot.

I'm finding it hard to argue with her.

The small bedroom is cluttered with a single bed, a treadmill, a set of free weights, a computer desk, and stacks of cardboard boxes. It's obviously his catch-all room.

Jason sets my suitcase on the floor at the foot of the bed. "Sorry about the mess. I'll clear most of this stuff out of here in the morning. We can go shopping tomorrow to get whatever you need, like a nightstand and a dresser. At least there's plenty of room in the closet for your clothes."

"Thanks," I say, forcing a smile. Inside I'm aching. This isn't what I expected. I assumed we'd be sharing a room.

That's because you're an idiot. He doesn't want to share a room with you. How can you be so stupid?

Jason comes up behind me and wraps his arms around my waist. "Is everything okay?"

"Yes."

"Layla, come on. I know you well enough to know when something's wrong."

"It's nothing, really."

Tell him. Tell him you're an idiot. Tell him how stupid you are.

"Are you having second thoughts?" he asks. "If you want to go home, just say the word, and we'll go. It's perfectly fine."

See? He can't wait to get rid of you.

"No! I don't want to go home. I like being here. I like meeting your friends."

He turns me to face him and studies me. I can tell he doesn't believe me.

Tell him how stupid you are. Tell him you want to sleep in his bed. Tell him. I dare you.

I can't do that. He'll think I'm needy.

You *are* needy. You're such an idiot.

"I'm fine, Jason. Honest. Why don't you unpack your stuff while I unpack mine?"

He doesn't look convinced. Glancing around the room, he says, "I know this isn't quite what you're used to. Tomorrow I'll clean this up, I promise. We'll get this room fixed up nice, however you want it. If you want it a different color, I'll paint it. And we can get you new furniture and a bookcase. We'll get you anything you like."

I smile to hide my disappointment. "That sounds great."

When he leaves me to unpack, I stare at the single bed and try not to let the hurt get the best of me. I'm sure he has his reasons for wanting us to have separate bedrooms.

Yeah. He doesn't want to sleep with you.

You don't know that.

But the more I think about it, the more it hurts, and the more I'm afraid she's right.

When I'm finished unpacking, I go in search of Jason and find him in the kitchen staring into a sparsely stocked refrigerator. "What are you looking at?"

"An empty fridge." He straightens and faces me. "How're you doing?"

"Fine."

"You don't seem fine."

My problem is, I don't understand exactly what our relationship is. He said we're dating. Doesn't that mean we're *together*—as in girlfriend and boyfriend? And yet we have separate bedrooms. He's affectionate—he puts his arms around me, and he's kissed me before—but lately it's been platonic between us.

He's not truly interested in you. Trophy fuck, remember? How many times do I have to say it?

Jason casually pulls out his phone and studies the screen. "Your sugar level is getting low. We need to eat soon." He opens the pantry door and digs around until he finds a single-serving little bag of Skittles. He rips open the pouch and pours the brightly-colored candies into my hand. "That should tide you over. How about we go grab some dinner and then go grocery shopping?"

I pop one of the candies into my mouth and chew. "Sounds good." It's perfect timing as I'm starting to feel a bit woozy.

We leave the apartment and take the elevator down to the parking garage. As we step out of the car, he reaches for my hand and pulls me close as he walks me to the car.

Before I slide into my seat, he gives me a friendly peck on the cheek. Is this typical for boyfriends and girlfriends? Honestly, I wouldn't know because I've never had one before. It just seems awfully... platonic.

That's because he's not really into yo u. Why can't you get that into your thick skull?

37

Jason Miller

Cohabitating with Layla is turning out to be a helluva lot harder than I ever imagined. Where do I draw the line between bodyguard and boyfriend? I want to keep her safe, of course; but I also want to make her happy and just love her. Being so close to her all the time—just the two of us in such tight quarters, with no chaperones, no parents under our roof, no staff, no one to walk in on us—is pure torture.

I'm trying to take this slowly for her sake. She's so young and so inexperienced. I don't want her to rush into a relationship and end up regretting it later. We have all the time in the world to get to know each other and for her to decide if I'm the right one. I already know how I feel. The heart wants what it wants, right? I don't believe in fate or destiny, but when I met her, something clicked inside me. And now, I feel like I'm a planet orbiting her, and she's the sun. She's the center of everything for me. I'd feel lucky to spend the rest of my life trying to make her happy.

I'm doing my best to keep my hands off her, but it's not easy. I have to fight the constant urge to reach out and pull her to me. To *touch* her the way I want to. To *kiss* her the way I need to. I don't dare do any of these things because one thing would lead to another, and then we'd be sliding down a slippery slope. I only have so much control.

We started off as client and bodyguard, and we quickly became friends, which led to tiptoeing into boyfriend/girlfriend territory, and now we're living together. *Under one roof.* Granted, we'll be sleeping in different bedrooms. But I honestly don't know how I'm going to handle this.

I'm trying to do the right thing by her; I'm trying to take things slowly. She's hardly been kissed. She's sure as hell not ready for sex. And I refuse to do anything that might set her back emotionally. I don't want to rush her. This needs to happen at her pace, when she's ready for more. I'll just have to take my cues from her.

We end up grabbing a quick bite at a sub shop that's located right next to the market. Then we hit the grocery store, which turns out to be a rather entertaining experience for me. I struggle to keep a straight face as I watch her attempt to navigate the workings of the fresh produce department. Clearly, she's never set foot in a grocery store in her life. And why should she? She's grown up with *staff* doing everything for the family, including the food shopping.

When she stops and stares at a bin of tomatoes, I stand quietly at her side and observe, curious as to how this is going to go. She doesn't say anything, doesn't ask for help, doesn't ask any questions. She just stands there watching. When a guy walks up to the bin and pulls a produce bag off the reel, she observes him closely as he selects a few tomatoes, puts them in the bag, and ties the bag closed. She's practically taking notes like she's studying for a quiz.

When the guy walks away, she copies his actions. Then she turns to me with a grin on her face, and I swear to god, I want to give her a gold star for effort.

"That wasn't so hard," she says as she sets the tomatoes in our shopping cart. "What else do we need? Onions? Potatoes?"

I nod. "And lettuce."

"And cucumbers and carrots," she says. "We can make a salad."

"We should also get you some low-carb snacks to keep in the apartment."

I stand back and watch her select the rest of our produce with the same degree of scrutiny that one would use when buying a car. She's so damn serious, it's sexy as hell. And also very endearing.

Apparently, I'm not the only one who thinks so. I've noticed several guys checking her out. Finally, one of them has the balls to approach her. A yuppie corporate guy in a suit walks up beside her as she's examining the avocados. He's standing close enough that his arm brushes hers—accidently, I'm sure. *Yeah, right.*

Immediately, my territorial instincts kick in, but instead of barging in between them, I wait and watch. She seems completely oblivious to his interest, but I catch him sneaking glances her way. I can't really blame him—I'd be checking her out too if I were him. But still—*not cool, pal.*

"So, what are you making?" he asks her, as he nods to our grocery cart.

"I was thinking tacos," she answers.

"I love Mexican food," he says. "I could eat it every day. What's your favorite Mexican restaurant around here? I'm new to the area and still trying to find my way around."

Oh, no you don't, buddy.

Having heard enough, I step up behind her, put my arms around her waist, and pull her back against my chest. *Yeah, I'm staking my claim. Damn right I am.* "Hi, honey. Find what you're looking for?"

She smiles back at me. "I think so. How about tacos for dinner tomorrow?"

"Sounds perfect."

Her admirer frowns at me as he walks away.

Layla whispers to me, "How do you know if an avocado is ripe?"

"It's easy." I pick up a couple and test their readiness, then put them back. When I find one that's perfect, I hand it to her. "Here, squeeze this one. See how it's not too hard and not too soft? You want one that gives just a little, but isn't mushy."

She nods as she slips that one into a produce bag, then carefully chooses another one.

"What's next?" I ask.

"If we're having tacos, we'll need taco shells, ground beef, sour cream, and shredded cheddar. Oh, and salsa. Do you know where we can find those ingredients?"

"Follow me." As I steer the cart away from the avocados, her admirer watches her go with a wistful expression on his face. "Asshole," I mutter under my breath.

"Did you say something?" Layla asks.

I smile innocently. "No. Nothing."

* * *

After we get home and put the groceries away, Layla smiles at me. "Grocery shopping's not that hard, is it?"

I can't help grinning because she's just so damn adorable. "Nope. Piece of cake." And then, impulsively, I drop a kiss on her lips—just a quick one—because I can't resist.

Her eyes widen in surprise. When her tongue darts out to

lick her lip—right where I just kissed her, my dick hardens.

She gazes up at me, her eyes searching mine, and I know what she's looking for. She's looking for *more*.

"I forgot," I say quickly, hoping to redirect her thoughts. "I need to put clean sheets on your bed." And then I walk past her and out of the way of temptation. Just being near her is dangerous for my mental and physical health. If she knew the things I wanted to do to her, she'd probably run away screaming. And after everything she's been through, I wouldn't blame her one bit.

I grab a fresh set of bedding from the hall linen closet, strip the twin bed in the guest room—I mean Layla's bedroom—and quickly make up the bed. I know she's watching me from the doorway because I can feel her gaze on me. When I finish and step back to look at her, I see the range of emotion flitting across her face.

Disappointment. Confusion. Hurt.

Damn it.

I walk over and pull her into my arms. "Layla."

But she slips out of my hold and walks away.

I follow her down the hallway. "Layla, wait."

But she keeps walking, through the living room, and then she turns the corner and disappears into the kitchen. She's gone as far away from me as she can possibly get without leaving the apartment.

I follow her as far as the living room, but then I stop at the patio door and gaze out toward the lake. Being with Layla is new territory for me, and I'm trying to do the right thing. I'm trying to take the high road.

How much time do I give her? How much space?

The last thing I want to do is take advantage of her. And yet I'm disappointing her. *I'm hurting her.*

She's probably as confused and lost as I am right now.

I find her in the kitchen staring out the window. From this vantage point, we can see the lights of Navy Pier off in the distance. The Ferris wheel is lit up like a beacon. "Have you ever been to the Pier?"

She nods. "Once, when I was little."

"It's changed a lot since then. Would you like to go sometime?"

She shrugs.

I move in beside her and look down at her profile, not missing the shine of tears in her eyes. My throat tightens. I reach for her hand and link our fingers. "Layla."

"Yes?" There's a hint of tremor in her voice.

"I think we should take it slow, you know? I'm trying not to rush you."

"Or maybe you're not really interested."

Her quiet statement is like a blow to my chest. I squeeze her hand. "Trust me, it's not that. Quite the opposite, actually. I'm trying to give you space."

"Maybe I don't want space."

"Look, you're out of your parents' house for the very first time—even if it's just for the weekend—and you've never been in a relationship before. These are all huge first steps. I'm afraid if you take on too much too soon—"

She turns to face me, her eyes radiating pain. "How do you feel about me, Jason? Be honest, please."

My heart slams into my ribs, and I bite back the words I want to say—*I want you to be mine.* Instead, I dial it down and say, "I think you're amazing."

"No, I mean, you know..." She breaks off suddenly and looks away, wincing. When she shakes her head, I'm pretty sure there's an argument going on inside. One I'm not privy to.

I'd give anything to hear what she hears. "Layla?" I turn her to face me. "Tell me what's going on in here." I tap her head. "What's she saying?"

She swallows hard, and the sheer level of pain I see in her eyes makes my heart hurt.

"Tell me, please," I say. "Word for word."

She shakes her head. "She's my problem, not yours."

"That's where you're wrong. Anything that's a problem for you automatically becomes my problem, too. Now, tell me what she said."

The words spill out of her, tumbling over each other in a mad rush. "She says you're just humoring me, that you don't really want me, and that's why you put me in the guest bedroom, because you don't want to be with me, and you don't want to hurt my feelings, so you won't tell me the truth, because you're too nice to hurt someone, so you *pretend* to like me, to want to be with me, but you really don't. I told her she's wrong, but how do I know, because this is all new to me. She says I'm too crazy for *anyone* to want—"

I can't bear to hear another word, so I pull her into my arms and kiss her, shutting off the slew of lies and hurt. "She's so fucking wrong, honey," I say against her lips. We're both breathing hard, our shaky breaths mingling. I stare hard into her eyes. "She's wrong, Layla. Dead wrong. Do you hear me?"

"Yes," she breathes.

I thread my fingers into her hair. "Who do you trust, Layla? Me or her?" I'll repeat this as many times as I need to, to get through to her.

She answers without hesitation. "You."

"Then you pass this message on to her: I'm crazy about you. You're the most exciting woman I've ever met. I think about you day and night, and I can't stop imagining what it would be like for us to be together. I can't wait to kiss you—really kiss you. I want to taste every inch of your body. I want to feel your bare skin, hot and sweaty, pressed against mine. I think you're the most amazing woman in the world. Period. End of story. And anything less than that is a straight up lie."

I gently grip Layla's chin. "Is that clear enough for you? For *her*? *I want you.* I want you in every way a man can possibly want a woman. I want you to be *mine*, and only mine. I'm just so damn scared of doing something wrong, of hurting you, or pushing you too far, too fast. I don't want to screw this up."

Fat tears roll down her cheeks. "Then please don't treat me

like I'm a special case, or like I'm damaged or fragile. I want you to treat me like you'd treat any other girl. Jason, please. That's what I want—to be *normal*. Is that too much to ask?"

I cup her beautiful, teary face in my hands. "But you're not just a normal girl, Layla. You're the girl I'm falling in love with, and I've never been in love before, so I don't know how to act. You matter more to me than anything on this earth, and I can't risk messing up, or hurting you."

Her fingers circle my wrists, and she holds on to me. "Don't handle me with kid gloves." Her hands cover mine, and she links our fingers together. "Please let me be normal for once."

38

Layla Alexander

I see the indecision in Jason's expression, the fear and the worry. And his concern for me only strengthens my resolve that he's the right one. I know love at first sight is a fanciful idea, but I honestly feel like I *know* him. Like my soul recognizes his. And even though we haven't known each other for that long, I do know this—he'd never intentionally hurt me. There's no one in the world I trust more.

He kisses me, and I'm surprised to find he's breathing as hard as I am. There's so much at stake here, for both of us. His lips glide against mine, somehow both soft and firm at the same time. Then his mouth nudges mine open, and his tongue slides inside. My heart thuds in my chest as my pulse starts racing.

This kiss is hot and hungry, as if his restraint is slipping. His fingers burrow into my hair, tightening on my scalp, as he deepens the kiss.

My belly quivers deliciously, and my knees go weak. There's a tingling heat between my legs as my body begins to throb. This is all new territory for me, and it's thrilling. I want this. I want *him*.

His hand slips around to the back of my head, and he cradles it in his palm. He's holding me to him, his touch protective, just like I knew it would be.

He breaks our kiss. "I'm trying so hard to be careful and do the right thing."

I shake my head. "I don't want careful. I want *normal*. What would you do with me if I was just some girl you met at a bar and brought home with you?"

He laughs. "I'm not going to answer that."

"Why not? Because that's what I want."

"Are you sure about this?"

"About you? About *us*? Yes, I'm sure."

"Once we do this, it'll change everything."

I laugh nervously. "I certainly hope so. That's kind of the point."

Grinning, he says, "I just meant it'll complicate our relationship."

I grab hold of his T-shirt. "I'm sure."

Without warning, he swings me up into his arms and carries me out of the kitchen and down the hallway into his bedroom. My head is spinning as he sets me on my feet beside his bed. My nerves are spiraling.

He stares down at me, his expression tense. "At any time, if you want to stop, just say so." His voice has grown rougher, deeper, and I can tell he's as affected as I am.

I nod.

His brow furrows. "You're not on the pill, are you?"

"I'm not. Because of my psych meds, I can't take regular birth control pills. I'd have to use something else, something nonhormonal. And since I've never been sexually active, it just didn't seem important. Until now, that is."

Nodding, he says, "Condoms are nonhormonal." Then he opens a nightstand drawer and removes a condom packet. He lays it on top of the nightstand.

Reality is starting to sink in, and my stomach drops. We're going to take our clothes off, and that means… *oh, crap.* He'll see my insulin pump and my glucose monitor.

He tips my chin up. "What's wrong?"

I lay my hands on my top, right over the devices attached to my body, one on each side of my belly button. "My pump."

"Hey." He sits on the side of the bed and pulls me forward to stand in front of him. "You have absolutely nothing to be concerned about. Your pump and monitor are part of you. We'll be careful, I promise. But trust me, I'm going to be staring at *you*, not at your pod. I have a confession to make. I read up on precautions to take with type 1 diabetics during sex so there wouldn't be any surprises. I know your glucose level will probably drop, so we'll keep some apple juice boxes by the bed. It'll be okay."

Jason leans forward and kisses my belly right through my top.

I look away, embarrassed. "I'm sure you've never dated a girl who had to stop and check her blood sugar level when you're about to have sex."

"I never dated a girl who meant as much to me as you do." He links our fingers together. "Diabetes is part of your life, Layla, and that makes it part of mine." He lays his phone on the nightstand. "The monitor will alert us if there's a problem. So, for now, we won't worry about it."

He remains seated on the bed, and for a change, I'm towering over him. I think he's doing it on purpose, to give me a sense of control. But the truth is, I feel totally out of control and very self-conscious.

He captures my hands and brings them to his mouth to kiss. "What's wrong?"

"I've never undressed in front of someone before. It's a bit nerve-racking."

"You're not the only one who's nervous here." He holds one of his hands out to show me it's shaking.

I laugh. "You are *not* nervous. I don't believe that for a second. This isn't your first time."

"Well, no, it's not. But it's my first time *with you*. And that makes all the difference. I never cared so much about making a good impression on a woman before." He grasps the hem of his T-shirt, whips it over his head, and tosses it on the floor.

My gaze drops to his chest, and I can't look away. The lines and ridges of his body are stunning, his chiseled muscles well-defined. Now my heart is pounding for a whole new reason. I know I'm staring, but I can't help it.

He places my hands on his chest, right over his pecs. His golden skin is taut and smooth. A thin line of dark hair travels from his abs downward, disappearing beneath the waistband of his jeans.

All of this is so unfamiliar. Butterflies are rioting in my belly, and I feel dizzy, and for a change, it's not from low blood sugar.

He tugs lightly on the hem of my top. "Now it's your turn."

Take my top off? Seriously?

My heart lodges in my throat. The thought of taking my shirt off in front of him terrifies me. I still have bruises, not to mention my Omnipod and glucose monitor. And I'm not fit and tone like he is. I've never lifted a weight in my life.

He takes my hands in his. "You don't have to do anything you're not ready for."

"But I am ready. I want this. I'm just nervous. I don't want to disappoint you."

"Disappoint me?" He laughs. "My god, you seriously have no idea. I could never be disappointed. I've never wanted anyone so much in my life."

He's lying.

Go away.

"Layla, you take my breath away. You have no reason to be nervous." He stands up and pulls me close, his arms slipping around me. I can feel the heat radiating from his bare chest. And his scent does something deliciously wicked to my body.

His hands slide up into my hair. "How about we take this one step at a time? Rome wasn't built in a day, you know. There's no rush."

"I'm not chickening out, Jason."

"I didn't say you were. I just meant maybe we should slow this down." He pulls me closer, and now my breasts are pressing against his chest. One of his hands grips the back of my head while the other one slips down the side of my torso, settling on my hip.

He kisses me, his mouth coaxing and gentle, covering mine and nudging it open. I gasp when his tongue slips inside my mouth, sliding against mine. The whole time he's kissing me, I can feel his hardness right through his jeans as it presses into my belly.

Feeling encouraged by his physical reaction, I step back impulsively and pull my top off before I lose my nerve. Cool air washes over my heated skin, making me shiver.

He gazes down at my peach-colored silk bra. At the sight of the rounded tops of my breasts, Jason sucks in a sharp breath and swallows hard, his Adam's apple bobbing. "You're so beautiful."

With his gaze fixed on mine, he reaches around me to unfasten my bra. The cups spring loose, and my bra straps slide down to catch on my elbows. My breasts are exposed now, for the most part. He peels my bra off me and tosses it onto our growing pile of discarded clothing.

As he cups one breast, his thumb strokes my nipple, which puckers tightly. "Your skin is so soft, it's like silk."

Lightning rips through me, from my nipple to the hot wet place between my legs. When a plaintive sound escapes me, his expression darkens and his nostrils flare.

The next second, he's kissing me again, his lips traveling from my mouth to my jaw and then down the side of my neck. His warm hands are splayed wide on my back, stroking my skin and causing more shivers to ripple through me.

Without warning, Jason sweeps me up into his arms and lays me on the bed. He unfastens my jeans and slowly lowers the zipper. When he sucks one of my nipples into his mouth, my back bows off the mattress and I cry out sharply, caught off guard by the intensity of the sensations.

My hands work their way up his arms, past his taut shoulders to his hair. He groans when I run my fingers through the short strands, tugging lightly. The rough sound makes my insides melt and my knees turn to jelly.

Jason lays his forehead against mine, breathing heavily as he chuckles. "I'm not sure I'll survive this."

When he tugs my jeans down my hips and legs, I'm definitely having an out-of-body experience. It's so unreal, part of me doesn't recognize that this is even happening.

I'm practically naked now, lying on the bed in just my panties. I never dreamed this would happen. And the way he's looking at me takes my breath away. He's looking at me like I'm—

Beautiful.

Her one word, spoken almost reverently, shocks me to the core. I don't think she's ever said anything kind to me before.

"She said I'm beautiful," I say, in complete awe.

Jason smiles at me. "That's because you are."

His hands grip my waist, and his gaze slips down to my panties. My breath catches in my chest as he gently tugs on the waistband, signaling that he's going to pull them down. If he thinks I'm going to put on the brakes now, he's wrong.

I'm reveling in the throbbing ache between my legs. My body is responding like it knows exactly what to do, even if I don't. My body is normal—it's just waiting for the rest of me to catch up.

Jason starts peppering my abdomen with kisses. Then his mouth travels downward, to my belly button. And then farther down, his nose rimming the waistband of my panties.

My breath catches in my throat, and I can't breathe.

He grins up at me. "How much *normal* do you want?"

Swallowing hard, I answer without hesitation. "All of it."

39

Layla Alexander

Without warning, Jason presses his nose to the front of my panties. I gasp, shocked at the intimacy. As he inhales deeply, his hands tighten on my waist. Then he slowly tugs my underwear down my hips, past my legs, and tosses them aside.

Oh my god, I'm naked. And he's staring at me. "This doesn't seem fair," I say, laughing shakily.

"What doesn't?" His expression is amused, as if he's enjoying this way too much.

"I'm naked, and you're not."

He laughs. "Well, let's just say I'm playing it safe." He presses his hand to the front of his jeans, palming his erection.

When I feel his fingers slip between my legs, I tense all over. The sensation is too much.

"It's okay. Just relax," he says.

I shake my head. "That's easy for you to say."

"Do you want me to stop?"

"Don't you dare. Did I say stop? No, I didn't."

He nudges my legs apart, and the air feels good against my heated flesh. I jump when his fingertip teases my opening, gently searching. He groans. "My god, you're so tight."

His jaw clenches, and I watch the muscles in his cheek flex. His finger slips up to my clitoris, and he starts rubbing gentle circles there.

"Oh, my god," I groan as my body stiffens. I've read plenty of romance books before—explicit ones—but until it actually happens to you, it's all sort of esoteric. This is *really* happening.

"Just relax and let me make you feel good," he murmurs. His finger continues teasing and circling my clit. He trails kisses above my pubic bone, then down below. When his tongue slides between the lips of my sex, I nearly come out of my skin. I dig my fingers into his scalp so hard he grunts.

Soon his tongue is joined by a finger. I'm soaking wet and swollen with desire. His finger slides easily through slick arousal, teasing me. His tongue flicks against my clit, relentless and demanding. My legs are shaking uncontrollably, and shameful sounds come out of me—high pitched, keening sounds.

"Shh," he croons. "It's all right."

He continues to tease me until pleasure sweeps through my body, up my spine to my skull, and I practically see stars.

"That's right, honey, come for me," he murmurs. His lips cover mine once more, and he tastes like me, warm and salty. It's shocking and arousing at the same time.

My thighs tighten and my breath catches in my throat when I cry out loudly, my back arching, as my orgasm sweeps through me. It's not the first time I've come—I know all about self-love—but it is the first time I've come in the presence of someone else.

But I don't even have time to feel embarrassed because suddenly, he reaches down to unfasten his jeans, lower the zipper, and shove them and his underwear off, leaving him naked too.

For a moment, I stare at his body, transfixed by all the sharp planes and well-defined muscles. His body is so different from mine, and it's beautiful.

When my gaze lands on his erection, my face heats. I've seen pictures of naked men before, but that doesn't prepare you for the real thing. He's thick and long, much bigger than I thought it would be. It's intimidating, to say the least. I'm not sure how *that's* going to fit in me.

Hesitantly, I reach for him. "Can I touch you?"

He intercepts my hand, kisses it, and shakes his head. "Not

this time."

"Why not? I want to touch you."

Shaking his head, he laughs. "Honey, if you touch me right now, I'm liable to embarrass myself. I've thought about this moment way too many times, wanted this, craved this with you, for too long. I don't want it to be over before we even start."

Jason lies down beside me and sweeps my body with a heated gaze. "You are so beautiful."

He skims his fingers lightly from my collar bone, down to my breasts, to my belly, and lower. I have goosebumps from head to toe.

Holding my gaze, he slips a finger between the lips of my sex, gliding slowly through the slick wetness. "Open your legs," he murmurs.

I do as he says, and his finger starts teasing my opening. He leans down and kisses me, and our heated breaths mingle. Then he reaches for the condom, rips the package open, and quickly sheathes himself.

Oh, my god. It's happening.

As Jason kneels between my thighs, I can't stop shaking. He meets my gaze, studying me for a long moment as if he's making sure I'm still okay.

I'm more than okay.

He reaches down and grips his erection, positioning himself at my opening. Gently, he rubs the head of his cock against me, sliding easily through the wetness. My thighs are shaking, partly in anticipation and excitement, partly in fear of the unknown.

And then, leaning forward, he grits his teeth as he slowly pushes into me. Wincing, I gasp at the sudden pinching sensation, followed by a slight burn. He sinks deeper and deeper, so slowly, and I revel in the feel of his hardness sliding into my body. He's trying so hard to be gentle, and I love him for it. My heart swells as my breath catches in my chest. Any discomfort I feel from losing my virginity is eclipsed by the emotions welling up inside me.

I love him.

I can't imagine anyone more considerate. I can't imagine how this moment could be more perfect.

When he's all the way inside me, his body pressed against mine, he stops moving, dips his head and touches his lips lightly to mine. "You are exquisite. I feel like the luckiest man on Earth because you chose me."

No, I'm the lucky one. I lucked out and got a true knight as a protector.

My eyes tear up, and I feel the wetness streaming past my temples.

He wipes my face. "I hope those are happy tears."

I nod because I don't trust myself to speak.

And then he starts to move, so slowly, so carefully. His body slides in and out of me, and with each stroke I heat up all over again. Pleasure shoots through me as his thumb slips between us, and he begins stroking my clit. Everything feels so good, the heat and the friction, and his strength as he surges into me, over and over. Gradually, he picks up his pace. His jaw is clenched, and the muscles of his shoulder and neck stand out in stark relief. Suddenly, his gaze locks onto mine, and without warning, he arches his back. His muscles and limbs strain as he cries out, his voice deep and guttural. The sound sinks deep into my soul.

His movements slow after that, and he glides gently in and out of me a few times before he finally withdraws.

"How do you feel?" he asks a little breathlessly as he settles down beside me and pulls me close.

"Perfectly wonderful." I can't help smiling. *I feel normal. I've never felt more normal in my life.*

You're not normal. You'll never be normal.

I ignore her. I'm not going to let her ruin this moment for me.

After dropping a kiss on my shoulder, Jason moves to sit on the side of the bed, removes the condom, and ties it off. "I'll be right back."

He disappears across the hall, and I hear the water running in the bathroom. A moment later, he returns to sit on the side of the bed. The first thing he does is grab his phone and check my sugar level. "It's low. I'll be right back."

I'm not surprised. I'm starting to sweat, and I feel clammy. I'm surprised the alarm hasn't gone off yet.

Jason pulls on a pair of sweatpants and walks out of the bedroom. When he returns, he hands me an apple juice box and helps me sit up and lean against pillows propped against the headboard. "Drink."

After I finish the apple juice, I head to the bathroom to take care of business, wash up, and brush my teeth.

When I return, he's just coming back to the bedroom holding another juice box. "Just in case you need it," he says.

He crawls back into bed and snuggles with me beneath the covers. "It's only nine-thirty. Do you want to watch a movie?"

There's a large TV hanging on the bedroom wall across from the bed.

I grin. "How about *Pride and Prejudice and Zombies*?"

He rolls his eyes. "You've got to be kidding. Jane Austen and zombies?"

"It's a fun movie. And the ending is absolutely swoonworthy."

I lay in Jason's arms and watch a movie with one of the most romantic endings I've ever seen. My knees go weak every time I hear Mr. Darcy proposing to Elizabeth.

But Mr. Darcy has nothing on my real-life hero.

* * *

When I wake in the middle of the night to find the bed empty, I call Jason's name, but there's no answer. So I get out of bed and pull his discarded T-shirt over my head and go looking for him. He's not in the bathroom, or in the living room or in the kitchen. Where else is there? My heart starts pounding because he should be here. He couldn't have gone anywhere this time of night, at least not without telling me. He wouldn't just leave me here alone.

A chilly breeze wafts in through the open balcony door. "Jason?"

"I'm out here, honey."

40

Jason Miller

I knew I'd have to face this eventually. Now that we're sleeping in the same bed, she's going to find out about my insomnia real quick. Layla steps out onto the balcony wearing nothing but my T-shirt, her long legs bare. She's not even wearing underwear. "Honey, come here. You're going to freeze."

I hold out my hand to her, and she lets me pull her onto my lap. I'm wearing a pair of sweatpants and a sweatshirt, so I'm perfectly comfortable out here in the cool night air. I tuck her bare feet onto my lap and wrap her up in the fleece blanket that's draped over the lounge chair.

She nestles close to me. "Why are you out here so late? It's three-thirty."

I sigh and face the inevitable. I don't like talking about my PTSD. "I couldn't sleep."

"Is it because of me?"

"Goodness no. It has nothing to do with you, I promise." I wrap my arms around her, and she lays her head back against my shoulder. "I'm sure you know what PTSD is."

"Of course. Is that why you can't sleep?"

"That, plus insomnia. I hate going to sleep because I dream about people I lost in the line of my work—soldiers in war, civilian casualties from when I was a paramedic. I have nightmares, and they keep me up at night. I didn't want to wake you, so I came out here to try to clear my head."

"Do you want to talk about it?"

He chuckles. "Definitely not."

"But maybe if you did—"

"Trust me, you don't want these memories in your head. You have enough to deal with without adding my issues."

"Have you tried counseling? Or medication?"

"Yes to both. It helps some, but the memories are still there. I saw things I can't unsee. I saw tragedies that haunt me to this day—broken lives, broken families, and a lot of broken hearts."

She turns toward me and kisses the side of my neck, the touch of her lips gentle and soothing. "Tell me a happy story.

Tell me about someone you saved."

I smile, touched by how she's trying to help me. "I saved my commanding officer's life in Afghanistan. We were travelling with a convoy, taking supplies to a forward unit. My CO brought me with him because there were some soldiers with minor injuries that needed treatment. On the way, the truck driving in front of us hit an IED—an Improvised Explosive Device. It detonated and practically destroyed the truck. Shrapnel from the explosion hit our vehicle, and my CO ended up with a jagged piece of metal in his neck that just barely missed his carotid. If it had struck him another couple inches over, he would have died instantly. I was able to patch him up, stop the bleeding, and keep him stable until we could medevac him to a field hospital."

"Did he have a family back home?"

"A wife and two sons—eight-year-old twins."

"So, because of you, because of your knowledge and training, your commander lived to see his family again."

"Well, yes. He has since retired from the Army and is stateside now, working as a private consultant."

"Focus on the positive outcomes, like this one. Try not to think about the unfortunate ones." She rests her head back on my shoulder. "Believe me, I know it's not easy. Tell me another one."

"There was a time when I was out on patrol in Afghanistan and my best friend was hit in the leg by sniper fire. He almost bled out right in front of me. I was able to slow the bleeding and keep him alive until we got him to a hospital."

She frees one arm from the blanket and wraps it around my neck. "You've probably saved more people than you can count."

"I suppose that's true."

"And the families and loved ones of all the people you saved probably thank God for you every day of their lives."

Her words make me smile. "When you put it that way, I guess so. I have a tendency to dwell on the ones I lost, not the ones I saved."

She yawns. "Come back to bed with me. I know a secret trick that will help you sleep."

"Oh, really?" I chuckle at her optimism, but nonetheless, I lift her into my arms and rise from the lounge chair so I can carry her inside.

Once we're undressed and settled back in bed, she rolls me onto my belly. Then she runs her fingers through my hair, so gently all I feel is a light tingling that sweeps over my scalp, down my neck and spine. I shiver at her touch.

"Just relax," she whispers. "Close your eyes and let your mind float."

Sighing, I do as she says. I don't think it will help, but having her fingers playing with my hair is heavenly, and I don't want that to end. She continues stroking my hair and whispers softly in the darkness. I'm practically hypnotized by the sound of her voice, by her gentle words.

Her fingers slide down to my back and she starts drawing

shapes on my skin. Flowers, hearts, random little squiggles… it's soothing.

* * *

I wake feeling refreshed, and I have Layla to thank for that. She lulled me to sleep last night with her soft touches and random finger painting on my back. I turn to face her and find her still sound asleep. She's turned toward me with her hand tucked beneath her pillow.

Her face is soft and relaxed in sleep, and I find myself just staring at her in wonder. My god, she's beautiful. And for some reason, she wants me. That blows my mind.

Last night was incredible. I tried to take it slow and easy. I didn't want to rush her or scare her. I think things are moving way too fast, but I couldn't deny her last night when she just pleaded for normalcy.

Maybe we *are* moving too fast. She's so young, she can't possibly know yet what she wants in life. She may want me now, but she's never been in a relationship before. Once she has some experience, she may decide she wants something different. Someone different.

I do know one thing—I'll do anything and everything in my power to protect her and make her happy.

I reach for my phone and check her blood sugar.

As if she can sense me watching her, she starts to wake. Her eyelids slowly flutter open, and she smiles. "Good morning."

"Good morning to you, too."

"Did you sleep well?"

I nod. "I did, thanks to you and your magic touch."

Layla grins. "My mom used to rub my back when I was little and had trouble falling asleep. She'd sit with me and tell me stories and draw pictures on my back. It was the only thing that relaxed me enough that I could sleep. So, I thought it was worth a try."

I lean closer and press my lips to her forehead. "Well, it worked. You're a miracle worker." I sit up. "I need a shower. Then how about we make breakfast?"

"That sounds wonderful."

I nod toward the bathroom, which is directly across the hall from my bedroom. "Want to join me?"

Her dimples appear. "I'd love to."

41

Layla Alexander

I hate leaving Jason's apartment Sunday evening to head back home, but I know I need to be patient. He's worrying so much about me being overwhelmed. I'm not. I had the most wonderful weekend imaginable, and I can't wait until we come back here, hopefully on a permanent basis.

When we arrive back at the house, Jason carries our bags up to our rooms.

While I'm unpacking, my mom raps on my door. "Hi, sweetie. Can I come in?"

I've been expecting this. "Hi, Mom. Come on in."

She sits on the bed and watches me as I put my things away. "So, how'd it go?" she asks.

"It was wonderful. We went grocery shopping, we made tacos last night for dinner. Jason made me breakfast this morning. I met some of his friends who live in the building. There's a girl my age, Erin, who seems really nice. She's the manager of Clancy's Bookshop, downtown."

"That all sounds wonderful," Mom says. "How did it go between you and Jason? This was a big step for you... being alone with him."

My face heats as I recall all the things we did together over the weekend, and the fact that I slept with him and not in the guest room. I walk over to the bed and sit beside my mom. "Can I ask you a question?"

She puts her arm around me and gives me a hug. "Of course, sweetheart. What is it?"

"Do you believe in love at first sight?"

She smiles. "Well, let me tell you about the first time I went out with your dad. We met in law school, in a course on tort reform." She pauses to smile to herself, as if she's recalling something special. "One day, at the end of class, he asked me out to dinner, and I said yes." She reaches for my hand and links our fingers together. Then she leans close and lowers her voice as she speaks. "I knew by the end of that first date that he was the one."

"But how did you know?"

She shrugs. "I could just tell. I felt like I knew what kind of man he was, that he had integrity. That he was honorable. I knew in my gut that he'd be a good husband and a good father. And my instincts were right. We've been married for thirty-eight years, and I'm glad to say I was right." She stifles a grin as she pats the back of my hand. "Why do you ask?"

"I feel that way about Jason. I feel like he's the one. But how can I know for sure? I've never really dated anyone before."

You're so gullible.

"There are no guarantees in life, sweetheart. But sometimes we get lucky and meet the right one. Only time will tell, but it's worth a chance, isn't it?"

I nod and sigh. "Yes. He's worth taking a chance."

"So? How did it go? Did you guys—"

"Mom!" I can feel my face heating. "Yes. And before you ask, it was amazing."

She smiles. "You'll know in time if he's the right one. Just don't rush into anything until you're sure."

I nod. "I think he is. Deep in my heart, I just know."

She hugs me to her. "I'm so happy for you, sweetheart. That's what I want for you. Your father and I both want that… for you to find someone who truly knows you, knows what you need, and is there for you."

A moment later, Jason pokes his head through my open door. "Hi, Ruth," he says to my mom. Then to me, he says, "I'm done unpacking. Do you need any help?"

"Nope. I'm good."

He nods. "I thought I'd run down to the fitness room to

run a bit and lift weights. Do you want to come with me?"

"I'd love to."

"I'll run back to my room and change my clothes. Come get me when you're ready. No rush."

"Truthfully," I tell my mom after he's gone. "I'm not that much into working out. I just like to watch him lift weights."

Rising from the bed, she grins. "I don't blame you. Go have fun."

* * *

That night, after I've washed up and brushed my teeth, I climb in bed. A few minutes later, there's a knock at my door. "Come in."

Jason walks in and closes the door behind him. He's dressed in a pair of gray cut-off shorts and nothing else. He climbs onto my bed and slips beneath the covers. Then he pulls me to him, his legs entwining with mine. "I figure since we shared a bed at my apartment—and your parents didn't kill me—it's okay if we do it here. If I promise to be good, can I sleep in your room?"

I wrap my arms around his neck and kiss him. His warm skin is slightly damp from his shower, and he tastes like mint. "I would love that."

He spoons me, wrapping me in the safe cocoon of his embrace.

"Jason, do you believe in love at first sight?"

My god. You're so gullible.

Oh, be quiet.

Jason's arms tighten around me as he sighs. "I do."

I place a kiss on his firm bicep, which is just inches from my mouth. "Me, too."

He chuckles. "So, have you met your true love yet?"

"I have," I say as I feel his lips in my hair. "I've never been so sure of anything in my life."

"Me too," he says as his lips dip down. He kisses me behind the ear, making me shiver.

He's lying.

No, he's not.

I smile as he pulls me closer. Whatever the future holds, I know it'll be all right because we have each other. And even if I sometimes stumble, I know he'll be there to catch me.

* * *

Thank you so much for reading Layla and Jason's story. I hope you enjoyed spending time with them as much as I did. I'm sure you'll see more of them in future books.

The next release in the *McIntyre Security Protectors* series is Liam McIntyre's story, *Damaged Goods*.

* * *

If you'd like to sign up for my newsletter, download my free short stories, or locate my contact information, visit my website: www.aprilwilsonauthor.com

* * *

For links to my growing list of audiobooks, visit my website: www.aprilwilsonauthor.com/audiobooks

* * *

I interact daily with readers in my Facebook reader group (Author April Wilson's Reader Group) where I post frequent updates and share weekly teasers. Come join me!

* * *

Books by April Wilson

McIntyre Security Bodyguard Series:

Vulnerable

Fearless

Shane (a novella)

Broken

Shattered

Imperfect

Ruined

Hostage

Redeemed

Marry Me (a novella)

Snowbound (a novella)

Regret

With This Ring (a novella)

Collateral Damage

Special Delivery

McIntyre Security Protectors:

Finding Layla

McIntyre Security Search and Rescue Series:

Search and Rescue

Lost and Found

A Tyler Jamison Novel:

Somebody to Love

Somebody to Hold

Somebody to Cherish

A British Billionaire Romance:

Charmed (co-written with Laura Riley)

Audiobooks & Upcoming Releases:

For links to my audiobooks and upcoming releases, visit my website:

www.aprilwilsonauthor.com

Printed in Great Britain
by Amazon